AF575618

SIN EATER

GREG MORGAN

Copyright © 2024 Venturi Press

All rights reserved. No part of this publication may be reproduced, stored in a retrieval system, or transmitted in any form or by any means – by electronic, mechanical, photocopying, recording, or otherwise – without prior written permission from the author or publisher.

ISBN: 978-1-7349657-7-3 (Paperback)
www.greg-morgan.com

This is a work of fiction. Yep, that means it ain't true and didn't really happen. More specifically, it is historical fiction, which also means the story that ain't true occurred in a historical period of time that did happen. Most of what's written here are the products of the author's imagination and/or used in a fictitious manner. Then again, several of the characters were, in fact, true historical figures of the nineteenth century, but the roles they play in this narrative are entirely fictional, and so is their dialogue. Yep, the author made it up, all in his imagination. Any resemblance to actual living persons is purely coincidental, and since this narrative took place in the mid-nineteenth century, if you think I'm writing about you, you're crazy! Oops, I'm sorry, I mean peculiar.

To my daughters,
who inspire me
with the beauty
of their being.

PROLOGUE

1871

The sin eater rode toward the farmhouse perched atop a mule like a scarecrow on a fence post. His long legs dangled low enough for his boot heels to nearly scrape the dusty path. A tangled gray beard cascaded over his chest, matching the unkempt mane that shrouded his shoulders. The air around him hung heavy with the pungent musk of stale sweat, a vapor that preceded him like a foul herald.

Shadows pooled beneath the brim of his open-crown hat, a black void that seemed to swallow what little light dared venture near his eyes. He pulled it even lower as he reached the farmhouse fence. With a grunt, he swung his leg over the mule's back and awkwardly slid off.

The mourners standing outside stared at him, making him nervous. From the depths of his pocket, he retrieved a brown cloth, its edges frayed with time and use. He pressed it to his nose and mouth, inhaling deeply. The cloth, a token of a moment stolen in time, had been spirited away from his late wife on the second day of their acquaintance. She had used it then to cleanse her hands and arms, a simple act rendered intimate through memory's lens. The scent of it, the essence of that moment, soothed the ever-present anxiety that gnawed at his edges. With a sigh, he allowed the cloth to fall from his face, his fingers twisting and weaving it in a dance of nervous energy, a habit he could not stop even if he wanted to.

Shoving the cloth back into its home, he silenced the murmuring crowd as he lumbered toward them. They parted for him, pushed back and aside by the sin he carried like dirt from a plow. Children darted behind their mothers' dresses and fathers' legs. A woman fell back, tripping on someone's shoes behind her. He paused patiently as a man pulled her up.

The sin eater breached the farmhouse threshold without wiping the mud from his boots or removing his hat from his head—such niceties held no sway over a sin eater. The interior greeted him with a somber embrace, every window and mirror shrouded in black linen, a traditional gesture of mourning. Flickering flames from the hearth and scattered candles waged a gentle war against the gloom. He stopped in the center of the crowded room, not confident where to go. Those still standing outside pushed in behind him, sucking the air out of the space.

The crowd parted like a black sea, revealing the deceased lying face-up on a long table. With the hesitant gait of a chastened child, eyes fixed on the worn floorboards, the sin eater threaded through the crowd and plopped down on a bench, back to the wall. Before him lay the corpse, and he settled in to wait, as patient and inevitable as death itself.

"Jenny?" A voice from the crowd summoned forth a woman, a plate of food in hand. She approached the table, positioning herself across from the sin eater. Her gaze, heavy with sorrow, drifted from the offering to the gaunt figure before her, finally settling on the still face of her husband—father of three, now dressed in his Sunday finest, shoeless for eternal comfort. With trembling hands, she extended the plate over her beloved's body.

His thin, bony fingers claimed it, hovering the dish above the deceased as he stammered out in an old, gravelly voice, "I give, I give peace and rest to you, rest to you, dear man. Go now, go now into the waiting arms of your savior. And for thy peace, I pawn my own soul. I pawn my soul, yes."

He set the plate down with reverent care and breathed in the smell of roasted chicken, its skin crisped to perfection, the warm, soft bread, and the mashed potatoes all covered with the bitter gravy of sin. His fingers, unburdened by the niceties of cutlery, tore into the meat with fervor, each piece disappearing into his mouth like a man starved for days. The gravy smeared over his lips, and crumbs of bread and tiny flecks of chicken found refuge in his unkempt beard.

The sin eater savored every bite and sucked the grease from his fingers before licking the plate. Slowly and delicately, he set the plate down before loudly belching a cloud of sin. The mourners flinched and stepped back in disgust. He wiped his mouth and beard with his shirt sleeve before he stood, pushing the bench back, its legs squealing across the aged floorboards.

His eyes landed on an unbuttoned button patiently waiting for him on the dead man's waistcoat. He needed to button it. He could not leave without buttoning it. He reached down and did so, eliciting a gasp from a woman in the corner. His eyes didn't leave the button until, after several moments, he pushed up the hidden spectacles on his nose and cleared his throat.

"Oh. Jenny, the bag," said a man in the crowd, his cue to begin walking out, the crowd parting for him again. Jenny used a broomstick to hand him the canvas bag as he made for the door. He swiped it off without a glance. The mourners filled the doorway to watch his stooped frame climb onto the waiting mule. As awkwardly as he dismounted, he pulled himself up on his stomach and threw a leg over. The sin eater cleared his throat again before giving the mule two kicks with his boots and two clicks from his tongue.

Ungracefully bouncing on the mule's back, the sin eater trotted toward the forest across the golden grass field. There, tall pines waited patiently for him like guards of the gallows. As he entered their custody, their trunks closed around him like the bars of a prison cell, swallowing his form from view.

CHAPTER I

1865

3 Years Prior

The bitter winds of March whispered through the trees and brush that hid Osborn Roche from sight. Beyond the brush obscuring him lay the expanse of a massive manicured green lawn and, two hundred yards beyond that, a grand mansion three stories high.

Sitting on a log with a telescope to his eye, Osborn leaned over and, with the back of his hand shielding his mouth, whispered, "He's letting the dog chase him." Next to him lay the final resting place of his deceased wife, Lou. The cross he had made for her read, "L. Roche, Embalmer," and beneath that, "Gone from the world, but alive again in our hearts."

In his lens, Ishmael, their six-year-old son, played ball with a dog. A gray-haired, elderly gentleman came from the house to the second-story patio above the lawn. "Oh, here comes Henry. He's calling him in. They'll be going to church soon." Osborn collapsed the telescope, the metal whispering as it slid into itself. He took his spectacles from his pocket, put them on, turned to the fresh flowers he had placed on his wife's grave, and declared, "Alright, let's be off now, off now." Dusting off his pants, Osborn descended the dirt path toward his secluded cabin forty-five minutes away. He undertook his journey every sunlit day unless the winter's embrace rendered the path impassable with snow.

The afternoon sun pierced through the trees, occasionally blinding Osborn as he approached his small, moss-covered log cabin nestled in the belly of the Pennsylvanian Appalachian Mountains. It stood solitary in a tiny clearing that nature was slowly claiming back, the encroaching forest threatening to swallow the structure whole with every passing season. On either side of the cabin stood two colossal pines, their trunks so thick it would take three men with outstretched arms to encircle them. These arboreal sentinels had grown in tandem with the cabin, their massive roots and expanding girth slowly reshaping the structure over decades. The roof, pushed askew by their relentless growth, now sat at an odd angle, as if the cabin were tipping its hat to passersby. Atop the slanted roof, a meadow in miniature had taken root. Thick grass, swaying in the breeze, grew to nearly a foot in height, creating a lush green carpet. The log walls, barely visible beneath a thick coating of lime-green moss, glistened with moisture from the river's ever-present mist.

He had stumbled upon it vacant, and luckily so. His beloved Romani Vardo camper wagon, from which he traveled the country, lived, and slept, had been destroyed in the river and swept away by the current.

At the end of the path, just before the cabin, Osborn passed by an unmarked grave beside the pathway. "Afternoon," he said to it before tapping his palm on the top of the cross at its head. Continuing past the small clearing of grass in front of his cabin, Hoady Junior, his faithful mule, grazed. "Afternoon, Junior," he said with a wave before entering the cabin. Junior only glanced up and shook his head at him.

As he pushed it open and entered, the old door creaked on its leather hinges. The interior was sparse; a small cot, covered by a moth-eaten green blanket, sat against one wall. Next to it, a bookshelf with six books, their spines worn and faded. A taxidermied boar's head hung high on one wall, and above the door was a Springfield Model 1795, a single-shot, flintlock musket. The cabin still had everything he needed: shovels, lanterns, oil, candles, and tools of all sorts.

He approached the hearth, prodding the smoldering remnants and coaxing them to life. The night settled around the cabin as Osborn lay back on his cot, the brown cloth clutched in his hand. Tomorrow, he would make the journey again to sit with Lou and watch their son from afar. But tonight, in this forgotten corner of the world, he allowed himself to remember and dream of a life that could have been.

Osborn reached for a book on a shelf close to the bed and opened it. He flipped through the pages, skimming the handwritten entries with dates—the diary of the previous occupant. From it, he had learned the man was a self-educated Susquehannock Indian who had taught himself mathematics, to read and write, Native American healing medicines, the stars, and the ways of the forest. As Osborn perused the journal, he discovered the most peculiar aspect of the previous inhabitant was a ritual the man referred to as "Sin Eating"—an unfamiliar spiritual tradition that piqued Osborn's curiosity.

On one of the first days after Osborn had found the cabin, he stumbled upon the man's skeleton. It lay at the start of the path to Henry's, splayed out beneath the gnarled roots of an ancient oak. The bones, bleached by time, still held together like a macabre jigsaw puzzle. He knelt beside it, his fingers hovering above the skull, where a spider had made its home within the vacant eye socket. Osborn felt no disgust, only a curiosity that brought an inquisitive gleam to his eyes. How long had this previous occupant of his cabin lain here, undisturbed but for the scavengers that had picked these bones clean? Osborn continued his examination. He noted how the skeleton's hand rested upon its ribcage as though it sought to hold itself together against some unknowable despair in life. A pang of kinship twinged within him.

"Who were you?" he murmured. "Thank you, thank you for the cabin," he added before rising. Osborn buried him the next day, where he found him. Until he had read the diary, the skeleton he had laid to rest that day was a mystery.

Tired, Osborn set the diary back on the shelf and lay to rest for the night.

With dawn's light seeping through the cracks of the worn cabin, Osborn Roche stirred from his cot. He filled the kettle and set it atop the stove before heading outside to relieve himself. The air held a perpetual chill, carrying the aroma of damp earth and old wood mixed with the faintest hint of decay. Junior grazed untethered in the small field in front of the cabin. "Morning, morning, Junior," he said with a wave. Junior ignored him, choosing to eat instead.

Osborn pulled up his trousers and walked down to the river to check for any fish he might have caught during the night within his fish trap. He had learned how to build it from a Cherokee friend while traveling across the Great Plains. She had taught him to create two walls of stacked stone that formed a V shape but opened into a basket at the bottom. Osborn approached the stone fish trap, hoping some errant trout or bass had swum into the basket overnight. The Cherokee woman who had shown him how to construct it said it worked best with a partner - one to frighten the fish into the V-shaped walls, the other waiting downstream to scoop them up. Fishing solo required more patience and luck. His heart sank when he saw the basket empty.

The kettle's whistle stopped Osborn from going further, a shrill intruder that demanded attention. Inside the cabin, he went to pour the steaming water over dried leaves, the aroma of dandelion tea filling the space with comforting familiarity. As always, breakfast was an affair as Spartan as his life now: dandelion tea brewed over the fire, the rarely caught fish or whatever wild berries he could scavenge from the encroaching woods. Not knowing how to hunt, he lost weight during the six months there.

His daily routine was an anchor, each task a lifeline tethering him to the present when the past threatened to drag him under. In his past, Osborn had led the life of a world-famous photographer, capturing moments of war and peace, a far cry from the stillness that now blanketed his existence. His new abode was void of the clattering sounds of human presence—no more did the voices of generals, political titans, or, thankfully for him, the cannon's roar vibrate within his ears. Instead, there was only the river behind or the creaking of the cabin as it settled further into its foundation and the rustling leaves that skittered across the porch like timid creatures. His existence here was simple, unadorned by the complexities that once filled his life. Yet within this simplicity lay a profound sense of abandonment—his life, now reduced to a mere echo of its former self. On the other hand, the quiet was a balm to his frayed senses, the kind that only someone who shied from touch and the gazes of others could genuinely appreciate.

His hand reached for a relic of his previous life: a leather-bound album, bloated with the metal daguerreotype and tintype photographs he had recovered from the riverbank a week after they had floated out of his submerged Romani Vardo caravan. Osborn's hands trembled as he held the photos, their images blurred from the many times he had handled them. He placed them aside, and his gaze drifted, unfocused, toward the cold hearth. The photos captured a world that now felt like a dream. It fell open to a page--a battlefield frozen in time, soldiers' expressions etched in silver nitrate. His eyes rambled through the pages, stepping into a past he could no longer touch, filled with faces he had memorialized in moments of glory and despair. A general mid-speech, his eyes alight with fervor, a vice president's weary countenance, and one of his wife, Lou. "Photography... fights time…" he murmured as he traced Lou's face with an absent touch, feeling the surface of the metal. "…by capturing a moment of it, like capturing one soldier, one soldier from time's endless army, time's endless army of soldiers, yes."

Osborn stepped out of his cabin, the door creaking shut behind him. A rustle in the underbrush caught his attention. He wheeled around, his body tensing. Instead of a threat, a dog emerged, its red coat gleaming in the dappled sunlight that filtered through the trees.

The thin, malnourished Redbone Coonhound trotted toward him, its tail wagging in a friendly manner. Junior, ever the stoic mule, merely glanced at the newcomer before returning to his grazing, unperturbed by the canine's presence.

Osborn, however, found himself intrigued. What was it doing out here, so far from home? The dog approached him, its nose twitching as it sniffed the air. Osborn hesitated, unsure of how to proceed. He had never been particularly fond of dogs, finding their boisterous energy and need for affection overwhelming. But something about this hound, a calmness in its demeanor, drew him in. The dread of a potential bite restrained him from caressing the inviting, soft red fur atop the dog's head, although it beckoned him as irresistibly as a siren's song. As if the dog felt his stare, it turned its eyes to Osborn with a panting grin.

Slowly, tentatively, Osborn extended his hand, allowing the dog to sniff it. The hound's tail wagged faster, pushing its head into Osborn's palm, seeking attention. Osborn ran his knuckles between the dog's ears, sensing the fur as soft as his beloved brown cloth. A small smile tugged at the corners of Osborn's mouth as he scratched behind the dog's ears. "Hello there, hello there," he murmured, his voice soft. The dog leaned into his touch, its eyes closing in contentment. "You're a long way from home, aren't you?" Osborn mused aloud, his fingers scratching behind the hound's ears. Osborn yanked back his hand after the dog licked it. "Ewww," he grimaced as he wiped his hand on his pants.

The dog's tail wagged in response before running off to the river behind the cabin. Osborn followed him to the river, where the dog's tongue lapped the water. Movement in the river caught the dog's attention, and it dashed across the water for it, its eyes sparkling. A school of trout scattered away from the hound, this way and that. When they headed toward his stone trap, Osborn ran for the basket. The hound chased them straight into it. Whipping up the basket, he could count at least seven trout. A triumphant smile spread across Osborn's face, and his hand went to pet the dog. "Good dog, good dog. We can both eat now," he praised.

As Osborn carried the basket of trout back to the cabin, the hound trotted alongside him, its tail wagging in satisfaction. Inside the cabin, Osborn set about preparing the fish. "You know, it's been a while since I've had a decent meal. I've been mostly eating berries, eating berries, yes."

Osborn continued to speak to the dog as he cooked the trout over the fire, the aroma filling the cabin. "I suppose I should give you a name, a name, yes," he said as he tapped his finger against his lips in thought. "How about Lincoln? Lincoln, yes." The dog wagged its tail in response. "A good, a good president's name for a, for a good dog. Lincoln, it shall be!"

CHAPTER 2

Osborn's feet traced their familiar path, each step a metronome in his daily pilgrimage to Lou's grave. Lincoln had been his silent companion for the last three months, and the occasional brush of his fur against Osborn's leg had become a comfort rather than an intrusion.

At their destination, Osborn claimed his usual seat on a weathered log, his gaze lingering on the distant mansion. Lincoln, nose twitching with canine curiosity, circled Lou's resting place before settling atop the soft mound, his preferred spot.

Osborn pulled out his telescope, focusing it on the house's rear door—minutes ticked by, the silence broken only by the rustle of leaves in the breeze. The butler emerged when the rear door opened, letting out their black labrador. Lincoln's ears shot up, and before Osborn could utter a word, the Redbone was off like a shot, racing toward his newfound playmate.

Osborn jumped up, and his heart raced as he watched the two dogs play, their barks and yips carrying across the lawn. He didn't know what to do. Should he call Lincoln back? Stay hidden? His decision was made for him when Ishmael stepped out of the house, a grin on his six-year-old face as he watched the dogs. He chuckled, shaking his head, and started toward them.

Ishmael reached down and petted Lincoln while the two dogs romped around him. Seemingly remembering his master, Lincoln ran back to the brush where Osborn hid, with Ishmael following.

"Ishmael, don't go too far!" the butler called, hurrying after the boy. Panic seized Osborn. He scrambled to his feet, leaving his telescope behind, and fled down the trail. His heart pounded in his ears as he ran, branches whipping at his face. He didn't stop until he reached the safety of the deeper woods, his breath coming in ragged gasps.

Minutes later, Lincoln caught up to him, tongue lolling. Osborn looked down at the dog, disappointment etched on his face. "You shouldn't have done that," he muttered. "Bad dog, bad dog. Shouldn't have done it, done it, no. I will not bring you again."

Osborn's nose wrinkled with irritation as he glanced at Lincoln on their journey back. Nearly there, a shadow of concern passed over Osborn's face as he approached the cabin. He sniffed the air and slowed his pace, noticing smoke as it rose from the cabin's chimney. The fire should have burned out. A white horse's rear peeked out from behind the cabin. Lincoln stopped and fixated on the log door before turning to Osborn, panting. Reluctantly, Osborn pushed the door open with its loud creak. Lincoln trotted in ahead as Osborn peeked in. A man sat at the small table in the corner of the small cabin, scratching Lincoln's head. "Good day, Pilgrim," he said. Osborn jumped back, eyes wide, and froze at the sight. The grizzled man appeared more bear than human, dressed all in furs patched up from years of wear. He appeared to be in his fifties with a weather-beaten face and a thick, unkempt beard going gray.

On the table lay a large knife next to his hand, and on the wall leaned a rifle. "If yous a good Pilgrim, there be no need to be fearin'. I ain't here to harm if no harm comes my way." The man's eyes hinted at a life filled with experiences as they studied Osborn. "What I be needing to know is to the which of the why about the ol' Injun that lived here 'fore ya?"

Osborn stuck his finger in the air with the thought. "Oh, oh, I buried him, buried him, yes."

The man studied Osborn for a time before saying, "Put your sitting britches on, sos I can get a feel for ya." Osborn cautiously sat on the cot across from him. "You have...," he paused for dramatic effect, "...something to do with his passin' on? The Injun's?"

"Oh, no, sir, no sir. I do not know how he passed on. I found his skeleton, his skeleton in the field. I stumbled upon it."

"So, ya say. I been watching ya for a day or two from yonder," he added. "How long ya been here?"

"It may be, it may be six months, yes."

Steam came from a coffee pot in the fireplace. The man swung it out from the metal rod it hung on. "Brought my own coffee if ya don't mind. Want some?"

"Why yes, yes. I have not had coffee in some time."

"Ya ain't from around here, are ya?"

"No, no. I was from Pittsburgh, Pittsburgh, yes. My name is Osborn Roche." Osborn weakly raised his hands and unenthusiastically said, "The world-famous O. Roche photography," as he spread his hands across the sky.

"World-famous, ya say? I wouldn't know no nothing 'bout that. Photo-phy, never heard of it."

"Photography is where we use a box we call a camera to make a portrait of someone or something from the light, from the light, yes, on the subject, yes."

"Oh, ya mean like them little tintype portraits I seen? I thought they just called tintypes."

"No, no, it is photography. Tintypes are the end product, the end product, yes. My portraits of the war between the states became famous."

"So, Pittsburgh, ya say. Ain't too far. Three day's ride or so, I'd say."

"Three day's ride, day's ride," Osborn repeated.

The man shoved the knife into its sheath on his hip. "Sos ya say ya been here six months, eh?"

Osborn's gaze fell to the floor. "Six, six months, yes."

The man took a sip of coffee. "Mind if I stay a few days? The old Injun used to let me stay when I passed through."

"Certainly, certainly. I have had no visitors," repeated Osborn.

"My cabin is way up yonder into the high hills. This cabin's your place now. You can have the bed. The name's Billy. Some call me Trapper Billy 'cause that's what I do, trap."

"Alright, alright, I will call you Trapper Billy, Trapper Billy."

"What'd ya say yourn was again?"

"Osborn, Osborn Roche."

"Osborn Osborn? Ya say it twice like that?"

"No, no. Just Osborn Roche."

Billy's eyes went to the rifle above the door. "You using his long gun?"

"I, I've never used it. I do not know how."

"That's a Springfield 1795. Can't find a Springfield 1795 no more. Scarce as hen's teeth they is."

Osborn pushed his spectacles up on his nose. "It's a beautiful gun, yes."

"It is. And the Injun rarely used it. He'd hunt with his hands, a rock, and a sling or a bow sometimes. Never seen him shoot it," Billy said as he stroked his beard in thought. "That one's cursed, it is."

"Cursed? I do not, do not believe in curses."

"I'm telling ya now, it is so. You see all the Injun carvings on its stock? They's curses. Years back, when I first came across this cabin, I was starving, and I knocked. No one home. I went in and found that gun. I'm now ashamed to say I stole it. Took it and skedaddled. That night, I was cursed with terrible nightmares, and after that, my traps went dry. Misfortune befell me in every way. I studied its wood stock and the carvings on it. I knew. I knew it was the gun. It had me in a spell. I brought it back to the Injun, knelt before him, and begged he take the spell off me. Just taking the gun from my hands brought relief, the likes you can never imagine. The Injun took pity on me, and we ended up as friends. Both us found solace in each other's company though infrequent that company was kept."

Osborn dropped his gaze to the floor. "I know loneliness, loneliness myself, yes."

"I see that. It hangs on your shoulders like a wet blanket. Ya get used to it after a time."

Rain pitter-pattered on the roof before it grew louder. Osborn rose from his cot and took a towel from a peg on the wall. He folded it and shoved it under the bottom of the door to keep the rainwater out.

"You know what that Injun did 'round these parts, Pilgrim?" Osborn shook his head. "You ever heard of a sin eater?"

Osborn's interest peaked. "I read, I read about it in his journal, journal, yes. I would like to know more. Was it, was it his religion?"

"No, not his religion. It was his profession. Made a bit of coin from it, got a good meal from it."

"His profession?"

"Yessum. A peculiar one most would say," Billy said as his eyes perused the room. "Not many would take the job on."

"Sin eating? How does one eat sin? Or is this a metaphor? I must declare, I rarely will understand a, understand a metaphor when one is, when one is used, no."

"I don't know what a metaphor is, but I'll learn ya what a sin eater is. It's a job unlike any other, takin' on the sins of the departed so their souls can rest easy. When someone passes, families call for the sin eater. He'd come to the house right before the dead would be laid to rest. The family would prepare a plate of food, and they'd pass the plate over the body to the sin eater sittin' on the other side of the dead. The food on the plate takes up all the sins of the departed as it's passed over the body. Each bite ya be takin' soaks up them sins, takin' 'em upon his own soul. It's a heavy burden, one that marks a man, sets him apart from the rest of us."

Osborn's gaze drifted to the cabin's weathered floorboards, worn smooth by countless footsteps. *Set apart,* he thought. As a boy, Osborn felt perpetually set apart and out of step with the world around him. The laughter of his classmates echoed in his ears, sharp and mocking. "Crazy, stupid, fool," they'd call him, their faces twisted in cruel amusement. He remembered the sting of exclusion, the cold dread of entering a room full of people who viewed him as an oddity. His father's voice, gruff with disappointment: "Can't you just be normal, boy?" The words had burrowed deep, festering like an old wound that never quite healed. "I've, I've been set apart, set apart from the rest, almost, almost all my life," he told Billy.

Billy cocked his head to the side, studying Osborn using his left eye. "Still, you don't want nothing to do with sin eating, Pilgrim. Folks around here respect the sin eater, but they keep their distance, too. You say you're lonely now? Thems got no friends at all. There's somethin' otherworldly 'bout one, like he walks in two worlds at once. That's why I was the Injun's only friend. Carrying the burdens of others is a weight most choose not to heft on the shoulders. Most times, it's the town drunk or an old whore. They's the only ones folk can convince to take the task. A fool that just don't care much about anything or anyone. The Injun weren't no fool, but the Injun just thought it was just a pack full of the white man's foolish thinkin'. He didn't believe no none of that. He just played on like he did. He ate the food and acted all solemn-like. It was quite a show. I seen him do it, playing the part like an actor on the stage." Billy grinned as he recalled the memory before his eyes flashed to Osborn. "You heard of the Susquehannocks?"

Osborn lifted his head. "Yes, they were a Pennsylvanian tribe."

"Were is right. They ain't no more, I believe. The Susquehannock that lived here was the very last one of 'em I know of. Anyhow, this ole' boy liked playing the sin eater. Good food, a bit of pay, even though he never went to town to use it. He just liked to take the money away from the white man, I 'spect. He didn't care no none about the loneliness of it all. He liked living up heres in these woods alone," Billy said before facing Osborn and asking, "So, ya say you been here about six months now?" Osborn nodded. "Ain't no one come by asking for the Injun?"

"No one has come by. I receive no visitors, no visitors, no."

"Hmm. Times be changing. Why I 'member the day a sin eater'd be 'round twice a moon's life or more. People changing. People don't be believing in no sin eaters no more suppose. Anyhow, if folk come a knockin' don't be takin' it on. Tell 'em to just move on."

"I would like a home cooked meal, home cooked meal, yes."

"I'd expect ya would. It's good eating too. But like I said, it ain't in your blood, Pilgrim. Ain't in your blood," replied Billy, looking about the room again. "You find a can 'round here? That's where that boy put his coin. I know that boy never did spend it. You find it, you might be shittin' in high cotton."

"Shitting in high cotton is a metaphor, it is a metaphor. As you say, I'm learning you now, as you say," said Osborn with a snort from the joke only he understood. "Everyone knows you don't shit in high cotton. Everyone knows."

Confused, Billy shook his head at Osborn as he continued, "Metaphors turn language into art. Ray told me. My nephew Ray told me, yes. I did not understand why people used them, but Ray told me. Language into art, language into art."

Billy cocked his head to the side. "Pilgrim, ya gotta interesting way of speaking sometimes."

Osborn stood to put another log on the fire. With a grin, he replied, "Some may say a peculiar way of speaking, way of speaking, yes."

Dawn broke, Billy's resonant snores jolting Osborn from his restless sleep. With Lincoln at his heels, he ventured into the crisp morning air. After tending to nature's call and a brisk river wash, Osborn set out on the well-worn dirt path.

At Lou's grave, man and dog assumed their customary positions. An hour crawled by before the butler emerged with Ishmael and the black lab in tow. Lincoln's ears pricked up, but Osborn's hand swiftly descended, a gentle barrier before the hound's muzzle. "No, Lincoln. Watch only." With a resigned huff, he seemingly accepted the command.

As Osborn raised his telescope, Lincoln's attention snapped rearward.

"Who's the little boy?" Billy's voice startled Osborn, but he kept his gaze fixed through the lens.

"My son, my son, Ishmael, yes."

"Who's in the grave?"

"My wife, yes, my wife lays in the grave. Lost my wife, yes, lost my wife. My best friend."

"Ya say it's your son?"

"Yes. We watch him together, my wife, my wife and I, yes."

Billy circled around to face Osborn with lips stained by wild raspberries. He extended a calloused hand, offering the fruit.

"Where did you find them?" asked Osborn as Billy poured some into his hand.

"Just off the path," said Billy before turning aside Osborn, gazing across the lawn. "So, what's the story? What's the which of the why ya over here spying on 'em?"

"Our son, our son lives with his grandfather, grandfather, yes. Henry, my wife's father, father, yes. He took our son from me, from me when Lou passed. He doesn't think I'm capable."

Billy's eyes narrowed on Osborn. "Took him, ya say? Is it because ya kinda cumfluttered, Pilgrim?

"Cumflut?"

"Ya got a twitch in the head or something? The war left many a man with the condition."

"No, no. I was a photographer in the war, not a combatant. They call me peculiar. I am peculiar, peculiar, yes. Not strange, not strange or cumflut, cumflut, or whatever that word was. I do not like the other words, no."

"Didn't mean to offend ya none. Just curious, is alls."

"Henry Cattell is, is a mighty powerful man, yes. Power with the government, the government, and the courts, yes."

"Hmmm, I can understand that," Billy replied before turning and peering out over the long green lawn to the back of the mansion in the distance. "Looks like they've gone in."

"Yes, yes." Osborn jumped up and abruptly headed back down the path toward his cabin.

Billy followed. "Got any other kin, Pilgrim?"

"Yes, yes. A nephew in Pittsburgh, in Pittsburgh, yes."

"Ever thought of heading that aways? Maybe he can lend a hand."

"Can't leave Lou, no. Can't leave Lou."

Billy shook his head. "Lou ain't going nowhere, Pilgrim."

"But I promised her I would watch for both of us. I would watch Ishmael."

Billy's gray eyebrows jumped. "Did ya mean every single day?"

Osborn stopped on the path in front of Billy. He paused in thought before answering. "I know, I know it is not logical, not logical. And I am a logical man. It has been a little over a year since Lou's passing."

"How'd she pass on?"

Osborn continued his walk down the path. "Giving birth to Ishmael, to Ishmael, yes. I had told myself that I would grieve for a year. One year of mourning, yes. But, I still find it difficult to leave both of them, leave both of them, yes. And I have adjusted to this life, adjusted to it."

Billy grunted with a smirk. "Not too well, I reckon. You need a pack full of learning, I reckon. Saw your fish trap in the crick. Catch much with it?"

"Recently, recently, yes, now with the help of Lincoln," replied Osborn as he glanced down to the top of Lincoln's head.

"That crick is chock full of trout. Seen 'em myself. You ever trapped game, Pilgrim?"

"Never, never."

"If ya let me stay through the winter, I can learn ya a few things if ya want. Ya looks like you could use some learnin'. Like the Injun done learned me."

"Learn me?"

"Trap, hunt, and the like. Make ya time here a bit more passable."

Osborn's head rose. "I would like that, like that, yes."

Approaching the cabin, Billy asked, "Mind if ya show me the Injun's resting place?"

"I'd be happy to, happy to. Please follow me."

Forty feet from the cabin, they approached a large oak tree with a mound of earth beneath it. Three logs forming a cross lay over it. "The first cross I made fell apart. I like that one better."

"Did ya say some words over it?"

"I did, yes, I did indeed. But I did not know his name, no, so I called him 'man,' man, yes."

"I never knowed it neither, truth be. Never did tell it to me." Billy contemplated the grave momentarily before adding, "Ya did a right fine job for the old boy."

"Yes, yes, I'm using his cabin. Least I can do, the least I can do, yes." Osborn pointed to a field across from it. "Found his bones right here, right here. Must've collapsed here."

Billy's voice carried a whisper of sorrow as he spoke. "Reckon so," he murmured, his gaze distant. Then, with a slight lift of his chin, he continued, "That old boy learned me plenty, he did. Learned me real good." His eyes refocused, meeting his companion's. "Just like I aim to teach you."

CHAPTER 3

The first whispers of winter danced on the wind as Osborn trudged up the familiar trail, his breath forming misty clouds in the crisp air. Three months had elapsed since his chance encounter with Billy, each day a lesson in wilderness survival. The snow-dappled ground crunched beneath his deerskin moccasins, a far cry from the city boots he'd once worn.

Osborn now had a thick, gray beard peppered with streaks of stubborn black along his jawline, which obscured much of his face. He wore a wolf-skin coat fashioned by his own hands under Billy's tutelage. Lou would never recognize him.

As he neared the cabin, Osborn paused, his keen eyes scanning the forest floor. "Rabbit's been through here," he muttered, noting the telltale tracks—a trick Billy had drummed into him weeks ago. Osborn allowed himself a small smile. He was no longer the lost soul who had stumbled into these woods. He had become something else entirely—part mountain man, part shadow, forever straddling two worlds.

As the sun dipped under the trees, Billy jumped behind a tree, bringing his rifle close. "Hide ya self, Pilgrim," he demanded in a whisper. Osborn did as told.

A distant voice called out, "I could smell ya a mile back! No need to hide yourself!" and laughed after he said it.

Osborn peered down the path from behind his tree—nothing.

"I can see ya there behind the tree!" yelled the voice.

Osborn ducked back behind his tree and looked over to Billy, peeking out. A grin came to Billy's face before he stepped out and opened his arms wide in greeting. "You're a long way from home!" Billy yelled with a laugh. Osborn walked out to a man approaching them from a distance wearing a hooded bear coat. Tassels ran down the length of his leather pants, and he wore moccasins on his feet. Long red hair flowed from the bear skin hood, and a bushy red mustache adorned his face. Billy gestured to Osborn. "I know this one. He's nothing to be fearin'."

"All these mountains are my home! I'm just moving from one room to another!" the bear-coated man yelled. After Osborn stepped out, he shouted, "Ah! It was him I smelt. You must've taken a bath for once!" The man opened his arms, wrapping them around Billy.

Anxiety grew in Osborn as he watched the two men hug, hoping the man wouldn't try that on him.

"You survived another winter," the man told Billy.

"We both did."

"Did indeed," said the man as he turned to Osborn, hand out. "The name's Mulvaney. Pleased to make your acquaintance."

Osborn stood staring at the hand, waiting for him to shake. "He don't shake no hand," Billy told him. "Don't take offense from it. Tell him your name, Pilgrim."

"Yes, yes, I'm sorry I do not like to touch, do not like to shake hands. My name is Osborn Roche, Osborn Roche, yes."

Mulvaney looked down at his hand before dropping it. "Well, then, I'm still pleased to make your acquaintance, sir."

"Yes, and I, and I as well," replied Osborn.

Mulvaney swiveled back to Billy. "Staying with the Injun, I assume?"

"The Injun's dead."

Mulvaney's face fell. "Ah, naw! Dog gone it! I came all this way for the boy," he said before stopping himself and turning back to Billy. "Oh! That's why I'm here. You heard about Old Dan?" Billy's forehead creased with the question as he continued, "Old Dan's dead. Passed on, he did. I come for the Injun. Wasn't thinking you'd be here."

Billy nodded. "I 'spected Old Dan be dead some time ago."

"No, sir. Just happened a fore' night ago. His old lady be wanting the sin eater."

"The Shawnee squaw? She believes in that?"

"Don't know, but it don't matter 'cause Old Dan did. He asked her to get one 'fore he passed on, he did, and she asked me to go find him."

Billy whipped up a smile and said, "We both know Old Dan's sin would need a pack mule to carry it," before they both burst into laughter.

Billy turned to the blue sky, sitting behind the canopy of pines. "Well, weather's good. I suppose I'll be paying my respects with ya. You headed back in the morn?"

"That's what I'm planning."

"Let's get ya something to eat. We'll head out together at daylight."

Billy and Mulvaney made their way back with Osborn bringing up the rear. Lincoln paced alongside Osborn's stride.

"You wouldn't believe the size of the elk I came across on the ridge over yonder," he said, gesturing broadly with hands that had seen many a winter. "Antlers like the branches of an old oak."

"Why didn't ya take him?"

"Well, ya see, I ain't got no horse. What d'ya 'spect? Carry him in on my back?"

"You're strong enough, ain't ya?"

Mulvaney cocked his head at Billy. "Why, of all folk, you should know I'm strong enough."

"That was twenty years back," replied Billy.

"At our age, twenty years is yesterday."

"I reckon you'd collapse under that weight before you took two steps," Billy jabbed, his voice a low rumble.

Mulvaney threw back his head and laughed, a sound as hearty as the river's flow. "I believe you are speaking the truth, but it'd be a pack more than you collapsing after taking no steps at all!"

Osborn cocked his head in confusion. The rapid-fire banter between the two men bewildered him, yet he found himself oddly captivated. These apparent long-time friends hurled insults at each other, their laughter punctuating each barbed comment. A strange dance of words he found fascinating.

The three men proceeded to the cabin. Once inside, Billy tended to the fire while Mulvaney slung his bear coat over a wooden chair and settled by the fire with a contented sigh. Osborn occupied himself with dinner preparations, cutting the salted venison. After he finished, he took up his usual place by the window, watching as twilight descended upon the woods. Billy continued preparations, slicing potatoes and onions with a practiced hand.

"So, Billy," Mulvaney said, nodding in Osborn's direction. "What's the story with this greenhorn here?" he asked before shifting to Osborn and saying, "No offense." Not understanding what a 'greenhorn' was, Osborn shrugged.

Billy set a pot of beans over the flames. "He's a greenhorn, that's for certain. But I been learning him. He's a fast learn."

Osborn nodded in agreement.

"How'd he end up here?"

"He's right next to ya. Ask him yourself."

Mulvaney faced Osborn. "How'd you end up here, Greenhorn?"

"Why are you calling me, calling me green…?"

Billy interrupted, "Ya know, it's a sad story, and I ain't gonna hear it twice on this fine eve, so the only thing ya gotta know is that the Pilgrim is a good sort. A bit cumflut—." He stopped himself and swiveled to Osborn, continuing, "A bit peculiar, but a good sort none-the-less."

Mulvaney nodded. "That's all that matters around here, I suppose. What happened to the Injun?"

"The Injun had no kin, and the Pilgrim found him first. He buried him proper and showed him respect. Law of the mountains says the place is his."

"Suppose," said Mulvaney, turning to Osborn. "I weren't saying it weren't, Greenhorn. Just curious is alls."

After the beans came to a boil, Billy handed the plates of food to Osborn and Mulvaney before sitting himself. Osborn threw a piece of venison to Lincoln. He swallowed it in one bite before smiling up at Osborn for more.

"Now ya done it," said Mulvaney. "He'll never leave ya now."

As the three men ate their meals, Osborn suggested, "I, I, I could do it. Could do it, yes."

"Do what?" asked Billy, his mouth full.

"I, could, could do the sin eating for the squaw, for the squaw."

Billy and Mulvaney stopped chewing, looked at each other, and then back to Osborn. "You don't wanna do that, Pilgrim," said Billy before returning to his meal.

Osborn continued, "The, the, the Injun left me his black hat and church clothes. And, and, and I do not, do not believe all that nonsense about sin eating, no."

"But others do, Pilgrim."

"Do you, do you?" Osborn asked Billy.

Billy shook his head. "Tell ya the truth, I ain't sure. But it's one of them things, ya know? One of them things that may be true, and if it is, you should stay clear of it."

"Mr. Mulvaney here said the squaw, the squaw is gonna be mighty disappointed if we arrive without a sin eater, without one, no."

Billy glared at Osborn before asking, "We? You don't even know Old Dan."

"No, I do not, I do not, but I know, I know the squaw."

Billy's head swiveled to Mulvaney, then back to Osborn, as he sat silently, staring down at his plate. "You know the squaw?" asked Billy with a raised voice.

"Well. Well, not personally, but I know her heart, know the loss in her heart, loss in her heart, yes. I know that. I could give solace, solace, yes."

Mulvaney finished his food, scraping the plate with his fork, and sat back in his chair, placing his hands behind his head before responding. "The squaw surely would be in your debt."

"A debt I do not want, I do not want it. I would like to give her a gift, a gift of being her sin eater."

Billy swung to Mulvaney with angry eyes. "Tell this Pilgrim the truth, Mulvaney! This ain't right convincing the man." Billy swiveled back to Osborn, shaking his head. "And I told ya, only drunks or whores do sin eating!"

"The Injun wasn't one of them," interjected Mulvaney.

"Shut your trap, Mulvaney!"

"Yes, yes, the Injun wasn't one of them. And I can have a fine meal. A fine meal with corn, with corn, hopefully. And gravy."

"And the squaw's a fine cook," he said, with a playful twinkle appearing in his eyes. "That's for sure."

"Better to keep your mouth shut and seem a fool than to open it and remove all doubt, Mulvaney!" Billy yelled. "You know he's a greenhorn. He don't know what he's getting himself into."

"I, I can provide solace, solace to a woman in need of it, and I, and I can have a good home cooked meal…"

"From a good cook," Mulvaney again interjected.

"…From a good cook, yes. I believe I am getting myself into, into something I want to get myself into, I believe."

The room fell silent. Billy shook his head and spat into the fire. It hissed like a snake as he disappointedly eyed Mulvaney. Mulvaney shifted uncomfortably in his chair.

"I… I think I'll go to bed now," Osborn said, standing and sitting on his cot. Billy and Mulvaney quietly sat as Osborn undressed to his long johns, removed his spectacles, and placed them delicately on the shelf before pulling the blanket over himself and rolling to his side away from them. Conversation over.

CHAPTER 4

The journey to Old Dan's homestead unfolded in silence, broken only by the rhythmic clip-clop of hooves on the well-worn backwoods trail. Osborn sat astride Junior wearing the Injun's open crown black hat, its weathered brim casting deep shadows across his face. The old black coat hung loosely on his frame as if reluctant to embrace its new owner. Its tattered edges fluttered, whispering secrets of its former master to the indifferent trees.

As they wound their way deeper into the wilderness, Osborn's figure cut a curious blend of the sacred and the profane - part sin eater, part lost soul. The forest seemed to hold its breath around them, the usual birdsongs and rustling leaves muted in deference to the solemn procession.

Osborn's mind wandered to the Injun, wondering if the man had felt this same sense of otherness, of being perpetually out of step with the world around him. There was a comfort in that thought. Here, finally, was a purpose that matched his innate sense of separation from the world. In these clothes, his differences weren't a flaw but rather a necessity.

Billy rode next to him on his horse. Mulvaney walked with Lincoln trotting alongside, occasionally veering off the path to chase fleeting shadows but always returning to Osborn's side.

Eventually, the path led them to Old Dan's home, where he lay. Dan's wife, a Native American of the Shawnee tribe, stood at the threshold for them.

"Where's the sin eater?" she asked.

"Sin eater's dead. Got a new sin eater here," Mulvaney told her, thumbing to Osborn.

"Ma'am," Osborn said as he removed his hat in respect.

Looking Osborn over, she replied, "Don't look like no sin eater."

"He's wearing the sin eater's old clothes. What's a sin eater supposed to look like?"

"I don't know, but not like him."

"Well, this is what ya got, and I got what I said I'd get, so let's get to getting to it," replied Mulvaney before pushing past her into the home.

"Ma'am, I am happy to do it, to do it and offer you solace, solace in your time of need," said Osborn as he held his hat to his chest.

She shook her head and said, "Don't talk like no sin eater either," before turning and heading inside. Billy and Osborn followed her in. Osborn stopped at the threshold and flattened his hand before Lincoln's face. "You stay here. Sit." Lincoln sat, and Osborn patted his head. "Good boy. Stay," he commanded before leaving Lincoln outside.

In the dim candlelight, the shadows danced upon the walls, creating an eerie tableau that matched the somber mood within the home. Old Dan lay on the dining table dressed in his best. Four children, aged five to fourteen, sat on a bench backed against the wall, with another older Native American woman seated near Old Dan's head.

Billy shuffled over to Old Dan, studying his face. Two coins sat on each eyelid. "I'd 'spect Dubois to be here."

"I ain't seen Dubois for some time now," replied Mulvaney. "He might be waiting for Old Dan up theres for all we knows."

"We all are getting old," replied Billy.

Osborn stood in the center of the room as the children huddled together, their small forms barely more than whispers in the gloom. The squaw readied the plate of food on a table in the corner with a stoic grace that seemed to be holding back a flood of sorrow. Osborn felt her gaze on him. "Does he know what to do?" she asked.

"Sit over there, Pilgrim," Billy told Osborn, pointing to the opposite side of

Old Dan. Osborn did as he was told and sat. The body lay inches from him, still and cold. Osborn shifted uncomfortably, his fingers reaching into his pocket to clutch at Lou's brown cloth. The familiar texture between his fingers soothed him.

Billy grimaced as he read Osborn's face. "You sure about this, Pilgrim? It ain't an easy thing."

Osborn's eyes went to the plate of food sitting on the table. "Yes, yes."

With a heavy sigh, Billy capitulated, moving to stand beside Osborn. "Alright, you gotta do this right, if you're gonna do it at all, so I'll learn ya here and now." Osborn nodded, and Billy continued, "First, you sit all quiet-like, just as you're doing."

Osborn did, facing Billy for the next step. "No, no. Close your eyes and think about the weight of what you're about to do." As Osborn did, a shiver ran through him - he wore more than just the Injun's clothes - he was donning an identity, slipping into the skin of a man who had walked between worlds. The fabric seemed to whisper secrets of countless sins consumed, of burdens shouldered in silence.

The squaw brought over a full plate of steaming bread, savory meats, potatoes, and gravy. The children surrounded her as she stood with the plate on the other side of her husband from Osborn.

Billy said, "Alright now, open your eyes. She's gonna pass ya the plate, and you're gonna take it." Osborn's bony fingers wiggled with either fear or anticipation as they took the food. "Now put the plate down before ya." Osborn had only inches remaining to set the plate as the body took up most of the table. Billy rolled his eyes. "Move him over a bit," he told Mulvaney. Staring at the food, Osborn salivated as they slid the body the few inches needed to put the plate down.

Billy said, "Now, before ya eat, ya gotta say, 'I give peace and rest to you...'"

Osborn focused on the food—delicious food he hadn't seen for quite some time. "There's no corn," he murmured.

"Ya gotta repeat after me, Pilgrim," demanded Billy.

Osborn shook his head. "Oh! Yes, yes, what was that again, that again, please?"

Billy started again, "I give peace and rest to you."

Osborn repeated, "'I give peace and rest to you, rest to you, dear man."

Billy glanced back to Mulvaney, trying to remember. Mulvaney stepped up and said, "Go, now, into the waiting arms of your savior..."

Osborn repeated, "Go, now, into the waiting arms, the waiting arms, yes, of your savior, yes."

"And for thy peace. . ."

"And for thy peace. . ."

"I pawn my own soul."

"I pawn my own soul. I pawn my own soul." Osborn stopped, looking to Billy with concern. "I pawn my *soul*?" he asked.

"Yep. Now you can eat, Pilgrim. Eat it all up."

Osborn shrugged before reaching for the first morsel. After the first delicious bite went down, he devoured the remainder without thought. Finishing the plate, Osborn faced Billy and Mulvaney, wearing a Cheshire cat smile.

Their heads swiveled to each other before Mulvaney broke the silence. "Now, ya gotta go, Greenhorn."

"Yeah, wait for us outside, Pilgrim," said Billy, opening the door for Osborn.

"Oh, oh, yes," Osborn said as he stood. The children parted the room for him as he headed for the door. Stepping outside, Osborn swung around to Billy with a questioning expression. "About that, about that pawn my soul part—"

"We'll be out in a bit," interrupted Billy before closing the door on him.

Osborn paced about as he waited for them with Junior and Lincoln. It was afternoon by the time they left the house. Mulvaney stopped just outside the door. "It's time to swap spit and hit the road."

Billy turned to him, "I ain't swapping spit with ya," he said.

"Ha! You'd be missing out!" replied Mulvaney.

"So you say. Where ya off to?" replied Billy.

"Trying new trapping ground, further north, I believe."

"Well, don't squat on your spurs," said Billy, climbing onto his horse.

"Good to see you, Billy," replied Mulvaney before looking at Osborn.

"Thank ya for taking that on, greenhorn. I'm sure she appreciated it."

"You're welcome, Mr. Mulvaney. But I'd like to ask—"

"You didn't do me no favor. You did her one," replied Mulvaney before turning and walking away.

Billy had already mounted his horse and headed toward the cabin. Osborn climbed onto Junior and kicked him to move. Lincoln trotted alongside, tongue lolling and tail wagging with each new scent that caught his attention.

Billy cleared his throat. "You did well back there, Pilgrim."

"I added the 'Dear man,' the 'Dear man' part."

"That was respectful, Pilgrim."

"And, and it was delicious, delicious."

His horse ahead of Osborn's, Billy replied, "I'm sure it was," with his back to him.

"Now, regarding the, the pawning my soul part?"

"Yeah?"

"Yes, yes, the pawn my soul part. I wasn't aware, aware of that part. No, who am I, am I pawning my soul to exactly?"

"Don't rightly know. God, I 'spect. Or the devil."

Osborn's eyes widened. "Now, now, would there be a way, a way to get it out, out of pawn? If I, if I would want that in the future?"

Billy's back still to him, he replied, "Don't rightly know that, neither. But I warned ya, didn't I? Told ya it'd make ya stand apart."

"You did, you did. But it was just the part about, about pawn my soul, yes. I wasn't aware."

"Well, you's eatin' sin, Pilgrim. What was ya thinkin'?"

"No, I'm not certain, not certain, no. And I, yes, and I would like to be with Lou again, Lou again, yes, someday. So, if there's a way, there's a way to get my soul out of pawn?"

"But you knew God don't like sin."

"Well, yes, yes, but Jesus, you see, Jesus, he died for our sins. We all, we all have sins. Jesus died for our sins, so we can, we can see the kingdom of heaven, yes."

"Well, then, there ya go! You won't need to get your soul out of pawn!

You'll see Lou again."

"You think so? It's not too much, too much sin?"

"Jesus is a might powerful, he is."

"But Mulvaney and you said, you said, Old Dan had a pack full, a pack full."

"Just an expression. Like a meta-whatfor. Art of language. And ya know, it ain't an easy thing eating up the earthly burdens of another. God will surely see that, he will. You doing folk a might service. Folk around here need that peace of mind. Knowing their loved ones are going to the Lord unburdened. God will see that kindness."

"I suppose, I suppose, yes," replied Osborn, almost convinced.

"But I have to warn ya. Like I said, you'll be treated different now that ya did that service. You should know that."

"I remember, I remember you told me. I am acquainted with being alone. I've never had many friends, many friends, no. And, and I do not like to touch."

"Yessum. I was about the Injun's only friend. Not that you'd get many folk visiting ya way up here."

"Is that why Mr. Mulvaney parted ways with us?"

"I believe," Billy replied.

"What I don't understand...," Osborn said slowly, "...is why folks would turn their backs on the sin eater. If it's such an important job, shouldn't they, shouldn't they be grateful?"

Billy let out a humorless chuckle. "I believe they are grateful, but after you're done with the meal, best get used to your own company. Ain't many folks will want to cozy up to a man who makes his living swallowing sin. They'll come to you when they're desperate, when they need those sins taken away. But don't expect no invitations to Sunday dinner or the church social."

"I never did, never did. Until I became famous, of course."

Lincoln let out a sharp bark, startling a rustle in the undergrowth. He ran over to it to investigate before returning to Osborn, unsuccessful. Pressing his warm body against Osborn's leg, he scratched the dog's ears. "You will be my friend, won't you, Lincoln?"

"Yessir, you got old Lincoln there, and I'll be stopping by every now and then. If there comes a time I don't, it probably means I'm dead."

Evening light slanted amber through the cabin window, the kind of light that turns everything it touches to gold and memory. As Billy worked the knife through the speckled trout, its scales scattered like tiny mirrors across the wooden counter, catching what light remained of the day.

Billy's eyes kept drawing up to the Springfield mounted above the door. That old rifle. Dark walnut stock with all manner of strange markings cut deep into the wood, symbolizing some story he couldn't read but felt in his bones. The firelight caught the metal parts and made them dance like the gun was alive and watching. He knew the rifle's history. Knew what it could do to a man who carried it without proper right.

Still, his gaze couldn't let the rifle sleep. Something the old Susquehannock had told him years ago started working its way forward in his mind, like a fish moving slow through deep water. Billy's eyes flickered between Osborne and the rifle. "That's a mighty fine piece," Billy said finally, gesturing with his bloody knife toward it.

Osborn grunted, not looking up. "Shame about the curse on it," Billy continued, watching Osborn carefully as a man testing ice. "Though I been thinking on something the Injun told me about it." He set down his knife and wiped his hands slow and deliberate on his pants. "Said the curse never touched him, not once. And he told me why."

It caught Osborn's attention, and he looked up, his eyes dark and questioning in the failing light. "He told me curses ain't nothing but sins gone wrong. Like bad intentions that got stuck to a thing, poisoning it," Billy continued. "Reckon if you was to do your sin eating over that rifle, might be you could draw that poison right out."

The cabin grew quiet then, save for the soft spitting of the fire and the eternal wind in the high places. Osborn studied Billy's face like a man reading signs in the weather. He scratched his chin, considering. "You, you think that would work? Eating the sins, the sins of a gun?"

"What's a curse but a sin that won't let go? We got the ritual. Got the power of a sin eater. All we need's a proper meal to pass over it."

"Why yes, why yes," Osborn replied. "The curse is just another kind of sin, isn't it? It is, yes."

Billy returned to his fish, working the knife with renewed purpose. Osborn rose and began gathering what they'd need - herbs from the dried bundles hanging from the rafters, cornmeal, the last of the wild greens. The cabin filled with the smell of cooking fish, familiar and holy as incense. Outside, night gathered in the hollows between the hills, and somewhere in the darkness, a raven called out three times, like a question being asked and answered all at once.

When the meal was ready, Osborn carefully laid out two tin plates, piling each high with the fragrant fish and a side of wild greens. He placed the plates on one side of the rough-hewn table, then reverently lifted the Springfield from its place on the wall and set it before him.

"All right," Osborn said. "Pass the plate over the gun, and I'll take on, take on its curse."

Billy did as instructed, wafting the aroma of the trout across the rifle's stock and barrel. "You 'member the words, Pilgrim?"

Osborn held the plate above the gun and said, "I do, I do. I give peace, peace, and rest to you, rest to you, dear gun. Go now, go now into the waiting arms of your new owner. And for thy loyalty to him, I shall pawn my own soul. I pawn my soul, yes."

Osborn set the plate down in front of him and took a large bite of the trout, closing his eyes as he savored the rich flavor. If the fish carried any hint of the gun's sin, he could not taste it.

Across the table, Billy smiled at the Springfield before digging into his fish with equal enthusiasm. They ate in contented silence, the only sound the crackle of the fire and the distant hoot of an owl in the woods beyond.

When the plates were clean, Billy picked up the Springfield, running a hand along its smooth stock. "Well, I'll be. It does feel different. Cleaner, somehow." He sat back with a satisfied sigh. "Reckon it's safe for me to take now."

CHAPTER 5

The black buggy creaked along the rutted mountain road, its wheels carving twin trails in the dust. Once a chestnut brown, the horse that pulled it now bore a coat as dark as a moonless night, dye staining its flanks. Black - the color of grief and mourning, perfectly suited to their somber calling.

At no more than six summers old, Dierdre walked beside the horse, one small hand grasping its bit. A wisp of a girl, her raven braids swung with each step, and her slate-gray eyes, far too knowing for her tender years, swept the path before them.

Within the buggy's shadowed confines sat her grandmother, known to all as "The Missus." The name hung in the air of every holler and ridge, whispered with reverence and fear. Charlotte Fenn was her true name, a secret guarded as fiercely as the family's ancient traditions.

For generations, the Fenn women had been the keepers of grief in these mountains. Mothers, daughters, grandmothers - all bore the mantle of The Missus in their turn, their faces forever hidden behind thick black veils. They came to weep for the dead, to bear the weight of sorrow that the living could not carry alone.

Clad in garments dark as sin, The Missus was more shadow than substance. The veil that shrouded her features served to conceal and blur the very concept of time. None could say with certainty whether the figure beneath the cloth was young or old, for in these hills, the Fenns had become something more than mere mortals.

Tales passed from mouth to ear spoke of impossibilities - perhaps there was but one Missus, a single weeper who had cheated death itself.

"Why, looky there," Charlotte murmured.

Hearing her from within the buggy, Dierdre turned. "What?"

"The sin eater."

Dierdre's eyes opened wide, scanning. "Where?!"

"Riding the mule over yonder." Charlotte's hand popped out of the window, pointing to a tall and lanky man with a gray beard riding his mule away from the farmhouse.

Dierdre slumped her shoulders. "Ah, I never get to see one," she said, disappointed.

"A youngin' shouldn't be around no sin eater, child. Don't want any of that sin to rub off on ya." Charlotte squinted hard at the sin eater. "Don't much recognize that one, though."

"Don't recognize him?"

"The sin eater I know is an old Injun," Charlotte murmured as her gaze followed him across the field. "You ain't never seen one?"

"I ain't, and I wanted to," Dierdre replied. "He's never at the remembrances when I'm with Momma."

"That's for the best, I suppose."

"What's they like, Grandma?"

"They's in the same line as us, get as much respect as us, but they's got a darkness around 'em."

"Don't weepers have a darkness around 'em?"

"Suppose folk may think that, but with sin eaters, you can feel it. No one wants to be around a sin eater."

"No one wants to be around us, neither."

Charlotte thought about it. "Hmm, suppose you may be right about that, too."

"That's 'cause I'm smart. What's this sin eater like?"

"Don't know much 'bout that one, but it's been years and years since I seen the one I know. That one must've taken over, I suppose. Thought that boy be dead 'bout now. Maybe I should be checking on him."

Dierdre perked up. "Can I go with ya, Grandma?"

"Lord, no, child. You're too young to be around that kind of blackness."

"You do."

"I'm a weeper. When you're old enough, you'll be a weeper, and you can see one. But never get too close to one. I always keep a distance. Shush now. Can't be talkin' no more."

Dierdre guided the mule to a halt before the weathered farmhouse, its clapboards gray with age and mountain winters. A somber gathering of mourners stood in the yard, their faces etched with curiosity. Dierdre paused, her small form dwarfed by the looming adults, and offered a smile tinged with an otherworldly sadness.

"Might someone help The Missus down?" Dierdre's voice rang out, clear and sweet as a mountain stream, yet carrying an undertone of age-old sorrow. "And her chair needs fetchin', if you please."

Her words stirred the crowd, and a young man, barely more than a boy, stepped forward. His Adam's apple nervously bobbed as he circled the buggy, eyes straining to pierce the veil that shrouded The Missus. With trembling hands, he unlatched the buggy door and lowered the folding steps.

Extending a hand, he waited. The Missus gathered her skirts and accepted his offered palm. She descended with a grace that belied her years, her movements fluid as water over stone. Once on solid ground, she released his hand without a word of thanks, leaving the young man to wonder if he'd touched flesh or merely shadow.

Swallowing hard, the youth pivoted to the buggy's rear. There sat The Missus's chair. It was an ancient thing. Its wood darkened by time and countless vigils. The back was a marvel of craftsmanship, covered in intricate carvings of angels in flight. Their wings seemed to undulate in the light as if poised to bear away the souls of the departed.

The young man lifted the chair with reverence, feeling its weight – not just of wood and nails but of tradition and unspoken power. As he carried it toward the house, whispers rippled through the crowd.

The young man stooped before Dierdre. "I shall secure for The Missus a most fitting place to sit," he assured her. Dierdre accepted his gesture with a silent nod and trailed behind him into the home. Close at their heels, The Missus, her hands demurely joined at her waist, followed them in.

Dierdre searched for a spot next to the departed where the gathered mourners could witness the depths of her grandmother's grief. She pointed to it. "That'll be a fine sitting spot for The Missus to find her sorrow," she declared. Placing the chair down, the young man nodded to The Missus and walked off. Dierdre dragged another chair to a dark corner of the parlor for herself to sit.

As all the Fenn women did before her, The Missus withdrew a black handkerchief from the folds of her dress. Her hand, pale as moonlight, disappeared beneath the veil before her gentle weeping filled the room.

The deceased man's name was Luka Smit, and he lived a life too short. A man cut down in the prime of life at eight and thirty years. He left behind Jenny, his wife, her face a map of grief, and three daughters with eyes wide and uncomprehending in the face of their loss. The Missus knew of the family but did not know them well until two days prior.

As was the custom, the Smit family had sat with The Missus, and they had spun out the tapestry of Luka's life - his first steps on these mountain paths, the day he'd first hefted his daddy's axe, the stolen kisses with Jenny behind the schoolhouse. They spoke of his laugh, which could chase away the dreary mountain mists and his hands, always busy and creating.

Charlotte had listened, her face hidden behind the veil, but her mind drank in every detail and nuance. She had committed each precious memory to heart. A sacred trust passed down through generations of Fenn women.

Now, as Jenny's shoulders shook with silent sobs and the little ones clung to their momma's skirts, The Missus let Luka's life wash over her anew. She wept for the boy who'd climbed the tallest pine to see the sunrise. She mourned for the man who'd built his family's cabin with his two hands, singing as he worked. And she grieved for all the moments that would never be - the grandchildren he'd never bounce on his knee, the gray hairs he'd never earn.

Her tears, falling unseen behind the veil, were as real as the mountain streams. At that moment, The Missus was not just Charlotte Fenn but every woman who had ever loved and lost in these ancient hills. She was the vessel for a community's sorrow, a living link between the world of the living and the realm of those gone before.

The preacher's voice filled the room as it delivered Luka's eulogy. From behind her veil, Charlotte's gaze fixed upon him, her breath catching in her throat. He bore an uncanny resemblance to her one great love in life, Archer True. He stood tall and lean as a young hickory, his frame draped in a well-worn black suit that had seen its share of funerals and weddings alike. His hair was dark as a raven's wing, and Charlotte could almost imagine the trace of pine sap that had always clung to Archer's hair. The preacher's face, smooth-shaven for the solemn occasion, was a canvas of sharp angles softened by those eyes - big, brown, and soulful, just as Archer's had been.

As lovers, they hadn't been together long, and decades had passed since his untimely death, but she remembered him fondly, and the preacher's likeness brought back those memories.

After the eulogy ended, the preacher went to the door to see the mourners out. The widow announced, "Please stay for the potluck meal. It is set up on the lawn." After the preacher greeted the last of the mourners, The Missus nodded to Dierdre. Understanding, Dierdre nodded back and approached the widow beside the preacher. "It'll be time for us to be on our way now. The Missus hopes you be thinkin' she did a right fine job of weepin' for ya."

The widow produced a small smile. "She certainly did, young miss." A pleased smile rose on The Missus under the veil before she rose and stood behind Dierdre.

Dierdre added, "Would ya be so kind as to have someone bring her chair back to our buggy?"

Looking directly at the dark veil of The Missus, the preacher asked, "Why, of course, and would you and The Missus be wanting any fixings from the mercy meal to take along with ya?"

"Thank ya, kindly," replied Dierdre. "but The Missus will not eat while mourning."

The preacher bent down to her, winked, and whispered, "But what about yourself, young miss? How about a piece of cake?"

Dierdre grinned. "Why, I believe that would be nice."

As The Missus made her way to the buggy, a hush fell over the gathered mourners. They parted like water around a stone, their eyes following her black-clad figure with awe and unease.

With a rustle of fabric and the soft creak of wood, The Missus ascended into the shadowy confines of the buggy. The door shut with a soft thud, like the closing of a tomb.

The preacher approached the rear of the buggy. He lifted The Missus's chair with reverence. As he secured it, his eyes darted toward the buggy's curtained window, searching for a glimpse of the woman within.

Dierdre scampered back from the farmhouse, a bundle clutched to her chest. The aroma of sweet cake, a rare treat in these parts, wafted from her hands.

A voice called out from the crowd, rough with emotion and respect, "Lord be with you, Missus." The statement lingered, suspended between blessing and supplication.

Dierdre, her small face solemn, opened the buggy door. The interior was dark as a moonless night, the veiled figure of her grandmother barely discernible. She carefully placed the linen-wrapped cake on the seat opposite The Missus.

Dierdre's slate-gray eyes narrowed as they bore into the mysterious veil. "Don't be eating my cake, Grandma," she admonished with a whisper before closing the door with a decisive click.

Dierdre led the horse out the same way they came in. After passing out of earshot of the farmhouse, Charlotte said, "Don't you get snippy with me, young lady. I'll only have a bite." Dierdre huffed. "Ah, stop, it's only a bite," she added. "Not like I'm taking half."

As the buggy lumbered through the forest, Charlotte removed her veil. Her hair, once as black as a moonless night, now bore streaks of silver. Her slate-gray eyes, mirrored in her granddaughter's gaze, held depths of wisdom and sorrow that belied her forty-eight years.

Dierdre stopped the horse and, as she walked back to the buggy, asked, "Grandma, do you think we'll see the sin eater on the way home?"

Charlotte chuckled, "No, dear. He lives in a different direction."

Dierdre opened the buggy door and switched places with her grandmother, eager to taste the cake. Charlotte took the horse's reins and climbed to the driver's seat.

"But I suppose we should be paying him a visit shortly."

CHAPTER 6

The Fenn farm emerged from the twilight like a half-remembered dream. Five rooms of hand-hewn logs stood sentinel in a clearing carved from the wilderness, forty acres of defiance against the encroaching forest. Tall white pines stood guard on all sides, their branches reaching skyward like gnarled fingers. At the heart of this woodland sanctuary lay twelve acres of tilled earth, a patchwork quilt of crops and possibility.

Across from a garden, a weathered barn hunched against the coming night. Scattered about the property, three smaller cabins dotted the landscape, each a chapter in the Fenn family saga. They stood in various states of repair and decay, silent witnesses to the ebb and flow of generations.

The buggy's wheels crunched to a halt on the gravel path before the barn. Charlotte climbed down and gently patted the horse before meeting Dierdre's gaze. "You did well today, child."

Removing the harness from the horse, Dierdre replied, "Thank you, Grandma."

From the main house, a woman emerged. Her name was Little Miss, Charlotte's daughter and Dierdre's mother, the bridge between generations of Fenn women. At first glance, one might mistake her for a younger version of her mother - the same raven locks, the same piercing gaze. But upon closer inspection, her mismatched eyes, one green and one brown, hinted at a uniqueness all her own.

Little Miss strode purposefully toward her mother, wiping her hands on her apron. "Momma, you're back. How was the remembrance?"

"Same as always," Charlotte sighed. "But I did see something peculiar today."

"We saw it," Dierdre demanded.

Little Miss arched an eyebrow. "Oh? What's that?"

"A sin eater," replied Dierdre before running into the house.

Charlotte finished hanging the bridle on the barn wall. "Ain't never seen him before. Tall, lanky fellow with a gray beard. Riding a mule, no less."

"What about the old Injun?"

Charlotte shook her head. "Haven't seen him in years. Have you?"

Little Miss shook her head. "It's been a while."

"I reckon someone got this old fool into doing the task."

Little Miss followed Charlotte toward the house. "You think the old one's alright?"

"I don't know, but I aim to find out. Thought I might pay him a visit, see how he's faring, if he's faring at all."

"Want me to come with you?"

Charlotte waved her hand dismissively. "No, no. One of us checking on a sin eater is enough. I'm doing it only outta respect for the old Injun. But I'll keep my distance and keep my visit short."

A few days later, the night had already claimed the sky by the time Charlotte's silhouette appeared at the threshold. She paused in the doorway, her eyes adjusting to the dim room, half-submerged in shadow, illuminated only by the flickering dance of firelight and the steady glow of four tallow candles.

"There's a new sin eater up here now," she said as she entered the house and proceeded into her bedroom.

Little Miss sat rubbing her feet in a tub of hot water. "You're home late. Supper's cold by now. It's on the table."

Standing beside her mother, Dierdre said, "We ate without ya, Grandma."

Dropping to her knees, Dierdre massaged her mother's feet in the tub. "Feet hurt, Momma?"

"You're a sweet one. Yessum, a bit."

"Why your feet hurt, Momma?"

"Getting old, I guess."

"You're not old, Momma. You're beautiful."

Little Miss smiled. "And you're sweet as punch."

Charlotte came back into the room, wiping her hands on a cloth. Little Miss turned to her. "You already told me there's a new one. What about the Injun?"

"Injun's dead. New one is living in the Injun's place."

"This old boy didn't do nothing wrong by the Injun, did he?" asked Little Miss.

"I don't believe this ol' boy could burn a tick off a hound. He don't even look ya straight in the eye, he don't. He buried the Injun proper. Saw his resting place myself. Done right and proper."

"I figured that ol' Injun musta passed. He had to be a hundred if a day. Who's this fella? Some ol' carpetbagger?"

"Don't seem so. I didn't stay long enough to find out," Charlotte said as she sat at the table. "Why on earth would someone take on that trade?"

Little Miss dried her feet with a towel. "Sin eaters don't have a place in this world no more."

Dierdre looked up to her mother. "Why, Momma? They eat all the sin up?"

"No, there's more than enough sin to go around the world ten times over. I just 'spose there ain't no work for a sin eater no more. Folks 'round here don't even 'member what a weeper is, let alone a sin eater," replied Little Miss before bringing her curious eyes to her mother. "What's this one look like, Momma?"

"He ain't an Injun. Ain't no carpetbagger, nor a drunk neither. He is a strange one, though."

Dierdre asked, "The sin make him strange, Grandma?"

"No, darlin', this one was strange from the get go, I believe," she replied to Dierdre before redirecting her conversation to Little Miss. "This one moves his gaze about while talkin' to ya, wouldn't look me straight in the eye, something I find mighty peculiar. He's tall and lean, gray hair and a long gray beard. Repeats his words a bit."

Little Miss began to perk up as she listened, eyes narrowing. "Repeats his words, you said? Don't look ya in the eye?" asked Little Miss as she put down her towel and focused in on her mother's words.

"Yessum. And a nervous sort, ya know? Always movin' about." added Charlotte. Trying to recall, Charlotte said, "Said his name was Oz, Oz…"

"Osborn," interrupted Little Miss.

Charlotte faced her, nodding. "That's it. Osborn."

Little Miss's jaw fell. "Osborn Roche. I know that man. What's he doing up there, I'll never know."

Charlotte raised her head and looked down the bridge of her nose to Little Miss. "You know him?"

"I met him before. I know who he is," replied Little Miss as she faced the fireplace. "Osborn Roche is his name. He's a world-famous photoman. You know, those tintype makin' men." Little Miss glanced back to her mother. "He tell you that? That he's a world-famous tintype man? That ol' boy's takin' portraits of Presidents and the like. He did a portrait of President Lincoln's dead boy, Willy, if I recall."

"What's a photo, Momma?" asked Dierdre.

"It's called a photograph, and he uses a special box to like draw ya. Except it's the light of the day that draws ya onto this special metal he uses. It's real special. Makes a portrait out of ya. Something you can remember for a long time."

"World famous, you say?" asked Charlotte. "What's he doing being a sin eater then?"

"Don't know about that, but he is famous. Most famous man doing what he does."

"Surely won't be famous no more being a sin eater," said Charlotte. "How'd you meet him years back?"

"He passed through here a few years back."

Charlotte's eyes strolled over her daughter. "You have a recollection of everyone that passes through here?"

Little Miss shrugged. "Wouldn't you if you'd met someone world famous?"

"Suppose."

"He also had his nephew, Ray, with him. Ray took a shine on me. He was a good one," she said, nodding to Dierdre on the floor. "But your father took my heart."

"My father?" asked Dierdre.

"Yep."

Charlotte smirked and said, "Went down the wrong fork on that one."

Dierdre's head snapped toward Charlotte. "Why was it down the wrong fork, Grandma? Would I still be me if Momma had married this nephew fella?"

"No, suppose ya wouldn't," said Charlotte, displaying a grin for Dierdre. "Praise the Lord for small miracles."

"I suppose I should go on up theres to be seeing to the which of the why," said Little Miss.

"You gonna see the new sin eater, Momma?" asked Dierdre.

"Suppose I should. He and his nephew worked together. Hope nothing happened to that boy. Ray took care of Osborn like he was his father."

"Can I go with ya, Momma?"

"You can. I could use the company."

Charlotte slammed her hand on the table. "She cannot!"

Little Miss flinched before cocking her head and asking, "And why not?"

"She's too young to be around a sin eater. She ain't no weeper yet."

Little Miss waved it off. "Oh, poo! I do not believe in all that foolishness. Thane was a sin eater for a time."

"Thane! If I would've known that sooner, he would've been gone a might before that! Thane, spreading his sins all about the place without me even knowing! And you let him do it. Shame!"

"Shame on me, Momma? Shame on you for telling 'em to leave. Thane and Easter had been living here all their lives, and you go off and tell them to get off yo' land. That's a shame."

The room fell into a silence so thick you could cut it with a knife. The only sound was the soft crackle of the hearth fire for a full minute. Little Miss rose to her feet. "Momma," she began, her voice steady but with an undercurrent of frustration, "I don't see the harm in Dierdre coming along. She could keep her distance, just as you taught me when I was young."

Charlotte's face hardened, the lines around her mouth deepening. "She ain't been a weeper yet," she said, her tone brooking no argument. "Too young to be around all that sin. Besides, the horse is needed for plowing come morning."

Little Miss let out an exasperated sigh, rolling her eyes. "The field can wait a day. I'll plow it the day after tomorrow."

Sensing an opportunity, Dierdre piped up eagerly, her ponytails bouncing enthusiastically. "I can help her do it, Grandma!"

"Now you listen here," she said, her voice as sharp as a winter wind. "You ain't taking that horse at all if Dierdre's going. Not tomorrow, not the day after, not ever. This ain't up for discussion." She brought her hand down on the table with a resounding thwack. "I'm The Missus of this family, and my word is final. Dierdre's too young, and that's the end of it. You want to go traipsing off, you do it on your own two feet, but you leave that child here where she belongs."

At fifteen, Little Miss inherited the mantle of The Missus from her mother, a transition as inevitable as the changing of seasons. The art of lamentation had been woven into the fabric of her existence since childhood, a legacy passed down through generations of women in her family. Micah, their freedman whose weathered hands bore the marks of a lifetime of service, had guided her through the intricate rituals alongside her mother.

"You have a gift, child," Micah would often murmur, his dark eyes glinting with a mixture of pride and something deeper, more melancholic. "The spirits themselves weep when you keen." His words, tinged with the cadence of his homeland, would echo in Little Miss's mind long after he had spoken them, a haunting refrain that both comforted and disquieted her.

As she honed her skills, Little Miss began to understand that her role as a weeper was not merely a performance but a sacred duty. She was a bridge between the living and the dead, her tears a balm for wounds that ran deeper than flesh and bone. And with each passing day, each remembrance at which she keened and wailed, she felt herself being shaped by the weight of this responsibility, molded into something both more and less than the girl she had once been.

During her years of weeping, it was Thane who bore the burden of consuming the sins of the departed. Little Miss had observed him at a handful of remembrances, his presence a stark counterpoint to her own role in the proceedings.

As the fourth hour of her journey along the winding mountain path drew to a close, the melodious gurgle of the river reached her ears. The air grew heavy with moisture, carrying the earthy scent of damp leaves and rich soil. Rounding a bend in the trail, tendrils of smoke became visible above the treeline, weaving through the branches like spectral fingers. The path opened onto a clearing, and there, nestled against the riverbank, stood a sight like something plucked from the pages of Hansel and Gretel. As ancient as the forest itself, the log cabin seemed to have sprouted from the earth, dwarfed by towering red pines that stretched skyward, their uppermost branches lost in a canopy of green a hundred feet above. Its moss-covered walls blended seamlessly with the surrounding landscape, making it difficult to discern where nature ended and human craft began.

Little Miss pulled up the reins and climbed off. Leading the horse to the front, she heard a man's voice call out, "Hey bear, hey!" Little Miss froze before letting go of the reins and ducking behind a tree. Peeking around it, she saw him. It was the man she knew, Osborn Roche, his beard now longer and streaked with gray. He sat on his mule, staring into the open cabin door as the mule backed up. A hound dog near him growled at something inside the cabin. Osborn threw the reins over an arm and clapped his hands. "Hey bear, hey!"

A crash came from within the cabin before a red-eyed black bear peeked out the door, searching. The hound dog began hysterically barking as Osborn called out, "Hey bear, hey!" again before the bear ran straight out of the cabin toward him. His mule whirled around to its side as the bear leapt up. Osborn raised his leg and kicked the bear in the face, only stopping its advance for a second. With Osborn clinging on, his mule took off toward Little Miss with the bear in chase. With a swipe of her massive claw across its hind end, the mule stopped and kicked with its powerful rear legs, smashing into the face of the bear. The bear's head snapped back, and its mammoth weight followed, rolling across the dirt.

The mule hee-hawed over and over as the bear slowly rose. "Let's go, Junior, let's go!" Osborn demanded, slamming his heels into his side and trotting past Little Miss, hiding behind the tree. The dog barked and nipped at the bear as it shook its injured head, spun around, and limped away in the opposite direction. The dog trotted after Osborn only to suddenly stop upon seeing Little Miss. Fearing a bite, she froze as it smelled her for a second before continuing on its way.

Little Miss calmed herself, inhaling slowly before cautiously stepping out from behind the pine and walking toward the cabin. She stopped before the door, eyes scanning the direction Osborn rode off.

Crossing her arms, Little Miss stepped inside the dimly lit cabin. Her eyes searched the interior wide with curiosity as she took in the unfamiliar surroundings. She wandered around, running her fingers over everything.

As she settled on the cot, Little Miss drew in a long, steadying breath. "I guess I'll wait a bit."

CHAPTER 7

With Lincoln trotting next to them, Osborn returned to the cabin, Junior's head bobbing up and down. Osborn's fingers idly combed through the mule's coarse mane, a habit born of long companionship. "You never cease to amaze me, Junior," Osborn mused aloud. "Always finding your way home, no matter how tangled these mountain trails get. How do you manage it, old friend?" He chuckled. "You're a good mule. Yes, you are." Junior, true to his nature, offered no response to the praise. "Makes me wonder why I even bother with this bridle."

As they rounded the final bend, the cabin came into view. Osborn's easy smile faded, and his face pinched with concern. The cabin door still stood ajar, swaying in the mountain breeze, its hinges creaking.

"Oh no. Not again," Osborn muttered, pulling Junior to a stop. He cautiously guided Junior to the right, taking a wide path to peer into the open doorway from a safe distance.

Osborn clapped his hands, his voice ringing out, "Hey bear, hey!" Lincoln's ears pricked forward, his muscular body coiled and ready to spring to his master's defense. Osborn's hand instinctively moved to his hip, where his knife hung at the ready.

But instead of the lumbering form of a bear, Little Miss stepped into the sunlight, her mismatched eyes squinting against the sudden brightness.

"Mr. Roche?" Osborn knitted his brows as if he hadn't heard his name in years. "Mr. Roche, it's me, Little Miss. You met my momma yesterday." Osborn dismounted and removed Junior's harness. No one had ever entered his cabin except for Billy and Mulvaney. Everyone else was too scared to do it. "We've met before," she continued. "You came to our farm with your nephew, Ray."

Osborn patted Junior to walk off to the pasture. "I, I remember you, yes. That was your mother yesterday. Oh, alright. Yes, I remember you were a weeper too, a weeper too. Just like her, yes."

Little Miss's forehead creased with concern as she studied Osborn's gaunt face. "You remember?"

"Of course, I remembered. I have a good memory, a good memory, yes. Didn't put two and two together, though. Two and two about her being your mother, no. Two and two, no." With the precision of a military parade, Osborn spun on one heel and headed for the cabin. She followed him in.

Osborn busily prepared a pot of coffee. "I have coffee, coffee, yes. I traded a miner for it, a miner for it. He only wanted a tin cup. You may sit on the bed, on the bed, if you wish."

Little Miss sat on the cot, her eyes darting around the cabin, taking in the sparse furnishings and the layer of dust that seemed to coat everything. She couldn't help but wonder how long he had been living like this. She flinched at the sight of the mounted boar's head, its glass eyes seeming to stare right through her.

Through a side glance, Osborn turned to it. "Yes, yes, taxidermy is like embalming, like embalming. Lou was an embalmer, yes, Lou was, yes."

"Lou, was? Where is Lou, Mr. Roche?"

Osborn spread his hands across the sky again, saying, "Lou is gone from this world but alive again in my heart. I embalmed her. I did it. I embalmed her, yes. Lou taught me."

Osborn rotated to the cabinet, pulled out two tin cups, and set them on the table. Sitting on a stool, his eyes locked on the coffee pot as he waited for it to boil. "I'm sorry to hear that, Osborn."

Taking the coffee pot over to the fireplace, he set it on the metal hanger and swung it over the fire. "I'm sorry to hear that, too," he said as he stared at the flames.

"Is Lou buried around here?"

"Down the road a piece, I'd say. I'd say, yes, about a forty-five-minute walk or, or a little less with Junior, yes. I see her every sunny day, not rainy days or snowy days, no, but often and..." Osborn jerked his head away, avoiding eye contact. His hands rose to his stomach with his fingers nervously tapping each other.

"Mr. Roche, what are you doing here? Where's Ray?"

"Ray is in Pittsburgh. In Pittsburgh, yes. Ray would remember you, too. Ray was sweet on you, I believe, sweet on you."

An inkling of something - nostalgia, perhaps - crossed her face, quickly replaced by concern for the present. Little Miss smiled. "Ray was a good man."

"Ray was and is a good man, a good man, yes. He courted you, he courted you."

"We did for a short time, but someone else ended up in my life."

Osborn stood staring at the coffee pot, swaying his hips. "Oh, too bad, too bad."

"When was the last time you saw your nephew, Ray?"

Osborn faced her with a smile that fell as fast as it rose. "It's been some time, some time, yes. I was planning on one year of mourning, one year. But, yes, that has turned into five, into five, I'm afraid, yes."

A whistle of steam came from the pot. Osborn whirled around to it, picked up a rag, and brought it from the fire to the cups on the counter. He poured the coffee with precise motions and pivoted to Little Miss with two cups in his hands, handing one to her.

"Thank you." She took a sip, more out of politeness than thirst, her mind clearly preoccupied with the man before her.

"You are welcome. I'm glad you came. Yesterday, your mother, your mother, was the first visitor I've had for a while besides requests for sin eating, requests for sin eating, yes. I don't get any visitors. No visitors, no."

"You ain't gonna get no visitors being the sin eater, that's for sure."

"Yes, yes, because, because I have pawned my soul, yes. I wish to get it out of pawn, yes. But, Trapper Billy, Trapper Billy will visit. He came again last year.

Your mother would not come in for coffee. She would not. She would only speak to me outside."

"It's because you're a sin eater. How'd you get into that line?" she asked softly, leaning in closer. Her eyes were kind but probing, seeking to understand the path that had led Osborn to this solitary existence.

"Originally, it was to help a woman in distress, in distress, like me, like me, yes. I, I also thought sin eating might provide me a sense of purpose, sense of purpose, yes. And, and the food is good, yes."

"Someone teach you the trade?"

"Yes, yes. Trapper, trapper Billy, yes." Wisps of steam, carrying the smell of the coffee, swirled up and eased the peculiarity of the room. "The sin eater's clothes were here in the cabin, under the bed, under the bed. The pants are too short."

"Mr. Roche, does Ray know you're here?"

"No, no."

"Do you want me to tell him you're here?"

"Yes, yes, that would be nice. I would love to see Ray, love to see him. I have no visitors. I'm glad you came, yes."

"Why haven't you visited him? You still have that fancy red wagon?"

"The Romani vardo was shattered, shattered in the river. I saved Hoady Junior from drowning."

"Hoady Junior?" asked Little Miss.

"Hoady Junior, my mule. You remember Hoady, the first Hoady, when I met you, met you?"

"I remember your mule. Didn't remember his name."

"Hoady was his name. But he passed on, passed on, yes. It made me quite sad. Quite sad, indeed. But my new mule is just as smart. I call him Hoady Junior, yes. I call him Hoady Junior."

"Why don't you take Hoady Junior to see Ray?"

"I can't leave Lou. Can't leave Lou, no. I had told myself that I would grieve for a year. I know, I know it is not logical and I am a logical man. One year of mourning, I told myself, yes. But I still find it difficult to leave both of them, leave both of them, yes. And I have adjusted to this life, adjusted to it."

"Both of them?"

"I can't leave our son. No, no, can't leave our son too. We watch him together."

Little Miss's eyes opened. "Your son? You… you had a child? Is he buried next to Lou?"

"No, no, he is not dead. He lives in the house, in the house in front of Lou's grave. Her father's house, Henry Cattell's house."

Little Miss cocked her head, confused. "Your son is alive and living in Lou's father's house? Less than an hour from here?"

"Yes, yes. We see him on occasion, on occasion, yes."

"Oh, so Lou's father knows you live here?"

"Oh no, no he does not know. I buried Lou beyond the treeline, in a place Henry cannot see, cannot see from his house. Henry wanted to take Lou from me, take Lou, yes."

Little Miss shook her head, her mind reeling. "But Lou is gone now, and he has your son?"

"Henry is a powerful man, and Henry does not like me, does not like me, no. But he is a good grandfather. I see him. He is a good grandfather. Lou and I can be together and watch our son playing in the backyard. We see as he grows older and taller." Osborn dropped his head. "I see Lou in his face," Osborn said as his eyes welled. "Lou in his face, yes."

Ray Roche, Fotografer, Pitsburg, Pennsilvana

Dear Ray,

I hope Pitsburg ain't such a big city that this letter can't find you. Plees write me back so that I know you receeved it. I hope you're doing all rite. I know it's been a while since we seen each other, but I got somethin real important to tell you. Your Uncle Osborn has been living up in the woods not too far from my family's farm.

I reckon you know your uncle's been having a real tuff time since his wife passed on. Seems like losing her made him want to hide away from the world, and now he's living in a tiny cabin, keeping an i on Lou's grave.

I think your uncle could really use some family right about now. As his kin, you mite be the only one who can get him to come back home and be with fokes who care about him.

I know coming all the way from the city ain't no small thing, but if you decide to make the trip, I'd be more than happy to show you the way to your uncle.

Plees think on it, Ray. Your uncle's a rite talented and respected fella, and it just breaks my heart to know he's suffering all by his lonesome.

If you're fixing to come, just send word.

Your friend,

Little Miss

Little Miss squinted at the letter, chewing on her bottom lip. Before she could change her mind, she folded up the letter, sealed it, and wrote out the only address she knew: Ray Roche, Pittsburgh, Pennsylvania. Standing up from the table, she grabbed her shawl and headed out. Johnstown post office was a half-day ride.

CHAPTER 8

Little Miss strained against the harness that bound her to the horse and the plow. Her bare feet sank into the loose soil of the field as her calloused hands struggled to keep the implement steady. Dierdre followed behind, dropping seeds and punching them into the soil with a stick as Charlotte pulled stones from the nearby field.

"Almost done here," Charlotte called out, her voice strained from the physical exertion. "Then we can get cleaned up before the day gets too hot."

As they reached the end of the row, Little Miss and Dierdre paused to catch their breath. The horse snorted and stomped its hoof, eager to continue. A sudden movement in the distance caught Little Miss's eye – a figure approaching on the dusty path leading to the farm. She squinted against the sunlight, trying to make out who it was.

She recognized him as Ezra Jameson, a portly man with a bushy mustache. As he neared the garden, Ezra tipped his hat before holding a folded letter clutched in his calloused hand. "Mornin', ladies," he said, his voice thick with the twang of the countryside. "Got a letter here for the Little Miss, it says. The postmaster asked me to drop it off on my way."

Charlotte rose, brushing the dirt from her skirts. "Much obliged, Ezra," she said, accepting the letter with a warm smile. "We don't get into town much these days."

"Thank ya kindly, Mr. Jameson," said Little Miss.

"No trouble at all. You ladies have a good day now." Mr. Jameson tipped his hat and rode off.

Charlotte brought the letter over to Little Miss. "What is it, Momma? Who's the letter from?" asked Dierdre.

Little Miss turned the letter over in her hands, her heart skipping a beat when she saw Ray Roche's name on the return address. "Who's it from?" repeated Dierdre.

"From Ray, the sin eater's nephew," she absently replied before tearing open the envelope and reading.

Pittsburgh, Pennsylvania

August 10, 1871

My Dear Little Miss,

I was pleased to receive your letter telling me about my uncle Osborn. I will be coming up on Tuesday the 16th to see him. I would be obliged if you would be so kind as to show me where he is living. I look forward to seeing you.

Yours,

Ray.

Little Miss's eyes widened, a sudden realization dawning across her features. "'Momma," she breathed, "what day is it?"

Charlotte hefted and threw the stone in hand. "Two days after the Lord's day, so it be Tuesday," she replied as she bent down for another one.

"The 16th?" Little Miss pressed, a note of desperation creeping into her voice.

Exasperation colored Charlotte's expression. "Now, how would I know that?"

Little Miss glanced down at her attire, taking in the dirt-stained fabric with mounting horror. A wave of panic washed over her.

Charlotte, noticing Little Miss's distress, walked over to her. "What's the matter?" she asked, her voice low and tinged with concern.

"It's Ray," Little Miss said, her voice trembling. "He's coming today, and I'm not even close to being presentable."

Charlotte wiped the sweat from her forehead with her dress sleeve. "That the boy that took a shine to ya?"

"That was a few years back, Momma. Married by now, I 'spect."

Charlotte took the letter from Little Miss's hands and read it. "Well, then," she said, as her features softened into the beginnings of a smile. "You best get cleaned up. Can't have you looking like a field hand when a married man comes to call," Charlotte said with a mischievous grin.

Little Miss sneered at her mother. "You surely are pleased with yourself."

An inquisitive gleam appeared in Dierdre's eyes. "Why does Momma need to get all dressed up for the sin eater's nephew, Grandma?"

Charlotte chuckled. "Oh, my dear girl," she said, patting Dierdre on the head. "You'll understand when you're older."

"I can hear a horse a coming," said Charlotte as she exchanged a knowing glance with Little Miss, both women rising from their weathered porch chairs in unison. The heat from the late afternoon sun cloaked a man on a horse. Even at this distance, there was no mistaking that shock of flame-red hair.

"It's Ray," Little Miss breathed.

"You should go on in. I'll greet him," said Charlotte.

"No need for formalities, Momma. He's just an old friend."

"An old friend that you needed to get gussied up for."

"Shush, Momma."

"I'm guessin' you don't need no chaperon since he's married and all," Charlotte teased with a wink before rising and heading into the house.

Little Miss inhaled deeply, steadying her nerves as she tucked a wayward strand of hair behind her ear. Her heart pounded in time with the approaching hoofbeats as she made her way up the dusty road.

Suddenly, the screen door banged open. Dierdre burst from the house, her tiny legs furiously pumping as she raced to catch up. "That him, Momma?" she panted, her wide eyes glued on the approaching rider.

"Yes, the sin eater's nephew. His name is Ray."

Ray materialized before them, the setting sun casting a halo around his fiery hair. He cut a striking figure atop his mount, clad in a crisp gray suit and a canary-yellow vest underneath. His warm and familiar smile stirred long-buried memories in Little Miss's heart. "It's been a while, Little Miss," Ray called out. "How you been?"

She returned his smile as he dismounted. "I'd say it has been some time. Don't you look like a gentleman, Ray. A fine gentleman."

Ray smiled at Dierdre. "And who is this pretty young lady?"

"My name is Dierdre, young sir."

"Young sir? What fine manners you have, young lady. I can see you didn't get your mother's eyes, but you surely took on her beauty."

Dierdre grinned as Little Miss smirked. "Ah, Ray, there ya go with those compliments again. Like they never stopped from all those years back."

Ray shrugged. "Compliments aren't compliments if they's truths. I'd say they were truths, is all."

"Come on, let's get you something to nibble on. I'm sure you're hungry."

"I'm hungry too, Momma." Dierdre started off in front of them.

"Is Augustus around?" asked Ray.

Dierdre spun around, "You knew my daddy?"

Ray quickly glanced at Little Miss, a question on his face. "I'm sorry."

Little Miss swung her head back to Dierdre. "Ray met him once. Now, Dierdre, I gotta speak on some matters with Mr. Ray for a bit. You run on in and help Grandma with fixing the table."

"Momma…" she pleaded.

"Go on now."

Dierdre grimaced and ran off. Ray dropped his head. "Something happen to him?"

Little Miss stopped and faced him. "Nothing happened to him. After you left Johnstown, it didn't work out with Augustus and me. Ray. I, I, I just can't tell ya, Ray. It ain't good, and I just can't tell ya. As far as Dierdre knows, her father died in the war before she was born. Now come on in and put something in your belly." Dierdre waited for them on the veranda step in the distance. "She's sure pleased we have a guest," said Little Miss. "What about you, Ray? You have any children?"

"Ever since I got to Pittsburgh, I never had time to court. My daguerreotype shop kept me busier than a funeral home fan in July."

"That's surprising. You were such a charmer when I met ya."

"I still am, but only to the fillies that suit my taste."

"I'm certain there are plenty of fillies in the big ol' city."

"Why can't I go, Momma?" Dierdre stood on their veranda with her hands on her hips and pursed lips. Charlotte stood behind her, silently disapproving.

Little Miss shook her head at her mother before kneeling down to address Dierdre. "Now, you know I'd let you come if I could, but we're taking Mr. Ray's horse to get there before noon." As she spoke, Ray brought his mare up to the porch.

"I can run alongside."

"No, you can't. You'd have a hitch in your get-along just past the farm."

"We can take our horse, and he can ride his horse," explained Dierdre.

Little Miss smiled at her daughter. "Grandma needs our horse today. You heard her. Now, that's enough." Dierdre frowned and stomped into the house.

Ray settled into the saddle, then extended his hand toward Little Miss. "Stick your foot in the stirrup and take my hand."

She returned his smile with a doubting smirk. "I believe I'll fetch a stool." Little Miss walked off to the house, returning moments later with a wooden stool. Setting it next to the porch railing, Little Miss stepped up onto it, then climbed further onto the edge of the porch. Carefully turning, she held her back against the railing, only her heels gripping the porch edge. "Come on over and get me."

Ray led the mare over to her and pulled alongside. Little Miss stood at eye level with him. "I suppose that'll work," he said.

Little Miss put one hand on his shoulder and, with a small jump, threw one leg over and plopped behind him on the horse's rear. "I suppose it did," she replied, putting her hands on the back of the saddle to steady herself.

The forest enveloped them like a living, breathing entity, its ancient boughs stretching overhead to form a verdant canopy that dappled the sunlight into shifting patterns on the forest floor. Ray and Little Miss followed a narrow trail that wound through the wilderness, a ribbon of earth leading to the cabin.

"When I met ya, those years back, I thought your momma had passed," Ray recalled. "You were the lady of the house back when we passed through."

"I was," replied Little Miss as she moved her hands from the back of the seat to rest lightly around Ray's waist. "When I was young, about Dierdre's age, we moved from this farm to live in West Virginia for a time. When I was fifteen or so, my momma and her husband were planning to move to Petersburg, Virginia. He had a gun making business. Because of the war, they sent me back here to the farm. I took over the weepin' from my cousin, Janey, who I believe you met."

"I don't recall."

"Yeah, she was living here then. But after the war, my momma came back here."

"With her husband?"

"Naw, he was dead."

As they rode deeper into the heart of the forest, the trail narrowed further, forcing them to duck beneath low-hanging branches. The undergrowth grew thicker, a tangle of brambles and young saplings fighting for space and sunlight.

"Ray, I always wanted to tell ya," Little Miss began, trying to find the right words. "I was awful sorry about…well, maybe the way I treated ya back then."

"You mean how you tossed me aside for Augustus?" His face swiveled to her with a mischievous grin.

Little Miss replied with a smirk and a slap to his shoulder. "Now, you! I was trying to be earnest."

"I'm just playing. I know you can't win 'em all. Besides that, it made me move back to Pittsburgh, where I should've been. I don't think my business would've grown as large as it has without that. Providence, maybe."

Little Miss encircled her arms around his waist again. "Well, that's fine then, but I just wanted ya to know I apologize for my manners back then. I always wanted to tell ya."

"You couldn't help your feelings for him. I get that, and for my part, I saw that flicker in your eye for him. I ignored it, though. That was my fault," Ray said before changing the subject. "So, how long did my uncle say he has been living here?"

"He didn't say."

"He went missing after Lou passed. That was six or seven years back."

"You know he has a son? He told me so, Ray."

"I know. It's how Lou passed on, bringing him into the world. Henry Cattell, Lou's father, is raising him now. Abigail, Abigail is the one who wrote me."

Pleasantly surprised, Little Miss slapped his shoulder. "Oh, Abigail. How'd she fare? Sweet little thing."

"She is a good one. I believe my uncle and Lou became her family, like the parents she never knew. She felt close to both of them. I asked her to keep an eye on them, and she did, traveling the country with them. She ended up marrying a Cherokee man and now lives with the Cherokee. Quite an extraordinary story."

"I'll be! Married a Cherokee man. I'll be."

"Yep, sure did," replied Ray.

"Good on her," said Little Miss, feeling the warmth of his body through his coat. "She deserves to be happy."

The forest seemed to close in around them, a world unto itself where the concerns of civilization felt distant and insignificant. Little Miss held her breath at times, half-expecting to catch a glimpse of some magical creature darting between the trees.

"I want to thank you for finding my uncle and writing me that letter."

"Least I could do, Ray."

"You know, Little Miss, in its way, it's quite fortunate that you found my uncle. If it weren't for that, I might have never heard from you again, and I'm mighty pleased I have."

Little Miss smiled, a warmth spreading through her chest. "I'm pleased to see you again as well, Ray. So tell me about city life. What's it like in a big city?"

Ray let out a small laugh. "City life is a world away from what we have here. It's busy, always bustling with people and noise. Pittsburgh has become a mighty big town."

"I can only imagine."

"My business there is booming, and I owe that to my uncle. It's his fame that has helped the business grow into what it is today, I tell you. Nobody knew who Osborn Roche was in Johnstown. Everyone knows his name in Pittsburgh. What about you? How's life been treating you?"

"Oh, you know, tending to the farm, there's always something to keep ya busy."

"Still weeping?"

"Occasional. Momma does it mostly, but the family trade is slowing. Folk don't have no need for weepers no more. My daughter might be the first Fenn that ain't a weeper, I believe."

Arriving at the cabin, Ray put his hand back to her. "Give me your hand, and I'll let you down."

"This sure is a tall horse," she said. "Two hands taller than ours."

"I got you. Come on down." Little Miss took a breath before swinging her leg off and sliding down the horse's rear. "Why, you're just a wisp of a thing now, aren't ya?" he said as he lowered her gently to the ground. They walked over to the cabin door and knocked—no answer. He opened it—empty. "Where do you think he is now?" asked Ray.

"He visits Lou's grave every sunny day, he told me. He said he buried Lou right behind her father's house, and they watch their son together."

Ray whirled his head to her. "Henry Cattell lives near here?"

"Oh! I forgot to tell you. Yes, an hour's walk from here, according to your uncle. And he's been watching his son grow up."

Ray's eyes narrowed while shaking his head. "Watching him…?"

"Yessum, that's what he says."

"Does Henry know?"

"No. Mr. Roche says he hides behind the trees and watches through an eyepiece."

Ray walked to the open doorway and stared out. "What ya pondering on?" she asked.

Ray glanced back at Little Miss with a question on his face. "You ever met the Cattells?"

"Heard of 'em, but never had the pleasure. He's one of the high fallutin' folk in Johnstown. Rich enough to eat his laying hens, is what I heard. Why?"

"I'm just confused as to why my uncle is spying on him and hasn't taken his son back. It's *his* son."

CHAPTER 9

Osborn shuffled along the dirt path, his hands halfheartedly brushing at the grime on his pants. His daily trek had carved the trail into the earth over six years. Each step carried him from the loneliness of his cabin to the solemn ground where she rested. The journey there gave Osborn time to collect his thoughts and musings he'd share with her. On the way back, he would recall Ishmael's play time on the back lawn.

As the cabin came into view, Osborn approached the grass-covered mound that marked the Susquehannock's grave. An old cross stood sentinel at its head, its wood grayed and weathered by countless seasons. Without breaking his stride, Osborn's hand reached out, tapping the cross's peak – a gesture as natural to him now as breathing. "Afternoon," he said as he passed.

Lincoln bolted ahead, his canine energy propelling him toward the cabin. "What's the..." the words dying on his lips as he froze mid-step. At first glance, the well-dressed figure greeting Lincoln at the doorway was a stranger to Osborn's eyes: the height, the build, that unmistakable shock of red hair. Recognition dawned like the first rays of sunrise. Ray.

Osborn's feet moved before his mind could catch up, breaking into a run. Tears welled in the corners of his eyes, carving tiny rivulets through the dust on his cheeks. A smile bloomed on Ray's lips as he steadied himself for impact.

Osborn's arms rose, reaching out like a man grasping for a lifeline. He collided with Ray, enveloping him in an embrace that spoke of years of longing and loss. The force of their reunion sent them stumbling back into the cabin, nearly toppling over in a tangle of limbs and emotions.

"Whoa, Uncle! You almost..." Ray's words cut short as Osborn's tears soaked into his shoulder, the older man's grip unyielding.

"I missed you too, Uncle."

Osborn could only respond with sniffles, his emotions too raw and overwhelming for words. Ray's eyes flickered to Little Miss, who stood in the doorway, her own eyes glistening. She wiped at her cheeks, brushing away tears.

A full five minutes passed before Osborn's arms finally loosened their hold. He stepped back, his hands still gripping Ray's shoulders, as if afraid his nephew might vanish if he let go completely. His eyes, red-rimmed but shining with joy, searched Ray's face, drinking in every detail of the man his nephew had become.

"How, how are you, Ray?"

"I'm very well, Uncle."

"Would you like me to make some coffee? I traded a miner, a miner for it, yes." Osborn spun around to the counter.

"I would like some, yes," said Ray, following with Little Miss and Lincoln in tow.

Osborn turned to Little Miss. "Would, would you...?"

"Please," said Little Miss as she sat on his bed.

With a big smile, Osborn got to work making the coffee. "Uncle, I'm very sorry to hear about Lou. Very sorry."

"You should not be sorry, not sorry. You should be sad. Yes, sad. Like I am."

"Yes, I am sad. Very sad," said Ray with a look back to Little Miss. "Why didn't you contact me? Why didn't you come home?"

"I wanted to stay with her for a year of mourning, a year of mourning, yes. But a year passed, Ray and I was still here and became accustomed to life here. I cannot leave Lou, Ray. Cannot leave her and our son."

"Why don't you..."

"And, of course," interrupted Osborn. "I have become the sin eater, the sin eater for these parts."

Ray shook his head. "What's a sin eater?"

Little Miss flinched. "Oh! I guess, I mean, I guess we didn't talk about that."

"Talk about what?"

"Well, I'll be tellin' ya then. That's how we found your uncle."

"Yes, that's how they found me, Ray."

"My Momma was weepin' at a remembrance and saw there was a new sin eater, and she came up to see on the old sin eater..."

Osborn interjected, "He was dead. I buried him, I buried him."

"And she came back and described him, and I knew it was your uncle right off, just by the description."

Ray laughed. "Well, what is it? What is a sin eater?"

Little Miss's eyes fell to her lap. "It ain't something to laugh about, Ray."

Osborn brought the coffee pot to the fireplace. "No, I provide, I provide a solemn and necessary service, service, yes. With my sacrifice, I consume the darkness so others, so others might walk in light."

Confused, Ray faced Little Miss. "Well, then, how does he do that?"

"Well, you know how I'm a weeper, or was, if I ever do it again, but anyhow, like a weeper, folks hire a sin eater for a remembrance. A sin eater will sit and eat a meal from a plate that is passed over the body of one who had passed."

"A dead body?"

"Yessum. And folks believe that as the plate is passed over, all the sins from the one who passed enter the food, and the sin eater eats the food. Do ya understand what I'm tellin' ya?"

"And *he* ate the food? *He* is the sin eater?" Ray asked Little Miss.

"Yes, I am, Ray," Osborn responded. "It's the last mercy for the living," Osborn reflected, "allowing them, allowing them to believe their loved ones depart unburdened, unburdened, yes."

Ray looked to the ceiling. "Well, that's quite a story. Was the food good, at least?"

"Delicious, delicious, yes."

Ray let out a small laugh as Little Miss put her hands on her hips. "This ain't funny, Ray! Your uncle has pawned his soul."

Ray stopped laughing and turned to his uncle. "Pawned your soul?"

Shame and sadness filled Osborn's features. "I am afraid so, afraid so, Ray. I would like to, like to get it out of pawn."

"How do we do that?" asked Ray, shifting to Little Miss. Not knowing, she shrugged.

Ray spun back to his uncle. Osborn shrugged as well. In a sad voice, Osborn said, "Jesus may, Jesus may fix it, yes. He died for our sins."

Ray studied his uncle's sadness. "Well, let's work on one thing at a time. I can help you get Ishmael back."

"Henry will not allow that. Not allow that, no."

"Why do you say that? He has no right. You are his father."

"But he is his grandfather, and he is a powerful man. Powerful man."

"Uncle, you are a powerful man. You are the most famous photographer the world has ever known."

"I am a very famous photographer, yes. Very famous. I've photographed Willy Lincoln and Vice President Hamlin and General Jeb Stuart and General McClellan and…"

"We know, Uncle."

"You know, but Little Miss does not know," replied Osborn.

"I am a powerful man now as well, Uncle. I have done very well with the business, carrying on your good name."

"Very good, Ray, very good. You have done well for yourself. I always knew you would, you would, yes."

"But my point is that I can hire the top lawyer in Pittsburgh, and we will get Ishmael back to you. Come back to Pittsburgh with me, and we'll talk to the lawyer about your rights with Ishmael..."

Osborn's eyes flashed. "I won't leave her, I won't leave her."

"We'd come right back up with the buckboard and bring her back too," Ray soothed. "Give her a proper burial in the family plot, next to Ma and Pa. It's what she deserves."

Osborn twisted his beard, considering. "I have never considered this option."

Ray met Little Miss's striking green and gold eyes, saying, "You'd also be doing me a huge favor because Little Miss is coming to visit, too." Little Miss's eyebrows shot up, surprised but pleased by the suggestion. Ray continued, "She's never seen Pittsburgh and would love it if you could show her around town."

"Yes, I think that's a wonderful idea," added Little Miss.

Osborn's head tilted, questioning. "Ray could show you around. Ray could."

Little Miss smiled shyly, a pretty blush coloring her cheeks. "He surely could, but I'd need a chaperone. My Momma would demand it. I wouldn't be able to go without one such as you."

"Also, I will be busy with the business, Uncle. You'd be helping me considerable."

"Wouldn't that be nice, Mr. Roche? To have some company on the trip?"

Osborn blinked, thrown by the idea but seeming to ponder it. Ray pressed on, encouraged. "What do you say, Uncle? Will you come home with me, just for a little while?"

Osborn took a shaky breath, fiddling with a loose thread on his sleeve. "What about Lou?"

"I told you, we'll get the buckboard and come on back as soon as we're able to get her."

"I did embalm her. But I will not, will not unwrap her, no. She is, she is resting comfortably, and I should not ruin the memory I have, I have of her."

"I believe that is a rational decision."

The cabin fell silent, the only sound the soft creaking of the floorboards as Osborn shifted his weight. Finally, he gave a jerky nod. "I will do that, yes. I will do that if we can bring home Ishmael as well, as well, yes."

"Yes, I know the best lawyers," replied Ray.

Osborn's gaze fell to Lincoln, lying on the floor asleep. "And I have to bring Lincoln, Lincoln, yes. He's a good dog."

Ray guided his mare along the path back to the Fenn farm, the rhythmic clip-clop of hooves breaking the afternoon silence. Little Miss sat behind him, her arms encircling his waist. Osborn ran his fingers through Junior's soft mane as he rode behind them, his boots inches off the dirt path. Lincoln happily kept pace beside them.

In the distance, Charlotte stood on the covered veranda, her eyes narrowing as they approached.

Little Miss released Ray's waist and brought her lips closer to his ear. "Ray, I gotta tell ya something."

Ray rotated his ear to her. "Yeah?"

"My momma, she ain't gonna like your uncle none."

"Why is that? She's already met him."

"She respects sin eaters, but she's a fearin' of 'em more. A might fearin'."

"And, so what's there for your mother to be fearing?"

"Well, ya see, a sin eater is believed to be full of sin, and I mean full. They take on all the sins of everyone they take over a plate of food from. And folks believe that person be a bad omen and shunned."

"And your mother feels this way?"

"I'm sorry, but she does."

Ray pulled the reins on his mare a short distance from the porch. Little Miss slid off the horse and hurried over, hoping to smooth things over before they got out of hand.

"Momma, I'm back," she said as she reached the bottom of the steps.

Staring down at her, Charlotte cut her off with a sharp glare. "And ya brought the sin eater." She crossed her arms, her mouth set in a thin line. "Now, why'd ya have to go and do that?"

Dierdre came running over from the field. "Momma!" she called as she ran up to her mother, wrapping her in a hug before spinning around to Osborn as he sat on Junior a safe distance away. "That the sin eater?"

"That is. His name is Mr. Roche, and he is Ray's uncle." As they spoke about him, Osborn felt like a circus freak, a feeling he hadn't had since he was a teenager.

Ray stepped forward, his most charming smile in place. "Mrs. Fenn, I can't thank you enough for helping me locate my uncle."

Charlotte barely spared him a glance, her gaze fixed on Osborn as he dismounted stiffly. "Mr. Roche," she said, her tone frosty as a winter's dawn. "I'm sorry, but I'm afraid I can't invite you into my home. It wouldn't be proper, you understand."

Little Miss's heart sank. She had feared this reaction, but it still stung. Osborn, for his part, merely nodded, his expression unreadable.

"Grandma doesn't like sin eaters," said Dierdre.

"That ain't it. It ain't that I don't like sin eaters. I respect ya, but the plain truth is, sin eaters is just full of sin," she said before raising her voice for Osborn. "Ain't that so, Mr. Roche?"

"That's what they say, that's what they say. I have pawned my soul, yes."

"And I don't believe it neither, Momma. Please, this is just foolishness," Little Miss insisted.

"Even if I wasn't sure myself, it's better to be on the safe side. And even if I didn't believe it at all, other folk do, and we's weepers. We don't want none of that sin spreading around. Especially with a youngin' around."

"Well, they'll be leaving in the morning, but they need a place to sleep tonight."

Charlotte gave a withering glance. "Girl, you are so contrary you'd float upstream. Fine then, they can have the furthest cabin."

Little Miss bit back a sharp retort, knowing it would only worsen matters. Instead, she rotated to Ray and Osborn and pointed to a cabin. "See there, that cabin yonder? That's an empty cabin where the farmhands used to stay. Why don't you two get settled in, and I'll bring y'all out some vittles."

Ray raised a hand to Charlotte. "Much obliged, Mrs. Fenn," he called to her, hesitating briefly before addressing Little Miss. "We'll just keep to ourselves, don't you worry," he said as a distant rumble of thunder rolled across the sky.

Charlotte's eyes darted upward. "Storm's coming," she muttered, more to herself than anyone else. "Ain't natural, this time of year."

Little Miss felt a chill run down her spine that had nothing to do with the weather. She glanced back at the cabin where Ray and Osborn had disappeared, then to her mother's troubled face. "Momma," she began, "do you think—"

But Charlotte cut her off with a sharp wave of her hand. "Don't you go thinking nothing, girl. What's done is done. Now get inside and help me with supper."

Little Miss shifted uncomfortably in her seat as she, her mother, and Dierdre sat at the table, finishing a supper of ham, potatoes, and green beans. "Momma, Ray, and his uncle will be heading back to Pittsburgh in the morning. I... I thought I might go with them. Just for a few days, to see the city."

Charlotte's head whipped up, her eyes wide. "Absolutely not! Traipsing off with strange men, and one of them a sin eater? Have you lost your senses, girl?"

Little Miss felt her temper flare, even as a familiar weight settled in her stomach. She knew she should stand her ground, assert her independence, but the words stuck in her throat. The memory of sleepless nights wondering how she'd feed Dierdre without her mother's help flashed through her mind.

She glanced at Dierdre, then back at her mother, acutely aware of the delicate balance between the two. The thought of becoming the subject of town gossip, of seeing disapproving looks at church on Sunday, made her chest tighten. And wasn't there a part of her, small but persistent, that wondered if her mother might be right? After all, look how spectacularly wrong she'd been about Augustus...

"Momma," she began again, her voice softer now, caught between defiance and plea. "Ray is not a strange man. I told ya I already courted him for a bit." But even as she spoke, doubt crept in. *Did she really want to open that door again?*

Dierdre's jaw dropped as her eyes grew wide. "You courted him, Momma?"

"Oh, now ya done it!" exclaimed Charlotte.

Little Miss shook her head, embarrassed she had said that in front of her daughter. She closed her eyes, centering herself with a measured breath. "It was before your father and only for a small bit of time. Ray was always a gentleman with your mother. Now, you, go on now while I talk to your grandma in private." Dierdre did as she was told and walked off to her bedroom.

Charlotte rose, clearing plates from the table. "Ray is on the small side of the problem. I told you it's the darkness that'll rub off on you from the other'n."

"Osborn is the sweetest, kindest man you'll ever meet. The good in that man would gobble all the sin up and swallow it down in one bite. Ain't no sin in that man."

"That you can see."

Little Miss's posture stiffened. "I'm a grass widow, Momma, a divorced woman. Who would want a grass widow weeper? And I believe Ray still has a shine for me."

"You're a Fenn. Folk 'round here don't even know if you're hitched or not, let alone if you and yourn called it quits."

"Do ya want me to end up a spinster like you, Momma? Never having a man again? Remember who took that away from me the first time," Little Miss seethed.

Charlotte stood with her back to Little Miss as she cleaned the dishes in a pot of water. "That ain't fair," Charlotte replied quietly. "It was a necessity."

"I'm a grown woman," demanded Little Miss.

"Then think like one, girl!"

Secretly listening, Dierdre ran in from the hallway. "I want to go too, Momma! I've never been to the city before."

"Hush, child," Charlotte snapped. "You're too young to be gadding about."

Little Miss thrust out her chin and crossed her arms. "She is my daughter, and I will be making the decisions for her…"

Charlotte spun around, pointing her finger at Little Miss. "She will not go! You will not subject my granddaughter to a sin eater! No, ma'am!" Little Miss froze at her mother's anger. Charlotte's shoulders rose and fell with a deliberate breath before calmly saying, "You can go and be amongst that darkness if you so choose, but you take my granddaughter, and you will not be welcome to return."

The morning air hung heavy with dew as Ray and Osborn waited outside their cabin, the sun barely peeking over the horizon. Little Miss emerged from the house, Dierdre clinging to her skirts like a shadow. Her face was a canvas of conflicting emotions as she approached. "I'm afraid I won't be coming along with ya, Ray."

Ray shifted on his saddle, the leather creaking beneath him. "I'm sorry to hear that, Little Miss. Is there anything I can do to convince ya?"

Charlotte stepped out onto the porch, her presence looming behind Little Miss like a storm cloud. "Little Miss has a pack of chores to do, like we all do. Raising a child and farm life never stops."

Little Miss's expression fell at the words. Understanding, Ray held up his hand in a placating gesture to Charlotte. "Mrs. Fenn, I assure you, your daughter would be under my protection. We would never allow any harm to come to her."

Charlotte smirked as she replied, "And who's going to protect her from the likes of you?"

Ray flinched under the intensity of her glare. Desperate for an ally, he swiveled to Osborn, his eyes pleading for intervention, but Osborn merely shrugged. Ray's throat constricted with hesitant words as he forced himself to meet Little Miss's gaze. "Well then," he managed, "I suppose we'll be off now."

As Ray whirled his horse around, Little Miss's words spilled like water from a broken dam. "I'm sorry, Ray. I would have loved to go." Ray stopped with his back to her. "It's just that, well, he's a sin eater."

Ray's head bobbed in a slow nod before he clicked his tongue and kicked his heels. The horse sprang forward, carrying him away from the farm.

"Come on now," Charlotte said, her voice softer. "There's work to be done."

Little Miss released her breath in a slow sigh before allowing herself one last glance at the receding figures of Ray and Osborn, fading down the road like a dream upon waking.

CHAPTER 10

Ray and Osborn rode through the bustling streets of Pittsburgh, a city pulsing with life an d industry. Lincoln, panting, kept close to Hoady Junior. Having lived in seclusion for so long, their eyes darted nervously at the urban cacophony surrounding them. Storefronts and businesses lined the roads, their windows displaying various goods and services. Pedestrians hurried along the sidewalks as horse-drawn carriages and wagons clattered over the cobblestone streets.

Their two-story home sat on Crape Street, a residential dirt street lined with hazelnut trees. Two-story brick homes sat on either side of the road with a scattering of vacant lots. As they neared the back door, it swung open, revealing a middle-aged woman wearing a crisp black dress and a white apron. She had pulled her graying hair back into a tight bun, and her warm brown eyes crinkled at the corners as she smiled.

"Welcome back, Mr. Roche," the woman said. "I trust your journey was— " The woman's words died on her lips as shock rendered her momentarily mute. Her eyes widened, fixed upon the figure emerging from behind Ray like a specter materializing from the mountain mists.

Ray turned, following the woman's transfixed gaze, and found himself looking at his uncle as if seeing him for the first time. Osborn stood there with his beard thick and unkempt. Gray strands, matted and tangled, cascaded down his chest like some feral animal

"Oh, yes," Ray said to himself before turning back to the woman with a smile. "Our journey was pleasant, Mrs. Hawkins. Thank you." With his hand gesturing to Osborn, he added, "Mrs. Hawkins, I'd like you to meet my Uncle Osborn. He will clean up nice, I promise."

Mrs. Hawkins brought back her smile. "Pleased to make your acquaintance, Mr. Osborn. Your nephew speaks very highly of you."

Osborn tipped his hat, surprised by the presence of a full-time maid in Ray's household. "The pleasure, the pleasure is mine, Mrs. Hawkins."

Osborn followed Ray into the house. A bittersweet smile tugged at his lips as he realized how much had changed, yet how familiar it all remained. Memories washed over him like a gentle tide.

Ray turned to Osborn with a warm smile. "Uncle, why don't you take your old room? It's just as you left it."

Osborn nodded and climbed the familiar stairs, each c reak a whisper from the past. The door to his old room swung open, and Osborn found himself transported back in time. The faded wallpaper and the worn wooden floor were all as he remembered. His mind drifted to those early days when he first moved in, a young man suddenly thrust into the role of guardian to a grieving little boy—Ray at eight years old.

He remembered the nights spent comforting the boy, awkwardly trying to fill the shoes of the parents Ray had lost. There were moments of doubt, of fear that he wasn't enough, but also moments of unexpected joy - teaching Ray photography and watching him grow into a man of integrity.

Osborn made his way to his bedroom. He paused at the threshold, his hand resting on the doorknob. Taking the brown cloth from his pocket, he put it to his nose and mouth, taking a deep breath through it before stepping inside. The bed where he and his late wife had spent their wedding night stood against the far wall. He set his bag down on it and sat on the edge of the bed, running his hand over the quilt. Osborn rose and stood by the window of his old room, watching the hazelnut trees sway in the breeze. He thought about the years that had passed, and the roads traveled. But as he looked out at the quiet street, a stirring in his heart told him that perhaps it was time for a change again. The world was vast, and there were still so many stories to be part of and so many photographs to take.

The following morning, Ray stood in front of the house as Osborn exited the front door, bathed, clean-shaven, and wearing a new suit.

"Well, well," Ray said. "Very dapper. You'd never know you were a sin eater."

"Thank you, Ray. I don't know how I survived without a hot bath, without a bath, no."

The men headed down the sidewalk until they hit Liberty Avenue, a bustling street.

"Uncle, as you know, the daguerreotype business has been thriving, and a big part of that success is due to your reputation."

"Why, thank you, Ray. But you give me too much credit, Ray. It is also your talent from what, from what I have taught you, taught you, yes. And your success as a businessman, yes."

Ray shook his head. "That may be true, but having your name associated with the studio has opened so many doors for us. And that's why I wanted to ask you something."

Excitement built in Osborn's chest as they approached the impressive facade of Roche Photography and Daguerreotype. The large windows displayed an array of photographs and portraits.

"Here we are," said Ray as he opened the door for his uncle. The bell above the door jingled, announcing their arrival. Osborn's gaze darted about the room, never settling on any one point for long. His eyes flicked from the ornate picture frames adorning the walls to the polished wood of the counter, then to the gleaming brass fixtures of the camera equipment. He seemed to drink in every detail of the studio, his expression a mixture of wonder and unease.

They passed through the comfortable waiting area and into a larger room with several photography sets arranged throughout. At one of the sets, a photographer carefully positioned a well-dressed couple for their portrait.

A tall, well-groomed man in his early thirties approached them with a broad smile. "Mr. Roche, welcome back!" he said as he approached Ray.

"James, it's good to see you," Ray replied, returning the smile. "I'd like you to meet someone very special. This is my uncle, Osborn Roche."

James's eyes widened as he faced Osborn, his mouth falling open in awe. "Osborn Roche?" Osborn glanced briefly at the man's face before his gaze skittered away, settling on a point just over James's left shoulder. "The Osborn Roche? Sir, it is an absolute honor to meet you," he gushed, about to shake Osborn's hand. Osborn jerked it back.

Ray stopped him, "Uh, he does not shake hands."

"Oh, yes, yes, I remember you told me. I'm sorry, Mr. Roche. I understand."

A faint flush crept up his neck, coloring his cheeks with the unfamiliar heat of recognition and praise. "Thank you, thank you," said Osborn. "Yes, yes, I do not like to shake hands or touch at all, no."

"It is certainly not a problem," added James. "Your war photographs are legendary. In fact, most of the photographs we have hanging in the store are your works. They're absolutely breathtaking."

"Thank you, James. It's a pleasure to meet, to meet you as well. I must say, I must say, Ray has done an incredible job with the studio." The words tumbled out in a rush as if Osborn feared they might escape him if he didn't get them out quick enough.

"He has indeed."

"I'll show Mr. Roche around, James."

"Oh yes, do, and Mr. Roche, I mean, Mr. Osborn Roche, I'd love to discuss your photographs in detail later if I may be so bold."

"Certainly, certainly. I would like that, James."

"Come, let me give you the grand tour," Ray said as he gestured for his uncle to follow. "Two levels, one thousand square feet on each, twenty-eight dollars per week. They usually charge thirty-two, but I negotiated it down." As they climbed the stairs to the second floor, Ray continued, "Up here, we have my office and the lab where we develop and process the photographs. It's a bit of a mad scientist's lair." Ray opened the door to reveal a well-organized space filled with chemicals, trays, and drying racks.

Osborn walked in, closed his eyes, and pulled in the air through his nose. "I used to hate the smell, the smell of collodion. The ether, the ether in it. It took years, but now I, I love that peculiar smell."

Ray took a stool in front of the workbench and sat. "What I wanted to ask you…I want you to be a part of the studio, to work alongside me again. Like before."

"I, I believe I would like that too, Ray. But first things first. Ishmael and Lou, Ishmael and Lou, yes."

"Of course. But this is where you belong, Uncle. This is what you were meant to do. And I know that Lou would have wanted this for you, for us."

Pittsburgh, Pennsylvania

August 15, 1871

My dear Little Miss,

I hope this letter finds you in good health and spirits. The hustle and bustle of Pittsburgh is a far cry from the tranquil beauty of your farm, yet I find my thoughts constantly drifting back to our brief encounter.

I have been seeking the services of a reputable attorney to assist in the delicate matter of reclaiming my uncle's son. The intricacies of the law are as bewildering as the smoke that perpetually hangs over this steel town. Yesterday, I secured the services of Mr. Abernathy, a prominent lawyer known for his discretion and efficacy. He believes we have a strong case.

My uncle is leaning toward staying here with me and joining me in business, but he is becoming increasingly anxious in the desire to be near his wife's grave. We will be planning a journey back to your fair town in the coming weeks to reclaim her remains and bring her to rest in our family plot here in Pittsburgh so he can be close to her once again. If it would not be an imposition, I would very much like to call upon you. There is a particular vista I remember overlooking the valley, which I believe would make for a splendid photograph. Perhaps you might accompany me?

I eagerly await your reply and the possibility of seeing you again.

Yours sincerely,

Ray

Johnstown, Pennsylvania

August 28, 1871

Dear Ray,

Your letter arrived on a particular trying day, and I must admit it brout a welcome respite. I'm glad to hear of the progress with Mr. Abernathy. Legal matters can be so vexing; I hope it all resolves in your uncle's favor.

Regarding your proposed visit, you are always welcome here, Ray. The vista you speak of – I beleeve I know the very spot. It would be my pleshure to accompany you there. Perhaps we could bring Dierdre along? She's taken quite an interest in the wildflowers lately and has been pressing them in a book.

I must make a delicat request, Ray. While I hold no ill will toward your uncle Osborn, my mother's views on his former profeshun remain unchanged. For the sake of harmony, mite I sujest that he not accompany you on your visit? I hope you understand.

Do let me know when you plan to arive. I shall keep watch for you on the rode.

Yours truly,

Little Miss

Pittsburgh, Pennsylvania

September 12, 1871

My dear Little Miss,

Your last letter was a balm to my spirit. I shall be returning to you sooner than anticipated. My uncle's father-in-law has responded to our attorney and has requested a meeting in person prior to any court filings. We shall be there on the first Wednesday of next month, October 12th and staying in Johnstown. If time provides, and I can visit with you, I will come alone as requested.

My heart quickens at the thought of seeing you again.

Yours,

Ray

The blue sky was a welcome sight compared to the smoke-filled skies in the city. Ray approached the Fenn farmhouse, excited to see Little Miss wearing a beautiful yellow dress and waiting for him on the veranda.

"Ray," she called, "looking as dapper as ever."

"And you, as lovely."

He dismounted, a smile playing on his lips. "I hoped we might take that walk you promised me. The one to the vista point?"

"I've been waiting for ya."

Little Miss hesitated, glancing back at the house. "Dierdre—"

"I'll watch the child," Charlotte's voice carried from inside. "Go on, then."

Ray tied his horse to the trough as Little Miss took up a lunch basket. They set off on the path winding through the tall pines.

"I aim to talk to you serious-like today, Little Miss," Ray said, his voice carrying a trace of nervousness.

With a glance at him, a small smile rose on her lips. "Serious-like? Should I have worn a different dress?"

"I would request not, as that is the finest dress for a beautiful woman to wear on this finest of days," Ray replied, his eyes twinkling.

"Then what type of seriousness are we speaking of?" she teased.

"I believe you know."

"I assure you I do not."

"Or your humility assures you not."

The path continued up a hill thick with white pines, their scent heavy in the warm air. Ray pulled his handkerchief from his pocket and wiped his brow. "It's been seven years," he began, "seven years since we courted back then. It was a short time, but a time I still cherish."

"Cherish? That little ol' time?"

"I do. I do."

"Are you flirting with me, Ray?"

Ray took her hand to help her up a particularly steep embankment. "It seems I am. I hope you are not taking it as cavalier?" asked Ray, with a cheeky expression on his face.

"Why, yes, I am, but I like cavalier," she giggled.

"I was just a boy those seven years back, but I knew what I liked, and I liked you. I didn't win you, but that didn't defeat my heart."

The pair crested the hill and strolled to an overlook across the valley. The view stretched out before them, a tapestry of fields, forests, and distant mountains. They both stood quietly for a moment, awestruck.

Little Miss paused momentarily to take in the view, her eyes drinking in the familiar landscape. "Yessum, quite a sight. Been in my family for ages." Little Miss put down her picnic basket and spread out a blanket they sat on. Ray stared at her as she pretended to be concerned with setting out their lunch.

"At seventeen, when I first felt my heart stir for you, I had nothing but dreams to offer. But now, I've built something. My photography business is thriving, Little Miss. I have a home, stability... but it's empty without love, without family."

Little Miss's eyes widened. Ray continued, "Ever since I left you last time, I've been thinking about it. I've come to realize what I truly need next is a wife, a family. And when I think of that future, I see you, Little Miss. You and Dierdre."

The whisper of wind through the grass was the only sound until Little Miss spoke, "Ray, I feel I must be honest with you. Your words are beautiful, truly. But I fear you may be viewing our situation through rose-tinted spectacles."

"I don't believe it is," Ray insisted. "My house is large, with room for all. You, Dierdre, even your mother—you'd all be welcome. We could build a life together, a family."

Little Miss broke eye contact and lowered her head. "It's not that simple, Ray. My mother will never accept your uncle, and I could never leave my mother."

"She may change her mind when she sees Pittsburgh and my home, our home."

Little Miss shook her head sadly. "She's a woman of steel principles. She won't."

"He would never sin eat again, and he'd get baptized again or something."

Little Miss shook her head with sadness in her eyes. Ray's shoulders sagged, disappointment settling upon him. "Is there no way, Little Miss? No chance for us?"

She reached out, gently squeezing his hand. "I care for you, Ray. But our paths... they're just too different now."

CHAPTER 11

The Cattell mansion loomed before them, its weathered stone facade a testament to generations of wealth and influence. Osborn and Ray stood on the grand portico's granite floor before the mansion's imposing oak doors. Mr. Abernathy, their attorney, hovered just behind in his starched collar and polished shoes. Lincoln sat obediently at his master's feet, nervously panting.

Ray raised the brass knocker, its dull thud echoing through the house. Moments later, the door swung open to reveal a butler, his attire as crisp and formal as his demeanor. Ray stepped forward. "Hello, we're here to see Mr. Cattell."

The butler's eyes switched between the men. "Mr. Roche and Mr. Roche?"

"Yes," Ray confirmed, "along with Mr. Abernathy."

"You're expected. Please..." the butler's words trailed off as a shadow of concern crossed his features after his gaze landed on Lincoln.

Ray followed his line of sight. "Oh, he's fine. He will stay outside."

Osborn put his hand in front of Lincoln's muzzle. "Lincoln, stay."

"His name is Arthur," said the butler. "And he's been missing for... years."

The fact dawned on Osborn. "Oh, well, then," he said, putting his palm in front of his muzzle. "Arthur, stay."

The butler shrugged off his confusion and ushered them into the entry hall. Osborn's eyes swept across the cavernous two-story hall, his gaze cataloging details. Crystal chandeliers hung from coffered ceilings, each prism fracturing light into a kaleidoscope of colors. Osborn found himself entranced by a single droplet of light that danced on the wall, a fleeting moment of beauty he wished he could freeze in time. His mind raced with calculations of exposure times and chemical compounds that might capture such ephemeral brilliance.

The butler gestured toward an adjoining room as the door clicked shut behind them. "This way to the salon, gentlemen."

As they entered the salon, a crystal decanter on a side table caught Osborn's eye, not for its intrinsic value, but for how it distorted and refracted the world around it. Through its faceted surface, Osborn saw the room transformed - familiar shapes twisted into abstract forms, a glimpse into a reality just slightly askew from our own.

As they moved through the house, Osborn found himself cataloging textures - the plush pile of Persian rugs, the cool smoothness of marble busts, the intricate lacework of doilies perched on velvet-upholstered chairs. Each surface told a story, each shadow hinted at secrets, and Osborn's fingers itched for his camera, longing to preserve these fleeting impressions.

They followed, their footsteps muffled by plush Chinese rugs. Richly patterned wallpaper climbed the salon walls, broken only by windows draped in heavy silks. Ornate furniture dotted the space like islands in a sea of luxury. A collection of velvet sofas sat at the room's center, circling a fireplace that could have warmed a small village. The butler motioned toward them. "Please, make yourselves comfortable. I'll inform Mr. Cattell of your arrival."

As the butler's footsteps faded, the men exchanged glances, their eyes wide. "I've never seen a place this beautiful," Ray quietly said.

"Me neither," Osborn agreed, sinking into a récamier daybed. His fingers traced the plush red velour, marveling at its softness. Ray perched on a nearby settee while Mr. Abernathy remained standing, his bowler hat spinning absently between his hands.

The door opened again, and Henry Cattell strode in, his presence filling the room. At sixty, he moved with the vigor of a much younger man, his finely tailored suit a second skin. Gold cufflinks winked in the light, and a pocket watch hung from a chain that draped elegantly across his waistcoat. Osborn and Ray leapt to their feet.

Henry's eyes widened, a mix of surprise and curiosity dancing across his features. "Well, I'll be," he said. "Here you are. I must say, your correspondence came as quite a shock."

"Mr. Cattell," Ray acknowledged.

Mr. Abernathy stepped forward, hand outstretched. "Mr. Cattell, Armand Abernathy. A pleasure to meet you."

Henry clasped the offered hand. "Yes, Mr. Abernathy. Thank you for agreeing to this meeting." His gaze swept over the trio, assessing, before settling back on the lawyer. "Now, shall we get down to business?"

Osborn's words tumbled out, "Mr. Cattell, we've come to take Ishmael back home."

Henry's attention snapped to Osborn, his eyes narrowing. "Take him home? This is his home."

Ray stepped forward. "But Mr. Cattell, my uncle is his father."

"And I am his grandfather," Henry countered, each word precise and sharp. "This is his home."

Abernathy intervened. "Well, let's not get ahead of ourselves..."

"Yes, but—" Ray insisted, only to be silenced by Henry's raised hand.

The older man closed his eyes briefly as if gathering his thoughts. In a calmer, measured voice, he said, "Wait here. Let's discuss this in a rational manner." He paused, then added, "Shall we adjourn to the parlor for some tea?"

"Excellent idea," Abernathy agreed.

"I would like some tea," Osborn chimed in.

Henry rotated toward the doorway. "David," he called out. "Tea for four in the parlor."

The butler's response came from somewhere in the depths of the house: "Certainly, sir."

The parlor's two-story ceiling loomed above them as Henry turned, his eyes seeking Osborn's. "Please..." he began, then faltered, searching for words. "Before we go further, I must know. What happened to you, Osborn? What happened to my daughter?"

"Lou died. Lou died in childbirth, yes."

"I know she did, but what did you do with her body?"

"I embalmed her and buried her."

A tinge of pain crossed Henry's features. "Would you be so kind as to tell me where?"

"In your back acres," Osborn replied, then added, "May I see Ishmael, my son?"

Henry's eyes widened in disbelief. "In my back...?" The question trailed off, unfinished.

Ray stepped forward. "Yes, Mr. Cattell. To be close to Ishmael. Believe it or not, my uncle has been living in a cabin in the woods not far from here. Lou is buried just past your treeline."

Henry shook his head slowly, wonder in his expression. "Just past my treeline? All these years?" He spun around to Ray. "Did you know about this?"

"Until a few days back, I had no idea of his whereabouts," Ray admitted.

Osborn's voice cut through the tension, insistent and raw. "I had no means to reach Ray, and I did not want to leave Lou or Ishmael. May I see Ishmael?"

"Yes, certainly, certainly," Henry said, twisting to David, who stood at the parlor doors. With a simple nod, David walked out.

Henry shifted to Osborn. "When did you do this? When did you bury her there?"

Osborn dropped his head. "Six years ago, yes, six years."

Henry shook his head in amazement. "Six years ago," he repeated.

"In a place, in a place where we could be together and watch our son grow, yes, grow together."

Henry's eyes softened. "Would you be so kind as to show me this place?"

"I will. I wi—" Osborn's words died in his throat as the butler led a small boy with brown hair into the room. All heads turned.

"Ishmael," Henry said, standing and gesturing toward Osborn with an open palm. "I'd like you to meet Osborn Roche. This is your father."

Osborn slowly rose as Ishmael approached, his eyes never leaving the boy's face. Ishmael extended his tiny hand, his voice clear and polite. "Pleased to meet you, sir."

Osborn's eyes squeezed shut as Ishmael reached out. "I do not like to touch," he said, the words tumbling out in a rush. "I do not like it. Only Lou, your mother, your mother was the only one. And Ray, and Ray a little."

A smile spread across Ishmael's face. "That's peculiar," he said, his eyes sparkling with curiosity.

Osborn's eyes flew open, his head jerking in surprise. A smile spread across his face. "Peculiar?! Yes, yes, it is. It is peculiar."

Osborn cocked his head to the side. "You know, you know, we could try it, try it, yes," he said, bending down and sticking out his hand to Ishmael. Flashing a missing tooth smile, Ishmael slowly reached out as if playing a game of chicken. Osborn's eyes widened as their palms met, as did Ishmael's smile. He studied Ishmael's face intently, drinking in every detail.

"You do not have her eyes," he mentioned, a note of wistfulness in his voice. "I was hoping to see, hoping to see her eyes again."

Tears welled in Osborn's eyes, glinting in the parlor's soft light. Suddenly, he jerked to his feet, his voice choked with emotion. "I need, I need—" The words trailed off as he strode quickly from the room, leaving a wake of stunned silence behind him.

The others stood frozen, caught off guard by the abrupt departure. Ishmael remained still, his hand hanging where Osborn had released it.

"Hmm, well, should we continue or…?" asked Henry.

"Maybe wait for his return," said Mr. Abernathy.

Henry glanced down at Ishmael. "Ishmael, I have some things to discuss with Mr. Ray. Would you please go back to your studies?"

"I finished them."

"Well, then, whatever you would like to do," replied Henry. Ishmael grinned and skipped out of the room. Henry spun back to Ray. "Please sit." The three men took their seats. Henry tugged down his coat and said, "Until Osborn's return, I just want to reiterate that the boy has lived with me his entire life. This life is all he knows and, mind you, it is a good life with all of the finer things one could imagine. He does not go without and will be attending the finest in higher education."

"Quite true," said Abernathy.

Ray interjected, "Yes, but you are not his father. My uncle is. A boy needs a father."

"A father he has never known? I have been as good a father, and I have a grandfather, I assure you."

Ray stood, his jaw set in frustration. "Mr. Cattell, I'm afraid we've reached an impasse. It seems we have no choice but to let the courts decide Ishmael's fate."

Abernathy nodded solemnly, gathering his papers. "Indeed. We'll file the necessary documents first thing tomorrow."

Henry's face paled, his knuckles white as he gripped the arms of his chair. "You can't just—" Henry's gaze shifted to the window. "All these years he's been back there watching." When he turned back to them, they had already left the room. Henry ran to catch up.

"Gentlemen," he said, his tone measured, "surely there must be a way to honor both Ishmael's need for stability and Osborn's right to be a father."

As the trio reached the front doors, Abernathy pivoted to Henry. "Mr. Cattell, I'm sure this visit is a shock to you."

"It certainly is. And now I learned that my beloved daughter has been back there all this time? Is this true?"

Ray nodded. "It is."

Henry shook his head in disbelief. "If he only would have come to me. If he only could have spoken to me, I would've told him. I would've apologized for my previous behavior."

Ray's brows jumped. "Apologized?"

Henry turned to Ray with a soft expression. "I was wrong with what I spoke to you about those years ago. Wrong about your uncle and my daughter. So wrong. And I have read about his work and notoriety. If only he would have knocked on my door. He could have lived here rather than someplace in my back acres."

Ray's eyes opened wider. "You would have let him live with you?"

"Of course. He's my son-in-law, and he's the father of my grandson." Henry raised his hand, displaying the room. "And this home has eight bedrooms with only myself, Ishmael, and David living here."

Ray paused a moment to collect his thoughts, processing Henry's unexpected words. "Perhaps we should step outside for some air. It might do us both good."

With a distant expression, Henry said, "Yes, I think that would be wise."

Osborn stood on the grand portico, overlooking the front yard and gardens as they came outside. "You alright, Uncle?"

"Ishmael is the same age, the same age you were when I became your guardian," Osborn said.

"Yes, that's true," Ray agreed.

"I didn't need air, Ray. I needed to gather my emotions, my emotions. Yes, it was my emotions."

Ray grinned. "I know. We all understand."

Henry stepped beside Osborn, his voice gentle. "Osborn, perhaps a walk in the fresh air would settle your nerves. Would you be so kind as to show me the way to my daughter's last resting place?"

"I will, I will. This way, this way," Osborn replied as he descended the portico steps. Henry exchanged a meaningful glance with Ray before following.

As they crossed the lush expanse of the back acreage, Lincoln played on the lawn with Henry's black Labrador that bounded alongside him with puppyish enthusiasm. Henry's step faltered, his eyes widening in disbelief as he took in the scene. "My goodness!" he exclaimed, his voice a mixture of joy and bewilderment. "That's Arthur! We haven't seen hide nor hair of that dog for over—"

"Six years, six years," Osborn interjected, his words clipped and hurried. He ducked his head, avoiding Henry's gaze, and quickened his pace to avoid any further questions about it.

Henry called out, "Osborn, could you please slow down? My knees aren't what they used to be."

Osborn slackened his pace. "See those two red pine trees?" he asked, gesturing ahead. "With the goldenseal bushes and bloodroot flowers in front?"

"Yes," Henry confirmed, squinting against the afternoon sun.

"Lou is beyond that, resting beyond that."

"I wish I had known sooner."

Osborn's chest tightened as Henry's words hit his ears, heavy with regret. A familiar ache bloomed within him, a mirror of the pain etched across his father-in-law's face. Osborn's fingers twisted in the fabric of his coat, seeking the comfort of Lou's brown cloth hidden in his pocket. He longed to explain, to unravel the tangled set of circumstances that had led them here, but words failed him. Instead, he stood silent, a spectator to Henry's grief, acutely aware of the shared loss that bound them together in this moment, standing over the grave of the woman they had both loved so deeply.

They reached the end of the manicured lawn, where Osborn pushed through the delicate bloodroot flowers. Henry followed him to a mound of earth marked by a simple cross. Henry read it out, "L. Roche, Embalmer. Gone from the world but alive again in our hearts. So true and well put."

Henry sank to his knees before the grave. "I've missed her so," he sobbed, the words catching in his throat.

Osborn choked back tears. "I miss, I miss her every day, yes. Every day."

Composing himself, Henry said, "When she was little, she would play out here in these woods. I'd hear her talking to her dolls or lost in make-believe. With her condition, it was difficult for her to make friends. I'm sure you can understand that as well." Osborn nodded, a silent acknowledgment of shared pain. "I want to thank you for bringing her home."

"We plan, we plan on taking her back to Pittsburgh with us, back to..."

Henry's head snapped around, eyes wide with shock. "What?! You cannot—you cannot. I will not allow it."

"Ray says we can," Osborn insisted. "When we bring Ishmael to live in Ray's home. It is a very big home."

"Osborn," Henry pleaded, "Ishmael has lived here with me all his life. He's only six years old. It would be cruel to tear him away from everything he knows. Don't you agree?"

"I cannot leave Lou or Ishmael. I cannot. I will not leave Lou. I talk to her every day."

Henry stood, his expression softening. "Osborn, let me explain something. I was wrong about you. I was wrong about my own daughter. What I said in the past about the tragedy that would occur if you had a child—"

Osborn lifted his chin away from Henry, bristling at the thought. "I remember. I remember well."

"I was wrong, Osborn. Please forgive my previous intentions. I was so wrong. Ishmael is the smartest boy. Smart as a whip, that boy is. I was so wrong. I was the one that forced you to leave. Would you ever forgive me?"

"I never harbored ill feelings, never ill feelings."

Henry approached Osborn, about to grasp his shoulders. After Osborn slammed his eyes shut in anticipation, Henry stopped, remembering. "Oh, yes. I remember. I won't touch you, Osborn." Osborn opened his eyes to Henry, smiling.

"Osborn, you are my son-in-law," Henry said, his voice gentle but firm. "You've been living in these woods all this time. What if... what if you were to live here? With us?"

The question seemed to echo across the manicured lawns, bouncing off the imposing facade of the Cattell mansion. Henry pressed on, "Would you consider that? Tearing Ishmael away from the only home he has known and away from his grandfather would not be in his best interest. Our home is very large and comfortable, and we can raise Ishmael together and visit Lou every day, both of us, both you and I. I believe Lou would want this, and I believe it is best for Ishmael."

Osborn stood frozen, his weathered face a canvas of conflicting emotions. The proposition stood before him with seemingly no downside. He would be able to give Ishmael a life of opportunity and see his Lou every day. "But what about Ray?" he asked.

"Let's go ask Ray together. I'm certain he will agree."

CHAPTER 12

A heavy mist clung to the fields as Ray approached the Fenn farm, his mare's clip-clopping muffled on the damp earth. The air hung thick with the odor of impending rain, mirroring the tumult of nerves churning within him.

The farmhouse stood silent, its windows dark against the gray morning. Ray tied his horse to the hitching post before the water trough and walked around to the steps.

Before he could come up, the door swung open. Little Miss stood there, her eyes widening in surprise. "Ray? I didn't expect—" She stopped, noticing the intensity in his gaze. "What's wrong?"

"Nothing's wrong," Ray said, a smile breaking across his face like the first ray of sunlight through clouds. "I would like to speak to your mother."

Little Miss's shoulders slumped. "Oh, Ray," she said as she closed the front door behind her. "Ray, my momma ain't gonna change her mind. I know ya have feelings for me. I know you're fired up and determined, but it ain't no good. She ain't changing her mind. It ain't worth it to try."

Charlotte's voice rang out from within the house. "Let him try!" she called, her tone a mixture of amusement and challenge. Seeing Ray's grin, disbelief flashed across Little Miss's face.

Ray shrugged at her. "She says I can try."

Little Miss raised an eyebrow skeptically before opening the door for him. "You're climbing into your own casket," she said as she ushered him inside and waited at the door. In the kitchen, Charlotte looked up from her mending. "Mr. Roche."

"Missus."

Charlotte peered around Ray to Little Miss. "Close the door, honey."

Ray turned around to Little Miss. "Well, I believe due to the current set of circumstances, I should be speaking to your momma alone if ya don't mind."

Little Miss shook her head again. "Well, I believe you be putting nails in that casket of yours if I do, but, fine by me." With that, Little Miss walked out and shut the door behind her.

Outside, Little Miss sat under the shade of an apple tree as she patiently watched the front door. After almost an hour, the weather cleared up and became a sunny day. Dierdre poked her head out of the door. Spotting her mother, she grinned. Little Miss eyed her suspiciously. "What's got into you?" asked Little Miss.

"Something has," replied Dierdre with a giggle.

"They done in there? What theys talking about?"

"Theys—"

Ray emerged from behind Dierdre, the door creaking as he stepped onto the porch. The late afternoon sun cast shadows across the weathered planks. "Mind if we head on up to the vista?"

Little Miss's eyebrows arched. "To the vista? I'll have to make up a basket."

"No, ya don't," Ray replied, a grin tugging at the corners of his mouth. "We can take my mare for a quick look-see."

Little Miss shrugged and rose with a soft groan. Ray bounded down the porch steps, untied his horse, and led the chestnut mare to the side of the porch. The animal nickered softly, pawing at the ground.

In her usual fashion, Little Miss shimmied around outside the porch and climbed onto the horse's back. She settled behind Ray, wrapping her arms around his waist. With a gentle nudge, they set off at a gallop toward the rolling hills, the wind whipping through their hair.

Little Miss leaned closer as they rode, raising her voice over the horse's hooves. "Well, ain't ya gonna tell me? You're smiling. I don't know why you're smiling, but I'm guessing it's something good. Mind telling someone?"

Ray's shoulders relaxed visibly. "We met with Mr. Cattell and worked it all out. We won't be going to trial or doing anything legal-like."

"I'll be," Little Miss breathed, her grip on Ray tightening momentarily. "Good for you, Ray. That's wonderful news. Is your uncle pleased?"

"Perfectly pleased."

Her lips to Ray's ear, she asked, "There's more to it, ain't there, Ray?" His knowing chuckle sent an involuntary shiver down her spine, though she couldn't have said why. Little Miss knew there was something more, but instead of insisting, she held his waist a bit tighter and decided to enjoy the ride. The cool breeze whistled through the trees, carrying their unspoken words to distant places, leaving only the sound of a whippoorwill, a woodpecker, and the horse's hooves.

Time stretched like taffy, slow and viscous until they crested a small hill, revealing the vista across the valley. After climbing down himself, Ray took a hold of her waist and helped her down. Little Miss suspiciously glanced at him as they meandered out to the edge.

As the sun dipped low, changing its hue from gold to orange, they gazed across at the valley below, standing side by side, taking in the breathtaking view. Ray paused, gathering his thoughts before speaking, his voice soft but steady. "I spoke to your momma. I told her I have feelings for you." Facing her, he took both her hands in his. "Seven years ago, when we first met, I fell for you hard."

"You surely were spilling those compliments out like water."

"I meant 'em." Ray's eyes took on a distant, reflective gleam as he spoke, his voice softening with the memory. "You know, when I first met you, I was struck by something... something I'd never encountered in a woman before." He paused, searching for the right words. "The way everyone deferred to you, calling you 'The Missus' – it wasn't just a title. It was a recognition of your authority, your presence." Ray's lips curved into a small, appreciative smile. "You carried yourself with this... this quiet certainty. It was as if you could see the threads of fate stretching out before you, and you knew exactly how to weave them to your will." Ray's gaze locked with hers. "Most folks, they stumble through life, reacting to whatever comes their way. But you? You moved with purpose, with a confidence that seemed to bend the very air around you. That kind of inner strength – it was captivating. Still is, if I'm being honest." Little Miss felt a warm flush creep up her neck, coloring her cheeks as Ray's words washed over her. "You were more than just the lady of the house. You were its heart, its guiding force. And I... well, I was in awe of it. Of you."

Little Miss ducked her head, suddenly fascinated by a loose thread on her sleeve. When she finally looked up, her eyes shimmered with emotions - surprise, pleasure, and a hint of melancholy. "Oh, Ray," she said with a wry smile. "You make me sound like some kind of mystic." She paused, gathering her thoughts. "Truth is, I was just doing what needed to be done. When you're responsible for so many lives, you can't afford the luxury of uncertainty." She straightened her spine, unconsciously embodying the very poise Ray had described. "But I won't deny it's nice to be seen that way, especially by you." Her voice dropped to almost a whisper. "Sometimes I wonder if that woman still exists, or if she's been buried under years of... well, life."

Little Miss's gaze drifted to the horizon, her expression thoughtful. "It's funny, isn't it? How we can be so sure of ourselves in one moment, and then life throws you a curve that leaves you questioning everything." She turned back to Ray, her eyes searching his face. "Do you really still see that woman when you look at me, Ray? After all this time, all that's happened?"

There was a vulnerability in her question, a rare glimpse behind the composed facade she usually presented to the world. In that moment, she wasn't The Missus or even Little Miss - she was simply a woman, touched and a little overwhelmed by the portrait Ray had painted of her younger self.

"I still see it. It's still there. But it didn't work out for us back then, and when I asked you again two days ago, you told me we were on different paths. I understand why – your mother not wanting you near my uncle." He paused, his thumb tracing gentle circles on the back of her hand. "But things have changed. My uncle will be living with Henry Cattell now. So, you see, there's room now. Room for all of you in my home in Pittsburgh, if you'll come."

"Is this what you were speaking to my momma about? Does she know?"

"I asked her, and she's given her blessing."

Her jaw fell open. "My momma gave her blessing?"

"She did. And now, I'm asking you again, hoping that this time, the answer might be different." He inhaled slowly to calm her nerves, then slowly lowered himself to one knee. Little Miss gasped, her hand flying to her mouth. "Little Miss, I love you. I've loved you for seven years, and I'll love you for seventy more if you'll let me. Will you marry me?"

Little Miss's face lit up, joy radiating from every feature. Tears spilled down her cheeks as she nodded vigorously. "I will, Ray. I will."

CHAPTER 13

14 Years Later

1884

The rustle of fallen leaves betrayed the presence of ground squirrels in the underbrush, their furtive movements a counterpoint to the stillness that enveloped Ishmael and Osborn. They sat in silence on the familiar log beside Lou's grave, now part of a family plot encircled by a low iron fence. Marble benches stood sentinel on all four sides, pristine and untouched, while Osborn found comfort in the smoothness of the log, its surface worn by years of use.

Both men cut striking figures in their finely tailored suits, gold cuff links catching the sunlight that filtered through the branches above. Their pocket watches, tucked away in waistcoat pockets, marked the passage of time with muffled precision. This manner of dress had become second nature—a lasting legacy of Henry Cattell's refined tastes and the world they now inhabited.

Osborn twisted the brown cloth between his fingers as his eyes traced the familiar contours of the four graves before him: Lou, Henry, Lincoln and Rex,

Henry's black Labrador. Four names, four lives, four absences that had shaped his world in ways he still struggled to comprehend. The grief had mellowed into something softer, more bittersweet, like the patina on an old daguerreotype. Time had transformed his pain into a form of melancholic beauty.

On the brink of twenty, Ishmael had grown into a striking man. His dark, tousled hair framed his sharp features: high cheekbones, a straight nose, and a strong jawline. Deep, expressive eyes held a trace of curiosity about the family he'd never met.

At sixty-two, Osborn's silver hair lent him an air of distinguished sophistication. His newly acquired gold-plated spectacles rested on the bridge of his nose, their weight still unfamiliar, yet already indispensable.

"So, Ray's family is really coming?" Ishmael asked. "I can't believe I'll finally meet Dierdre and the others."

Osborn nodded, his gaze lingering on the graves. "Yes, yes. It seems Charlotte's resolve has finally begun to crack, to crack with age. Ray's letter mentioned how Melody, how Melody had grown weary of her mother's iron grip on their lives, yes."

"Charlotte? I'm pleased she's not coming. I never want to meet her."

"I don't, I don't believe you ever will, no."

Ishmael picked up a stick, absently tracing patterns in the dirt. "It's strange to think I'll be escorting a cousin I've never met to college. What if we have nothing in common?"

"Try your best, try your best."

"Mr. Roche!" David, the butler, called from the back porch in the distance. "Mr. Roche, I believe it's time!" Osborn and Ishmael rose and strolled across the green grass lawn. Hoady Junior meandered about the back lawn, watching them as they crossed. "We should be heading to the station now," said David as they came up the steps. Osborn pushed up his spectacles on his nose and quickened his pace ahead of Ishmael.

The family buggy rattled along the cobblestone streets of Johnstown, its polished wood gleaming in the late afternoon sun. David sat ramrod straight on the driver's bench, his gloved hands firmly gripping the reins.

The Johnstown train station's clock tower came into view before the red brick facade of the main hall. "We've arrived, sirs," David announced as he pulled the horse to a stop at the curb.

Osborn adjusted his hat, squinting at the clock and confirming it with his pocket watch. "We're early," he said.

Ishmael hopped out first and offered a hand to his father. Osborn regarded his son's outstretched hand for half a moment until, with a barely perceptible nod, he grasped it firmly, easing himself down from the carriage. David busied himself with Ishmael's luggage, unloading the trunks and bags.

They stepped into the station's cavernous main hall. Sunlight filtered through high-arched windows onto the polished floor. The ticket counter stretched along one wall, a line of impatient travelers fidgeting before it. Steam billowed from an idling locomotive, swirling around the bustling platform.

A sharp whistle pierced the air. Osborn's hand instinctively went to his pocket watch. "That'll be the 2:15 from Pittsburgh," he muttered. "Ray, Ray always arrives on the 2:15, yes, the 2:15 from Pittsburgh, yes."

Ishmael's gaze searched the arrivals board, its wooden slats clicking as they updated. He ran a hand through his graying hair as the station doors swung open. A flood of passengers poured in, their voices rising in a cacophony that echoed off the vaulted ceiling. Osborn stood on tiptoe, scanning the crowd.

A flicker of movement caught Ishmael's attention, and he raised his hand, pointing. "There," he said. Osborn's smile lit up as Ray and Little Miss emerged from the crowd.

Ishmael's gaze shifted to Dierdre trailing behind. He blinked, momentarily taken aback. With her slate gray eyes and black hair, she strolled up to them wearing a slim, dark red velvet dress. Her presence exuded confidence, and her beauty was undeniable. Ishmael found himself at a loss for words before regaining his composure. He smiled at her as he approached. She returned it with a quick jump of her brows.

Ray approached Osborn. "Good to see you again, Uncle," said Ray with an embrace. Spinning around to Ishmael, Ray said, "Ishmael, my, have you grown. Why, you're a full grown gentleman now, ain't ya?"

"Possibly, but only my family dares to label me by that appellation," he replied as they embraced. "Good to see you, Uncle Ray."

After embracing Ishmael, Ray gestured to Little Miss. "Ishmael, you've never met my wife—"

"Little Miss, I've heard so much about you," greeted Ishmael.

"Osborn, Ishmael, good to see you," greeted Little Miss. "But, it's Melody now. Melody Ann Roche. My real name."

"Is that right?" replied Ishmael.

Osborn chimed in, "Oh, oh yes, it's Melody now. Ray wrote me. Melody Ann, yes. Melody Ann Roche, yes."

Melody stepped up to Osborn. "Mr. Roche, how have you been? Ray tells me you are doing very well here since Ishmael has been at the university."

"Well, very well. But, I was, I was hoping to see, to see Clara and Alice, yes."

Ray and Melody's expressions fell. "I'm sorry, Uncle, they couldn't come up," Ray explained. "Schoolwork. You understand? Maybe another time."

Ishmael watched Dierdre roll her eyes after hearing the excuse. He grinned. It would undoubtedly be Charlotte keeping them away.

"Yes, I'm sorry they couldn't come. Clara is now five, and Alice is seven. Schoolwork keeps them quite busy," said Melody.

"About, about the age you started taking care of me, Uncle," Ray recalled.

"And me," said Ishmael.

"Yes, yes, I came into the lives of both of you, both of you about that age, that age."

Ray laughed, shaking his head, before whirling around to Dierdre, casually standing behind them. "Oh! I almost forgot the reason we are here," said Ray as he took Dierdre's arm and pulled her forward. "Dierdre, this is Uncle Osborn."

"Nice, nice to meet, meet you, Dierdre," Osborn said with a nod.

A ghost of a smile played on Dierdre's lips as she sauntered up. "We've met before, if I recall."

"You were so little, so little, yes."

Dierdre cocked her head as she studied Osborn. "You surely do not look like a sin eater to me," she said before turning to her mother. "What's grandma going on about?"

Melody bristled at her comment. "Dierdre! Don't start."

Ishmael fought back a grin at Dierdre's biting sarcasm. He found it oddly compelling. Moving on, Ray extended his hand to Ishmael with a warm smile. "Thank you for taking Dierdre with you to Swarthmore. We sincerely appreciate it."

"No trouble at all. Swarthmore College is on my way. My university is just a few more miles up the road," he said, his gaze shifting to Dierdre. "Have you visited the college yet?"

Dierdre's eyes met his. "We have not had the pleasure," she replied, her voice self-assured.

"Well, then, I'll have the pleasure to show it to you and help get you settled."

"Oh, would you, lad?" Ray interjected, relief clear in his tone. "That would certainly set our minds at ease."

Dierdre rolled her eyes. "My parents apparently think me incapable."

Ray chuckled. "You are quite capable, darling. It is your mother and I who are incapable of not worrying about you."

"I'm sure she is quite clever, quite clever, indeed," said Osborn. "She was clever enough to get into Swarthmore, yes, Swarthmore."

Melody turned to Ishmael. "Ishmael, will this be your second year at the university?"

"It is my second year attending, but I am in my third year of studies."

"Oh, my. That is remarkable," said Melody.

David walked over to Ishmael, handing him his ticket. "The porter has your luggage, sir."

"Thank you, David."

Facing Osborn, David said, "I will be with the buggy, sir."

"Thank you, David," replied Osborn.

As David retreated, his black coattails stark against the sea of colorful travelers, Dierdre's gaze followed him. Her left eyebrow arched with a mischievous glint in her eye. "I wouldn't mind having my luggage given to the porter," she murmured, her voice low but pointed.

Ishmael's head whipped toward her, his eyes widening. "Oh! Well, yes, certainly," he stammered, pivoting on his heel. "David!"

Dierdre's hand shot out, grasping Ishmael's sleeve. "No!" she said, laughter bubbling beneath her words. "I'm only teasing."

Ishmael's face flushed as he called out, "Never mind, David. My mistake."

Melody's eyes narrowed as she watched the exchange. "Dierdre," she said, her tone sharp, "this is hardly the time for such antics."

Dierdre's smile faltered, but she squared her shoulders and met her parents' gaze. "Of course. I apologize."

Osborn jumped as the stationmaster's whistle pierced the air. "I believe that is our train," said Ishmael before he picked up Dierdre's trunk. "I'll be your porter," he added with a smirk.

The group moved as one toward the waiting train, its steam hissing from the locomotive. Ishmael handed the trunk to a waiting porter as Melody embraced Dierdre, smoothing a stray lock of her daughter's hair. Dierdre let out an exasperated sigh at the primping. "Write often," Melody whispered.

Ray clasped Ishmael's hand firmly. "Take care of our girl."

Ishmael nodded. "You have my word."

With a final round of hugs and handshakes, Ishmael and Dierdre boarded the train.

Ishmael opened the door to their private compartment. Dierdre's eyes widened, drinking in the room as she entered. "A private compartment?"

"Only first class for the lady."

Seeing her parents outside waving at them, Dierdre opened the window and leaned out to wave as the engine lurched forward. She fell into her seat with a laugh. Ishmael sat across from her, kicked off his shoes, and put his feet up on her side. She looked down at them and back at him with a sarcastic grin. "Only first class for the man."

The door slid open, and the conductor entered. "Tickets, please?" Ishmael handed him two. Dierdre studied Ishmael as he validated them. The conductor handed them back to him, nodding. "Mr. Roche," he said, nodding and leaving the room.

"How did he know your name?" asked Dierdre.

"We reserved this compartment. Let me know if you get hungry. There is a dining car on this train."

"I will, thank you kindly. So, tell me, what is your major at the University of Pennsylvania?"

"We call it U Penn for short. Chemistry is my major. What is yours?"

"I am undeclared as yet. Chemistry? Do you enjoy it?"

"I do. My focus is on photography, like my father, except it is the chemistry within the photograph I find interesting."

Dierdre leaned forward, elbows on her knees. "Indeed, it is interesting."

Seeing her interest, he continued, "I am working on a new photographic film. Not the daguerreotype film my father uses. It's more of a gelatin emulsion."

She sat back. "Half of those words you used, I have no idea."

"What you should know is that the average person will be able to use a camera, I believe. There will come a time when everyone owns a camera."

"My, oh, my, I love your enthusiasm. I surely hope to find that enthusiasm for myself in college. Maybe I should steal some from you."

"I'm certain you will find it for yourself."

Dierdre landed a finger on her lips in thought. "I wonder, did my father ever mention me on his visits to you?"

"Of course. He would speak of you often. All of you."

"He would?"

"Yes, he told us about you learning the piano and performing at your family gatherings. You graduating primary school. Recently, you published a poem in the Gazette? He brought it to us. Very good."

Dierdre smiled and rocked back in her seat. "Why, thank you."

"I remember he even told us about your first formal dance and the beautiful gown you wore. Ray goes on and on."

"Were you smitten with me, Mr. Roche?" she teased with a pouty expression.

Ishmael chuckled at her bold attitude. "My, aren't you presumptuous. I was about thirteen, so I'm certain I was."

She turned to the window, pressing her fingertips against the cool glass as she watched the farmland roll by in a patchwork blur of greens and golds. "Don't you think it's interesting that we have the same last name?" she mused, her breath leaving a small fog on the windowpane.

"Why would that be interesting? We are from the same family."

"Well, not really." Dierdre turned back to him, twirling a strand of hair around her finger. "In our case, we have the same last name but are cousins by marriage, not blood."

"True."

She leaned forward conspiratorially, her eyes sparkling with mischief. "We could get married, and I wouldn't even have to change my name."

A low chuckle escaped Ishmael as he reached into his coat pocket, retrieving an intricately carved pipe. "Is that important to you? Not changing your last name?"

"I like my last name. And your last name," she added with a laugh that seemed to fill the small compartment. Her fingers traced abstract patterns on the velvet seat as she continued, "And it's an important last name. Your father is a very famous man. My daddy's studio is very busy because of your father being famous and all."

Ishmael began loading the pipe with tobacco. "That's good to hear."

"You know," Dierdre said, leaning back and crossing her ankles, "it's a shame my grandmother doesn't like your father."

The match flared to life in Ishmael's hand, illuminating his features for a brief moment before he applied it to the tobacco. "It is," he agreed, puffing gently to coax the embers to life.

Dierdre's gaze followed the curling tendrils of smoke as they rose toward the ceiling. "Why, we could've been family all this time."

"I agree." The pipe stem between his teeth muffled Ishmael's response.

"I believe being a sin eater sounds deliciously salacious. You know, I remember seeing your daddy when he was a sin eater."

Ishmael's eyebrows arched in surprise. "You did?" he asked, the pipe momentarily forgotten.

"I think I did. I was little." Dierdre's eyes took on a faraway look, as if peering into the depths of memory. "He came to our farm when we lived there. He surely didn't look like he does now. I remember him looking like a mysterious warlock riding a mule."

Ishmael's eyes lit up with interest as he took a long draw from his pipe, the cherry-red ember glowing. "A warlock riding a mule, you say? That's quite a specific memory for a child."

"It is, isn't it?" Dierdre nodded, her fingers absently tracing the pattern on her cameo brooch. "I've always wondered about that day. There was something... I don't know, almost mystical about it. Like I'd glimpsed something I wasn't supposed to see."

Ishmael tapped the stem of his pipe against his lower lip, lost in thought. "You know, my father doesn't talk much about his days as a sin eater. It's as if that part of his life is shrouded in mist."

A playful smile danced on Dierdre's lips as she reached out, boldly plucking the pipe from Ishmael's mouth. "Well then, Mr. Roche," she said, bringing the pipe to her own lips and taking a delicate puff, "it seems we have our family mystery, don't ya think?" She held the pipe aloft, studying it as if it held secrets of its own. "Perhaps we should make it our mission to unravel them together."

CHAPTER 14

Dierdre and Ishmael stepped onto the paths of Swarthmore College. Ishmael, his shirtsleeves rolled up and his dark hair tousled, pulled a cart carrying Dierdre's trunk. The late summer air hung heavy, rich with the fragrance of blooming wildflowers. Students milled about, their chatter filling the morning air. A group of young men in pressed trousers and starched collars huddled near a grand oak tree, their laughter carrying across the quad. "Did you hear?" one said. "They're considering allowing men and women to take classes together next term."

Dierdre's eyes darted to Ishmael. "That should be quite exciting."

"Distracting?"

"One could say."

Reaching the entrance of Women's Hall, Ishmael removed the trunk from the cart and set it down. Dierdre caught the furtive glances and barely concealed whispers of the other girls, their eyes drinking in Ishmael's tall frame and wind-tousled hair.

The matron, a stern-faced woman in a high-collared dress, appeared before the large double doors. Her eyes narrowed as she spotted Ishmael. "Young man, you may go no further," she declared, her voice as unyielding as the building's stone foundation.

Ishmael's shoulders slumped. "But her trunk—"

"I'll summon some of the girls to assist," the matron interrupted, pivoting on her heel.

Dierdre and Ishmael's eyes met, a silent conversation passing between them. An easy camaraderie had blossomed during their journey to Swarthmore.

"Well, cousin," Ishmael said, a smile playing at his lips, "it seems this is where we part ways."

"I suppose it is," she replied, tucking a loose strand of hair behind her ear.

The matron returned with two older students, who began to heft Dierdre's trunk inside.

Ishmael backed away from her, reluctant to turn away. "I'll be at U Penn, not far from here," he said. "Perhaps we could meet for lunch in the coming days?"

Dierdre nodded happily. "I'd like that very much," she answered.

"Miss," the matron called sharply. "What's your room number? These girls can't read your mind."

"Forty-four."

"Don't tell me, tell them. Now, go on and help them. Those are your things!"

Dierdre tossed her head dismissively before spinning back to Ishmael.

"Wait!" she called out. Ishmael stopped and spun back to her. "How will I know? How will I know when 'then' is?"

"I will correspond with you," Ishmael declared, his gaze flipping upward to the weathered sign above the door. His eyes traced each letter as if committing them to memory: "Dierdre Roche, Swarthmore College, room forty-four, Women's Hall." With a smile and a wave, he walked away.

As if trying to memorize the rhythm of his gait, Dierdre's eyes didn't leave him. As he finally disappeared from view, Dierdre released a breath she hadn't realized she'd been holding, and in no louder than the whisper of a falling leaf, she murmured, "Ishmael Roche."

Ishmael stood on the bustling platform of Philadelphia's Broad Street Station.

The steam engine's whistle pierced the air, heralding the train's arrival from Swarthmore. Ishmael adjusted his bowler hat, his gloved hands fidgeting with anticipation.

As passengers disembarked, Dierdre emerged, her burgundy dress a splash of color against the gray stone of the station. Ishmael's breath caught at the sight of her fitted bodice and bustle.

"Ishmael!" she called, waving her lace-gloved hand. He hurried to her side, offering his arm.

"Welcome to Philadelphia," he replied. "I trust your journey was pleasant?"

Dierdre's eyes sparkled with mischief. "As pleasant as one can expect. It was a quick half hour."

"How was that last exam of yours?"

"Which one?" Dierdre asked, tucking a stray curl behind her ear.

"The physics one you wrote about."

"Oh! Yes," Dierdre recalled. "Not as difficult as I expected."

"School going well?"

"I enjoy school. I like my professors."

"Meeting friends?"

"I am. But I was simply delighted when I received your telegram. Weekends at Swarthmore can be so dull. All my friends leave to see family. Would you promise to take me out every weekend, would you?" she said as she batted her eyelashes at him mockingly.

"I will certainly try."

They made their way through the crowded streets, the clip-clop of horses' hooves and the rattle of carriages filling the air. "I thought we might visit the Academy of Natural Sciences," Ishmael suggested. "They have a fascinating new exhibit on Darwin's theories."

Dierdre laughed, the sound bright against the city's din. "Only you would consider evolution a suitable topic for a Saturday outing."

He felt his cheeks warm beneath his neatly trimmed beard. "Well, I—"

"It's perfect," she interrupted, squeezing his arm. "I wouldn't have it any other way."

At the Academy, they wandered through halls filled with curious specimens.

Ishmael's eyes lit up as he explained complex concepts, his hands gesturing enthusiastically.

She took his arm in hers as they meandered to the next exhibit. "You are always so polite and ask how I'm doing, how my exams are going," she told him with a smile. "And I never do. So, how have you been? Please tell me."

"I've been well and excited to see you."

"With all of your friends, you are still excited to see me?"

"I know it's hard to believe, but yes. I am able to squeeze you into my busy schedule."

"Good, because I am always excited to see you. Sometimes, I think," she paused, gathering her courage. "Sometimes I wonder what it would be like if we weren't cousins."

A glimmer of a grin played across his lips, equal parts surprised and intrigued. Ishmael continued to the next exhibit, a taxidermied ape. "What do you mean if we weren't cousins?" His eyes locked with hers, searching for confirmation of what he thought - what he hoped - she was implying.

"Oh, now stop! You are making me blush. You know right well what I mean. You and I get along splendidly. We enjoy each other's company."

"That may only be because we are cousins," he replied.

"Cousins by marriage," Dierdre chimed in, her eyes brightening. "It's not as though we share blood," she added, tightening her grip on his arm.

Ishmael's free hand moved to cover hers where it rested on his arm. He paused, choosing his next words carefully. "I must admit, the thought had crossed my mind as well."

The ride back to Broad Street Station was quiet with both of them lost in thought. On the platform, Dierdre turned to Ishmael. "This was lovely," she said. "Remember, every weekend, you promised."

"Indeed, I did."

Dierdre leaned in as the train whistle blew, her lips brushing Ishmael's cheek. "Until next time," she whispered.

He watched the train pull away, his skin tingling where her lips had touched. As the smoke dissipated, Ishmael's mind raced with possibilities and complications. He knew their situation was delicate, fraught with potential scandal. But as he remembered the warmth of Dierdre's arm linked with his and the sparkle in her eyes as she laughed at his explanations, he couldn't help but wonder if some risks were worth taking.

The grand ballroom of the Philadelphia Hotel was awash in golden light, crystal chandeliers casting a warm glow over the crowd. Ishmael stood near the entrance, his tailcoat impeccably pressed, nervously adjusted his white tie. His eyes scanned the arriving guests, searching for one face in particular.

As if conjured by his thoughts, Dierdre appeared. Her emerald gown shimmered as she moved, the bodice adorned with delicate beadwork that caught the light. Ishmael's breath caught in his throat.

"Dierdre," he said, stepping forward to greet her. "You look... radiant."

Dierdre's cheeks flushed prettily. "Thank you, Ish. You're quite dashing yourself."

He offered his arm, and they made their way into the ballroom. A string quartet filled the air with music, accompanied by the gentle murmur of conversation.

"I must admit," Dierdre said, leaning close to be heard over the noise, "I was surprised by your invitation. A chemistry banquet doesn't seem like your usual choice for our outings."

Ishmael smiled, a shadow of nervousness in his eyes. "Well, I'm presenting my research tonight. I... I wanted you to be here."

Dierdre's eyes widened. "Oh, Ish, that's wonderful! Why didn't you tell me sooner?"

"I didn't want to make a fuss," he replied, ducking his head modestly.

As they mingled with the other guests, Ishmael found himself constantly aware of Dierdre's presence at his side. The way she laughed at the professors' dry jokes, the intelligent questions she posed about various research topics – it all served to remind him why he'd been so eager for her to attend.

When it came time for his presentation, Ishmael's shoulders rose and fell as he steadied himself. As he began to speak, his eyes found Dierdre in the crowd. She smiled encouragingly, and suddenly, his nerves melted away.

He spoke with passion about his research into the new type of photographic film he developed by "…creating a flexible base on a strip of celluloid, coated with a gelatin emulsion. It will replace heavy glass plates," he said, as his hands animatedly moved as he explained the concepts. From her seat, Dierdre watched with rapt attention, her pride evident in her beaming smile.

As applause filled the room at the conclusion of his speech, Ishmael returned to Dierdre's side.

"That was brilliant," she said, squeezing his hand. "Truly fascinating work."

"You understood it all?" he asked, surprised and pleased.

Dierdre laughed. "Most. I've had my basic chemistry class. Besides," she added, "I always understand things better when you explain them."

The Annual Chemistry Society Banquet was winding down, the grand ballroom now half-empty as guests trickled out into the cool Philadelphia night. Ishmael and Dierdre lingered near one of the tall windows, the city lights twinkling beyond the glass.

Ishmael's fingers nervously adjusted his cufflinks. "Would you care for a turn about the hotel gardens? I hear they're quite lovely, even at night."

Dierdre's eyes sparkled with curiosity. "I'd be delighted," she replied, taking his offered arm.

They went through the hotel's ornate lobby and into the manicured gardens. Gas lamps lit the path, and the air was fragrant with late-blooming roses. They strolled with the sounds of the banquet fading behind them.

Ishmael turned to her. "I... I've been thinking about what you said a few weeks back. About us."

Dierdre laughed. "Oh? What did I say, and when did I say it?"

"A few weeks ago, when we discussed how we are cousins—"

"You had no idea before then? I've known for some time," she teased.

Ishmael cocked his head with a smirk. "You tease."

"I do, and I apologize. Now, go on. I do remember the conversation. I said I wondered what it would be like if we weren't cousins, yes?"

"Yes, and I want to, and have wanted to for some time, well, to divulge that I have had similar thoughts."

They continued along the gravel paths of the gardens, passing other guests along the way. "Dierdre," Ishmael began, his voice thick with emotion. But before he could continue, they were interrupted by a colleague congratulating him on his presentation. As they stopped to acknowledge the well-wisher, Dierdre's hand found Ishmael's, their fingers intertwining.

Again left alone, they continued along the path, her hand in his. "I know our situation is... complicated," she began. "But being here with you tonight, seeing you in your element – it's made me realize something."

"What's that?"

Dierdre stopped and leaned in close, her lips nearly brushing his ear. "That some complications are worth facing. For the right person."

"You think so?" he asked.

"I do, and I think you do, too," she said, facing him. "At least, I hope so. These past months, our outings, our conversations – they've become the brightest parts of my life."

"I have similar feelings, I admit," he replied as he took her gloved hands in his, his thumbs tracing small circles on her palms. "And tonight, seeing you here, supporting my work, understanding it..." He trailed off, searching for the right words.

"Go on," Dierdre whispered, her eyes never leaving his face.

Ishmael squared his shoulders. "Dierdre, I know our situation is... unconventional. But I can no longer deny my feelings, nor do I wish to. I..." He paused, gathering his courage. "I would like to court you properly and openly. If you'll have me."

Dierdre's breath caught. "I thought you'd never ask, but our families, the potential scandal..."

"I will write your father and ask for his permission."

Dierdre's face lit up. "Will you?"

"A proper letter, yes. Very formal."

"Wonderful!"

"Is that a yes, then?" Ishmael asked, a tentative smile tugging at his lips.

Dierdre's gloved hand rose and cupped his cheek. The silk was cool against his skin. She leaned in, her breath a whisper against his ear, carrying with it the faint trace of champagne. "Yes," she murmured, the word seeming to hang suspended in the night air. Time slowed to a crawl as she moved her lips to his. The kiss was gentle at first, tentative, like the first hesitant raindrops before a summer storm. It carried with it the weight of their shared history and the thrill of forbidden fruit.

CHAPTER 15

The parlor of Ray and Melody's home in Pittsburgh echoed with raised voices. Charlotte paced furiously, her silk gown rustling with each agitated step. Melody stood by the window, a crumpled letter clutched in her hand.

"You cannot let this happen!" Charlotte exclaimed, her face flushed. "They are cousins from the same family. This will not be a good reflection on our family. We are high society now. No longer weepers from the country."

A troubled expression flashed in Melody's eyes as she reread the letter. "But they're not blood-related, Momma. Perhaps—"

"It doesn't matter!" Charlotte interrupted. "Cousins from the same family should not be together. How will that be explained to guests? To anybody? You gonna explain to everybody that they ain't blood related?"

Melody frowned. "Suppose not."

Continuing her pacing, Charlotte pointed at Melody. "And you, of all people, should remember we have a family history with this type of thing leading to tragedy."

Melody's eyes flashed at her mother. "I do remember, Momma. You'll never let me forget."

"This type of thing only happens in the mountains. We are no longer country bumpkins."

Melody sighed, her shoulders sagging. "You're right, of course. The scandal alone would be devastating. What should we do?"

Before Charlotte could respond, the front door opened. Ray's footsteps echoed in the hallway as he approached the parlor. "I'm home," he called, his voice chipper. As he entered the room, his smile faded, sensing the tension. "What's wrong?"

Melody and Charlotte exchanged glances before facing Ray with solemn expressions. Wordlessly, Melody held out the letter.

A crease appeared on Ray's forehead. "What's this?"

"It's from Ishmael," Melody explained. "It was addressed to you, but... well, I thought it would be alright to open it, given it was family correspondence."

Ray took the letter, concern etching his features. "What's the problem?"

Melody swallowed hard. "Just... read it."

As Ray's eyes scanned the page, confusion bloomed on his face. He looked up, bewildered. "Dierdre say anything about this?"

"Not to me," Melody replied.

"It was polite for him to ask me. I like Ishmael."

Charlotte stepped forward, her voice urgent. "We cannot allow Ishmael to court Dierdre, Ray. This cannot happen. They're cousins from the same family. Think of the scandal, the damage to your reputation and your family's."

Ray searched Melody's face for an answer. "I believe she's right, Ray. It would make family gatherings. . .odd," Melody agreed.

"You think so?" Ray asked

"We've worked too hard to establish ourselves in Pittsburgh society," Charlotte replied. "We can't risk everything over this... this infatuation."

Ray's shoulders sagged, the enormity of it all pressing upon him. He looked at Melody for reassurance, but he didn't receive any.

"If you believe that, I guess," Ray said. After a heavy sigh, he continued, "I'll... I'll write to Ishmael immediately. Make it clear that this cannot continue."

Ishmael adjusted his bowler hat as he walked up Parrish Hall's weathered stone steps, his heart quickening with each step. Dierdre stood at the top, surrounded by a cluster of friends who seemed to orbit her burgundy dress like celestial bodies around a star. Ishmael's breath caught at the sight of her in her fitted bodice and bustle.

Dierdre's eyes lit up as she caught sight of him. "Ishmael!" she called, waving her lace-gloved hand.

As Ishmael neared, Dierdre announced, "Everyone, this is Ishmael." She turned to him, gesturing to each person in turn. "Ishmael, meet Olivia, Beatrice, and Catherine." The three girls nodded in greeting, their curious gazes appraising him.

"And this fine gentleman is—"

"Jefferson True," Ishmael interrupted, sticking his hand out to him.

Jefferson took it. "Ishmael, how are you? This certainly is a surprise."

The others watched in bemused silence as Ishmael explained, "We went to the same school back in Johnstown. Jefferson was a few years behind me."

"Four grades, to be exact," Jefferson added with a grin. "You were something of a legend, Ishmael. Never thought I'd run into you here at Swarthmore."

Dierdre's eyes danced between the two, clearly delighted by this unexpected connection. "Well, isn't this a marvelous coincidence? It seems introductions weren't entirely necessary after all."

Another young man walked up behind Jefferson, slapping him on the shoulder before addressing the group, "Hello."

Jefferson spun to him. "Hugh!" he greeted before turning back to the group. "Everyone, this is Hugh Wrigley."

"Hugh!" said Dierdre, recognizing him. "I didn't know you knew Jefferson. This is another coincidence."

"Dierdre, this is a surprise," Hugh replied. "Yes, Jefferson and I are rushing Delta Sig together."

"And how do you two know each other?" Jefferson asked Hugh, pointing to Dierdre.

"Dierdre and I have world history together," replied Hugh.

Beatrice, quiet until now, said, "As fascinating as this reunion is, we should probably start heading over to the lecture. Wouldn't want to be late for Elizabeth Cady Stanton."

There was a general murmur of agreement as the group began to move, falling into step together. Ishmael found himself walking beside Dierdre, their shoulders occasionally brushing. She leaned in close, her voice low and tinged with excitement.

"I can't wait to hear what you think of the exhibit," she said. "And later, you simply must tell me more about your Johnstown days with Jefferson. I sense there are stories there."

The group made their way through the crowded campus and into Parrish Hall. Hugh noted when Dierdre took Ishmael's arm in hers as they wandered through the halls to the main lecture hall.

"Hey?" Hugh asked Jefferson with a nod to Ishmael. "She with him?"

"Dierdre? Don't know for sure. Could be friends."

"Don't look like it. Who is he?"

"Ishmael Roche. We went to school together in Johnstown."

"Oh," said Hugh, his expression relaxing. "Her brother?"

"No. He doesn't have any brothers or sisters. Must be a cousin."

"Looks like they are close family, the way they cozy up to each other. You know him?"

"Yeah, and if he is courting Dierdre, better forget about it. He's very wealthy. The wealthiest man in Johnstown. Goes to U Penn."

"Hmm. That's too bad."

"Why? You like her?" asked Jefferson.

"Who wouldn't? Look at her. She's a beauty."

"She is that," Jefferson confirmed.

Inside the lecture hall, Dierdre sat beside Ishmael with Jefferson next to him. Hugh sat behind them with Olivia, Beatrice, and Catherine.

As they waited for the lecture to begin, Ishmael leaned over to Jefferson. "How have you been, Jefferson?"

"Well, and yourself?"

"Good. How's your brother and your family?"

"Very well. What about yours? Your father? How's he been? The world-famous Osborn Roche?"

"Ah, my father is always doing well."

As the small talk continued, Hugh listened from behind them. His interest peaked when Ishmael leaned in close to Jefferson's ear, his voice dropping to a whisper. "Listen, old boy," Ishmael murmured, his eyes darting briefly to Dierdre, "Dierdre and I... We're distant cousins." There was a pause, pregnant with unspoken implications. "But if word got around to my father, it might get around to her father, and you see, that might cause... difficulties."

Jefferson's eyes widened almost imperceptibly before he schooled his features into a mask of casual understanding. He nodded eagerly, a conspiratorial smile playing at the corners of his mouth. "Of course, old chum, mum's the word with me. Dierdre's a friend, and so are you. No one will hear of it."

Hugh steepled his fingers and sat back in his seat. His brows jumped with a thought, a plan already beginning to form in the shadowy corners of his mind.

Students lounged in small groups on Swarthmore's lush green lawn, where their laughter and chatter mingled with the rustle of leaves in the warm breeze. Dierdre sat beneath the sprawling branches of an old oak tree, her deep red skirt spread around her like a pool of rich wine. She concentrated on a book in her lap, occasionally jotting notes in her leather-bound journal.

Hugh Wrigley approached, pausing momentarily to drink in the sight of her. With a deep breath, he plastered on a genial smile and strode forward. "Good afternoon, Dierdre," he called, his voice light and casual. "Mind if I join you?"

Dierdre looked up, her slate gray eyes widening in surprise before settling into a polite smile. "Oh, Hugh! Of course, please sit."

Hugh settled onto the grass, careful to maintain a respectable distance. He pulled out his textbook, but his eyes darted to Dierdre's profile. After a moment, he cleared his throat.

"I couldn't help but notice you and Ishmael at the women's suffrage lecture last week," he ventured, his tone carefully nonchalant. "You two seem... close."

A faint blush crept up Dierdre's cheeks, and she tucked a stray lock of hair behind her ear. "Yes, well, we are."

"Are you. . .courting?"

"We are."

Hugh nodded, his expression thoughtful. "He seems like a fine gentleman. Although..." he paused, feigning hesitation, "I couldn't help but overhear something about you two being related? Cousins, was it?"

Dierdre's head snapped up, her eyes flashing. "We're not blood-related, if that's what you're implying."

Hugh held up his hands in a placating gesture. "I meant no offense, truly. I was merely curious." He paused, then added softly, "He's a lucky man to have caught your eye." Knowing the answer, he asked, "Your parents approve of him?"

Dierdre's expression softened slightly, but a wariness remained in her gaze. Wearing a smile, she lied, "Yes, they do."

He nodded as his gaze veered away from her. "That's good."

"Ishmael is... special to me," she admitted. "He understands me in a way few others do."

Hugh nodded, his jaw tightening almost imperceptibly. "And what is it about him that you find so captivating?" he asked, unable to keep a hint of bitterness from his tone.

If Dierdre noticed, she gave no sign. Instead, her eyes took on a dreamy quality as she spoke. "He's brilliant, of course—studying chemistry at Penn, you know. But it's more than that. He has a kindness about him, a gentleness that belies his strength. And when he looks at me..." She trailed off, a small smile rising.

Though jealousy gnawed at his insides, Hugh fought to keep his expression neutral. "He sounds remarkable indeed," he managed, his voice strained.

A bell tolled in the distance, startling them both. Dierdre began gathering her books, her movements hurried. "Oh! We'd best be off to Professor Whitman's lecture. Wouldn't do to be late."

As they stood, Hugh offered his arm out of habit. Dierdre hesitated for a fraction of a second before taking it, her touch light and impersonal. They set off across the lawn, their steps in sync, but their minds worlds apart.

The warmth of early summer carried the delicate scent of blooming flowers and freshly cut grass. Ishmael settled on the blanket he'd spread beneath a sprawling tree on the Swarthmore campus lawn. Dierdre appeared on the path, her skirts swishing softly against the grass. She carried a wicker basket, its contents hidden beneath a checkered cloth. Her face brightened as she caught sight of Ishmael and quickened her pace.

"I told you I was bringing lunch," Ishmael said, gesturing to his picnic hamper.

Dierdre lowered herself onto the blanket, smoothing her skirts. "I didn't want to come empty-handed. I brought dessert." She glanced around, drinking in the scenery of students taking a break from classes.

Dierdre began unpacking their meal. She handed him a sandwich and said, "The Senior ball is next week."

"And you are a sophomore."

"Yes, but I am on the decorative committee and have two tickets."

After taking a bite of his sandwich, he said, "Ah, and…?"

"Well, I would like it very much if you would attend with me."

"Now, is this a social or a ball?"

"More of a ball."

"Formal?"

"Yes, formal."

"Dancing?"

"Yes, dancing," she replied with a teasing glint in her eyes. "You do know how to dance?"

Ishmael grinned, surprised by the question. "I know how to dance."

Dierdre plucked a blade of grass, twirling it between her fingers. "I'd have to buy a gown. I don't have one."

"I'll buy it for you."

She met his gaze, a slow smile spreading across her face. "Then, I'd love to accept your invitation," she said with a laugh.

Hugh and Jefferson approached them, books in hand, their voices carrying on the breeze. "Hugh! Jefferson!" Dierdre called out. "What a pleasant surprise."

The two men tipped their hats in greeting as they drew near. Hugh's eyes lingered on Dierdre for a moment before he addressed them both. "Dierdre, Ishmael. Lovely day, isn't it?"

"Indeed it is," Ishmael replied, his tone cordial but guarded.

Dierdre's face lit up with a sudden, mischievous gleam. "Oh, I simply must share the most wonderful news," she gushed, her eyes darting to Ishmael. "Ishmael has asked me to accompany him to the Senior ball. Isn't that marvelous?"

Ishmael's eyebrows rose, but he quickly schooled his features into a smile. "I believe you asked me."

"A lady never asks a man. It isn't proper," she said with a wink.

Hugh's expression flickered for a moment before settling into a polite smile. "How wonderful," he said, his voice carefully neutral. "I'll be there as well, of course, given my position on the committee with you, Dierdre."

Jefferson chimed in, "And I'll be escorting Marie Fredrickson. You remember her, don't you, Dierdre? She's in your Latin class, I believe."

Dierdre nodded, her smile never wavering. "Of course! How lovely for you both."

Hugh cleared his throat. "I'll be taking Elizabeth Thornton," he said, his eyes fixed on Dierdre. "Though I must admit, I had hoped..." He trailed off, leaving the implication hanging in the air.

An awkward silence descended upon the group, only broken when Hugh spoke again. "Dierdre, I wanted to ask you about the floral arrangements for the ball. I was thinking perhaps we could incorporate some of those lovely maroon dahlias—they'd complement your eyes so beautifully."

Ishmael's jaw tightened almost imperceptibly at Hugh's words, his gaze darting between Hugh and Dierdre.

Dierdre laughed lightly. "Oh, Hugh, you flatterer. We can certainly discuss it at the next committee meeting."

"Speaking of which," Jefferson interjected, "we should be off. Wouldn't want to keep Professor Whitman waiting."

Hugh nodded, his eyes lingering on Dierdre. "Until later, then," he said softly before tipping his hat once more and following Jefferson down the path.

As Hugh and Jefferson disappeared around a bend, Ishmael turned to Dierdre. "Hugh... He's always been rather fond of you, hasn't he?"

Dierdre waved her hand dismissively. "Oh, Hugh? He's just being friendly. You know how he is—always trying to charm everyone."

"Friendly, indeed," he drawled, one eyebrow arched in sardonic amusement. "Our dear Hugh has been practically combusting with unrequited passion since your arrival. Two years of silent longing - it's positively Shakespearean."

Dierdre's laughter rang out a touch too brightly. "Oh, Ishmael, really. You and your fanciful notions." But even as the words left her lips, her gaze caught them in the distance as she ate her sandwich. Dierdre's forced smile faded, her mind churning with the complexities of her situation. She knew Ishmael was right about Hugh's feelings, but acknowledging them would only complicate matters further.

"After I graduate next month," Ishmael continued, his tone lightening, "I imagine our lovelorn friend will swoop in to claim my place at your side with unseemly haste."

"How dreadful," Dierdre replied, affecting a theatrical shudder. "Whatever shall I do without my stalwart protector?"

Ishmael laughed. "Impertinent creature," he scolded fondly, shaking his head at her antics.

"Speaking of graduation," he began, his voice taking on a cautious quality.

"Yes?"

"Do you remember that job opportunity in New York I mentioned? The one with that new photographic company, Eastman Dry Plate and Film Company?"

Dierdre nodded. "Yes."

"We've been in discussions. They have a new invention. A camera that, if married with my cellulose roll film, could take one hundred photographs without reloading. They've offered me a position with patent rights on my roll film discoveries. It's an incredible opportunity, Dierdre. If cameras become as common in households as I believe they will, it could mean... well, it could mean a very comfortable future."

"But New York is so far," she pouted.

"I know. Believe me, the thought of leaving you behind..."

"When would you have to leave?"

"They want me to start the day after I graduate," Ishmael replied. "But sweetheart, I've been thinking. What if... what if you came with me?"

Her eyes widened. "To New York? But Ishmael, I've got to finish school."

A determined look crossed his face. "Then let's get married. We could do it before I leave. Start our life together in New York."

For a moment, Dierdre allowed herself to imagine it – a whirlwind wedding, a new life in the bustling metropolis, building a future with Ishmael. But she wanted to finish school, and the reality of her parents' wishes quickly reasserted itself.

"Our family," she said. "My father...What do we do?"

Ishmael's eyes flashed with determination. "We've been discreet these past two years, and I am tired of hiding. We're adults capable of making our own decisions. We need to convince them."

CHAPTER 16

Dierdre stepped out of the carriage into the evening air, her gloved hand resting lightly on Ishmael's arm. Parrish Hall stood before them, all its windows aglow and muffled sounds of music and laughter spilling onto the leaf-strewn lawn.

Dierdre smoothed the folds of her new gown, a deep blue creation that whispered against the ground. Ishmael, resplendent in his tailcoat, gave her hand a reassuring squeeze.

"Ready?" he asked, his breath visible in the cool night air.

She nodded. As they ascended the steps, the door swung open, bathing them in golden light and the strains of a waltz.

The foyer bustled with activity as couples shed their coats and exchanged greetings. Ishmael guided Dierdre through the crowd, nodding to acquaintances as they passed.

The grand ballroom of Swarthmore College was transformed for the night, its usual austere academic atmosphere giving way to glittering chandeliers and swaths of midnight blue silk.

Ishmael's hand rested at the small of her back, a warm anchor in the sea of swirling gowns and polished shoes. As they made their way across the parquet floor, Dierdre caught sight of her friends clustered near one of the Grecian columns.

"Shall we?" Ishmael murmured, his breath warm against her ear. Dierdre nodded, steeling herself as they approached the group. They exchanged greetings with a flurry of false smiles and brittle laughter. Dierdre felt Hugh's gaze upon her, his dark eyes unreadable in the flickering candlelight.

"Some punch, perhaps?" asked Ishmael.

"Please," she replied.

As they turned to the refreshment table, Hugh excused himself from his bewildered date and stopped Dierdre by touching her arm. "Dierdre," he said, "I must say, you look... radiant this evening."

"Why, thank you, Hugh. That's sweet of you to say."

Ishmael's fingers tightened around Dierdre's arm. "Hugh," he acknowledged, his tone perfectly cordial and yet laced with an unmistakable warning.

As he faced Ishmael, Hugh said, "I wonder," his voice carefully modulated, "if I might borrow your lovely companion for a dance?"

Ishmael's face was a study of conflicting emotions, jealousy warring with a stubborn pride that wouldn't allow him to object. "That's for Dierdre to decide," he began. "But after our first dance, of course."

"Of course," Hugh said with a wink. "As I must attend to my escorting duties as well," he said, shifting to Dierdre. "But I do hope you'll save one for me later, Dierdre?"

Dierdre glanced at Ishmael, who gave an almost imperceptible nod. "I would be delighted, Hugh."

As Hugh disappeared into the crowd, Ishmael turned to Dierdre. "Would you like some punch, or would you like to dance?"

"Dance."

"Shall we?" he asked, extending his hand. They joined the dancers, falling easily into step with the music. He led her confidently through the turns and hops of the polka, his hand steady at her waist. Ishmael had not exaggerated his dancing abilities. As they twirled past the punch bowl, Dierdre caught sight of Hugh watching them, a thoughtful expression on his face.

The evening progressed with a blur of dances, laughter, and introductions.

Dierdre found herself swept from partner to partner, though she noticed Ishmael always seemed to materialize at her side between sets, offering refreshments or a moment's respite.

During a particularly energetic quadrille, Dierdre found herself partnered briefly with Jefferson. He proved to be an excellent dancer, easily guiding her through the complex figures.

"You move like a dream, Dierdre," he said as they promenaded. "I daresay you're the belle of the ball."

Dierdre laughed, a bit breathless from the dance. "You flatter me, Jefferson. I fear I'm quite out of my depth among so many accomplished ladies."

Jefferson's eyes sparkled with amusement. "Nonsense. You outshine them all." The dance separated them before he could say more, but Dierdre felt his gaze follow her as she moved to her next position.

As the night wore on, Dierdre found herself by the punch bowl, gratefully accepting a glass from Ishmael. The cool liquid soothed her parched throat, tart with hints of orange and clove.

"Are you enjoying yourself?" Ishmael asked, his cheeks flushed from exertion.

Dierdre nodded enthusiastically. "It's wonderful, Ishmael. Thank you for inviting me," she teased with a sly grin.

A shadow passed over his face so quickly she almost missed it. Before she could inquire, Hugh appeared at their side.

"I believe you promised me a dance, Dierdre," he said, bowing with a flourish. "That is, if your escort still doesn't object?"

Ishmael's jaw tightened almost imperceptibly, but he forced a smile. "Of course not. Dierdre is free to dance with whomever she chooses."

Dierdre took Hugh's arm, allowing him to lead her onto the floor. As they took their positions for a waltz, she glanced back at Ishmael, standing alone by the punch bowl, his expression unreadable.

The music swelled, and Hugh guided her into the first turn. "I must say, Dierdre, you've been quite the topic of conversation this evening," Hugh said as they glided across the floor.

Dierdre raised an eyebrow. "Have I? I can't imagine why."

Hugh laughed. "Can't you? A beautiful woman appearing in a stunning dress? It's positively Cinderella-esque."

"Hardly," Dierdre demurred. "I'm no princess, Hugh. But you certainly are a flatterer."

"Why yes, and I beg to differ. If you are not Cinderella, then you are the wicked witch. You've enchanted everyone here, myself included."

Dierdre felt her cheeks warm at his bold statement. "You're a rogue, aren't you?"

His grip on her waist tightened as he leaned in. "I assure you, I am not. My mouth seems to have a life of its own in front of a princess. It is not my fault."

"And so does my mind, which has decided to return to my sweetheart," she said, releasing herself from his grasp. Hugh's smile dimmed slightly, but he bowed graciously. "Of course. I understand completely."

Dierdre curtsied and thanked Hugh for the dance. She returned to Ishmael, who stood in conversation with a group of other students. The music swelled, and couples began to move toward the dance floor. Ishmael held out his hand. "May I have this dance, Miss Dierdre?"

She placed her gloved hand in his. "I thought you'd never ask, Mr. Ishmael."

On a rainy Wednesday, the postman delivered the mail. Mail delivery had only started a week prior. Ray, on his lunch break from the shop, opened the door to him.

The letter had the return address of Swarthmore College, but no name on top, and the printing was not from Diedre's hand.

Charlotte stood by the bay window, her face a mask of rigid control as Ray sat on the sofa, rereading the letter for what must have been the dozenth time. Behind him, Melody paced in agitated circles.

Mr. Roche,

I pray this missive finds you in good health and spirits. I write to you today compelled by duty and concern for the reputation of your daughter and esteemed family.

It has come to my attention, through various whispers and observations about campus, that your daughter, Miss Dierdre Roche, has been engaged in a courtship with one Mr. Ishmael Roche. I believe you may be acquainted with the gentleman in question, as I have heard tell that he bears some relation to your own family, though the precise nature of this connection eludes me.

It is whispered among the student body that you, sir, would look upon such a union with great disfavor. While I cannot speak to the veracity of these rumors, I felt it my moral obligation to bring this matter to your attention, lest Miss Roche's reputation - and by extension, that of your family name - should suffer.

I hope you will forgive the anonymous nature of this correspondence. I assure you my intent is not to cause discord but rather to ensure that you are fully apprised of the situation so that you might take whatever action you deem appropriate.

May wisdom guide your hand in this delicate matter.

A Concerned Observer

"I simply cannot believe it," Charlotte hissed, her carefully cultivated composure fracturing. "Carrying on with Ishmael after you told her?"

Melody's jaw clenched, the paper crinkling slightly in his tightening grip. "Now, Momma," she began, her tone deceptively calm, "let's not jump to conclusions based on an anonymous letter."

Charlotte whirled on her, her eyes flashing. "Do something! Your daughter's reputation, her very future, hangs in the balance!"

Ray's gaze drifted to the family portrait above the mantle, Dierdre's painted smile seeming to mock him now. "It's not Ishmael that truly concerns me," he admitted, his voice low. "It's Dierdre's willful disobedience. We were clear about our expectations."

Clad in formal black tie and tails, Osborn sat beside Dierdre in the venerable Old College Hall, a relic of the University of Pennsylvania, its walls steeped in history. The graduation ceremony unfolded with speeches blending into a soft hum of applause, a cascade of formalities that barely registered in his mind. Time warped as graduates flipped their tassels, their faces illuminated by the promise of new beginnings. Osborn's gaze landed on Ishmael, threading his way through the throng, his expression aglow with triumph.

"Father!" Ishmael's voice rang out as he enveloped Osborn in an embrace. "How are you?"

"Wonderful, wonderful. It is a splendid day. Dierdre, Dierdre had excellent seats, yes."

Dierdre leaned forward, her lips brushing Ishmael's cheek. "Congratulations."

"Now," Ray interrupted, his voice slicing through the celebratory air as he strode forward, Melody trailing behind him like a shadow.

Dierdre's heart sank as her parents suddenly emerged before her. "Father? Mother? What are you—"

Ray turned to Osborn, his tone measured. "Uncle, I have discovered that Ishmael has been courting Dierdre against my wishes."

Shock rippled through Ishmael and Dierdre. "Father!" Dierdre implored, her voice trembling with desperation.

Ray cut her off, "Not another word." Ray's gaze locked onto Ishmael. "Ishmael, it's time we had a frank discussion about this."

Osborn squeezed his eyes shut, a wave of panic crashing over him as he flapped his hands, his instinctive gesture of helplessness. "Oh, dear, Uncle, why don't you step outside?" Ray suggested with concern.

"The yelling, the yelling..." Osborn whined, his distress rising like smoke.

Ray pivoted to Melody. "Can you take my uncle outside? I will handle this."

Melody reached for Osborn's hand, and he flinched as if stung. "Oh, dear, I'm sorry, Mr. Roche," she murmured in a gentle voice.

"Uncle, you need to open your eyes and follow Melody out," Ray urged.

As Osborn's eyes finally opened, he met Melody's reassuring smile, which allowed her to guide him outside. Ray turned back to Dierdre and Ishmael, the tension thickening.

Ishmael stiffened, meeting Ray's gaze with fragile courage. "Ray, I assure you my feelings for Dierdre are—"

"Irrelevant," Ray interjected, his voice icy, devoid of compassion. "This dalliance ends now."

Dierdre's voice emerged, a tremor of rebellion coursing through her. "Father, please! You don't understand—"

"What I understand," Ray replied, his tone implacable, "is that you have willfully deceived us, Dierdre. And you," he continued spinning to Ishmael, "will cease all contact with my daughter immediately."

Ishmael's complexion drained. "Sir, I—"

"Unless," Ray continued, now fixing his steely gaze on Dierdre, "you wish us to reconsider our financial support for your continued education?"

A horrified gasp escaped Dierdre's lips, the realization of the stakes crashing over her. Ishmael's eyes darted between her stricken expression and her father's unyielding face, the cruel reality settling like lead in his chest.

Tears welled in Dierdre's eyes as Ray gripped her arm. "Come, Dierdre. We're leaving. Now."

"No, please!" Dierdre cried, her protests fading into the din of the graduation crowd as Ray propelled her toward the exit, her voice swallowed by the tide of celebration.

Ishmael stood rooted, the diploma suddenly a hollow token of triumph in his hand. Around him, classmates reveled, laughter and joy ringing out, oblivious to the shattering of his world. Tomorrow, he would board a train bound for New York, a new life awaiting him, yet as he trudged back to his dormitory to pack, he thought the bright future ahead seemed dimmed by the shadows of his past, each step forward a painful reminder of what he was leaving behind.

CHAPTER 17

Ishmael stared down at the bustling streets of Manhattan from his window, ten floors up in the executive offices of Kodak. Each passing stranger reminded him of the one face he longed to see. Sitting behind his mahogany desk, he pulled out another sheet of paper, his fingers hovering over the crisp stationery before him.

"Deirdre, my darling," he began for the hundredth time. The words flowed from his pen with desperate urgency, each stroke a futile attempt to bridge the chasm of silence that had grown between them. As he wrote, the soft whir of film reels and the distant clack of typewriters faded into white noise, leaving only the scratch of pen against paper to punctuate his thoughts.

Ishmael paused, lifting his gaze to the framed tintype on his desk. Deirdre's smile, frozen in time, mocked him with its constancy. How long had it been since he'd seen that smile in the flesh? Since he'd heard her lilting laugh or felt the warmth of her hand in his? The days had blurred into weeks, the weeks into months, each one marked by another unanswered letter.

He returned to his letter, pouring out his heart in ink. Promises of a future together, reminiscences of shared moments, and pleas for some sign of her spilled across the page. With each letter, a piece of him seemed to drift away, carried on waves of uncertainty across the expanse separating them. Ishmael sealed the envelope and added it to the stack in his outbox, a tower of unrequited devotion that grew with each passing day.

Ray's study was a quiet room of dark wood and leather with the scent of his pipe tobacco. Charlotte perched on the edge of an overstuffed armchair, her fingers drumming an impatient rhythm on the armrest. Across from her, Melody lounged behind Ray's oak desk, idly toying with a letter opener.

Melody's face softened, worry crossing her features. "She writes to him every day. Sometimes twice. I..." she hesitated, her voice dropping to a whisper, "I read them, Momma. The things she says... her hopes, her dreams. It's heartbreaking."

"But necessary," Charlotte interjected.

Melody nodded, though the movement lacked conviction. "I know. It's just... seeing her in pain..."

"We're protecting her. From herself, if need be."

"I hope you're right. It's just difficult," Melody said. "How are you managing to intercept her letters?"

"Your husband asked Frederick to deliver any letter from New York to his shop instead."

"The mail carrier?"

"Yes. And when he takes our mail, any letter to Ishmael also goes to Ray's shop."

"What do we do after summer break is over? What if he writes the school or if she sends letters from there? She surely will."

"Your husband already covered that one. The school will intercept any letter from him or to him. She will have no idea."

"Clever," Melody murmured, a note of sadness in her voice. "Have you read any of his?"

"Yes. Declarations of undying love, promises of a future together." Melody's eyes met Charlotte's. "You focus on Deirdre," Charlotte said. "Keep her spirits up, keep her distracted. This will all be over soon."

Dierdre clutched her books to her chest, a shield against the curious glances and whispered conversations that seemed to follow in her wake. Dierdre spotted her friends near the library. Beatrice's copper curls caught the sunlight as she waved enthusiastically while Hugh's tall frame straightened at the sight of her approach. Jefferson, ever the quiet observer, offered a small smile.

"Dierdre!" Marion exclaimed, pulling her into a tight embrace. "We've missed you terribly. How was your summer?"

Dierdre's smile faltered for a moment before she composed herself. "It was... quiet," she said. "Ishmael... he's gone to New York, and he never wrote back. Not once all summer."

A heavy silence fell over the group as Hugh's eyes darkened with emotion. "I'm so sorry, Dierdre," Marion said, squeezing her friend's hand. "Perhaps there's been some misunderstanding?"

Dierdre shook her head, blinking back tears. "I don't know what to think anymore. It's as if he's vanished into thin air."

As the girls continued to console Dierdre, Hugh pulled Jefferson aside. "This is it, Jeff," he said, his voice low and eager. "My chance to court Dierdre properly. No more of this Ishmael nonsense."

Jefferson's brow furrowed. "Good man, but are you sure that's wise? She's clearly heartbroken. I'd wait."

Hugh waved off his concern. "I'll be gentle, of course. But I've waited long enough. You won't... interfere, will you?"

Jefferson looked at Dierdre, her raven hair catching the light, her eyes bright with unshed tears. For a moment, he allowed himself to imagine what it would be like to comfort her, to be the one to make her smile again. But he pushed the thought away. "No, Hugh. I know how much you've been pining for her. I'll stay out of it."

A week later, it started with a fever, followed by the telltale spots. Chickenpox swept through the school like wildfire, and Dierdre found herself confined to the infirmary, her skin itching and her heart aching for home.

"I'm sorry, Mr. Wrigley," Nurse Abernathy said, blocking Hugh's path.

"Only those who've had chickenpox before can visit. We can't risk further spread." Hugh's fingers curled into fists at his sides, nails digging into his palms as he fought the urge to argue, to plead for just a moment with her.

Behind him, a flash of guilty excitement came over Jefferson. "I've had it, Nurse. When I was a child. May I see her?" he asked, his eager voice barely masked by a veneer of sympathy.

The nurse hesitated, then nodded. "Very well, Mr. True. But be brief." The corners of his mouth twitched, threatening to betray the small, selfish joy rising beneath his composed exterior.

Jefferson's heart quickened at the unexpected turn of fate. He entered the dimly lit room, his eyes adjusting to find Dierdre curled up on a narrow bed, her face flushed with fever. "Dierdre?" he called softly.

She stirred, her eyes fluttering open. "Jeff?"

He pulled a chair close to her bedside, careful not to disturb her. "I thought you might like some company."

A weak smile crossed her face. "You're not afraid of catching this dreadful thing?"

Jefferson chuckled. "Already had it when I was seven. Besides," he added, his voice softening, "what are friends for?"

Over the next few days, Jefferson became a constant presence in the infirmary. He brought Dierdre her assignments, read to her from her favorite books, and sat with her when the fever made it hard to think.

"You don't have to do all this," Dierdre said one afternoon, her voice hoarse but her eyes clearer than they had been in days.

Jefferson looked up from the book he'd been reading aloud. "I know," he said. "I want to."

As Dierdre recuperated, she looked forward to Jefferson's visits more and more. His quiet strength, gentle humor, and how his eyes crinkled when he smiled began to stir something in her heart that she thought she had lost with Ishmael's silence.

Finally, the day came when Nurse Abernathy declared Dierdre well enough to leave the infirmary. As Jefferson helped her gather her things, their hands brushed, and a spark of electricity seemed to pass between them.

"Jefferson," Dierdre said. "I... I wanted to thank you. For everything."

He turned to her, his eyes searching hers. "Dierdre, I—"

"Would you..." she hesitated, then pressed on. "Would you like to go for a walk with me? When I'm fully recovered, of course."

A slow smile spread across Jefferson's face, lighting up his features. "I'd like that very much."

CHAPTER 18

December 1887

A light dusting of snow covered the platform as Ishmael stepped off the train in Johnstown. Ishmael scanned the crowd, his face breaking into a smile after he spotted his father, Osborn, waiting for him as he stood next to David. Osborn's tall figure, slightly stooped now with age but still commanding, stood out among the holiday travelers.

"Father!" Ishmael called, waving as he made his way through the crowd.

Osborn's weathered face creased with joy as he embraced his son. "Welcome, welcome home, son. The house has been too quiet, too quiet without you."

David, ever the proper butler, gave a formal nod. "It's good to have you back, Master Ishmael. Shall I take your bags?"

As David loaded Ishmael's luggage onto their waiting carriage, father and son climbed inside. Warmed by hot bricks wrapped in flannel, the plush interior provided a welcome respite from the cold. As they set off through the snow-dusted streets of Johnstown, Osborn studied his son's face. "You look tired, Ishmael. I hope you're not working yourself too hard in New York. I hope not."

Ishmael chuckled, running a hand through his hair. "It's been a whirlwind year, Father. But an exciting one." His eyes lit up as he continued, "The launch of the camera has been an unprecedented success. Have you seen our marketing?" Ishmael said before using air quotes. "'You press the button, we do the rest'? It has resonated with the public."

"I've seen the, I've seen the advertisements. It's quite remarkable how you've simplified the process, simplified it, yes."

"That's the key," Ishmael explained, his fatigue momentarily forgotten. "We're not just selling a camera; we're offering a complete service. The customer buys the camera pre-loaded with film, takes their pictures, and sends the whole thing back to us. We develop the film, print the photos, and return everything with a fresh roll of film."

"Ingenious," Osborn murmured. "You're following in my footsteps, but in your own way. Not by taking photographs, but by revolutionizing how they're taken, yes, how they're taken, yes."

Ishmael beamed at his father's understanding. "Exactly. And the financial returns..." He lowered his voice for only his father to hear, "They're substantial, Father. More than I ever dreamed."

Osborn giggled. "And you are already wealthy, yes, wealthy."

The carriage veered onto the long drive leading to the Cattell mansion. "I'm proud of you, Ishmael. Truly proud. I am, yes."

As David halted the carriage, Ishmael added one last piece of news. "There's more, Father. George is making me a partner. We're changing the company name to the Eastman Kodak Company."

Osborn's eyes widened, but David opened the carriage door before he could respond. "We've arrived, sirs."

The Cattell mansion stood before them, its windows aglow with warm light. A large wreath hung on the front door, and garlands framed the entryway.

The essence of old books and fine cognac greeted them as they entered the foyer. David took their coats and disappeared to prepare tea. Ishmael followed his father into the study, where a fire crackled in the hearth.

"How have you been, Father?" Ishmael asked, settling into one of the leather wingback armchairs. "Keeping busy, I hope?"

Osborn nodded, "Indeed. I have a book signing coming up next month –

for my books. There's been renewed interest in war photographs lately."

"That's wonderful," Ishmael said. "Your work deserves recognition."

"And the charity work keeps me occupied, yes," Osborn continued. "We've been, We've been offering free portrait sessions for poor families. You'd be amazed at how, at how much a simple photograph can mean to those who've never had one, never had one."

David entered with a tray of tea, set it down, and began pouring.

"David, may I have a brandy instead? It's been an arduous journey," asked Ishmael.

"Certainly, sir."

David walked out and brought back a tray with a bottle of brandy and a glass.

Osborn stood. "Shall we visit your mother and grandfather? The snow's let up, and the air might do us good."

Used to his father's 'visits,' Ishmael followed him out onto the expansive lawn behind the mansion. Tea and brandy in their hands, they strolled silently to the graves, their feet crunching on the fresh snow. As they entered the treeline, they stood before the three graves nestled among the trees, paying their respects.

Ishmael's gaze lingered on his mother's headstone. The wooden cross bore a name - Lou Roche - that should have evoked a lifetime of memories yet summoned only a vast, echoing absence. He'd spent countless hours at this spot, trying to conjure some sense of connection to the woman who had given him life but found only the hollow weight of obligation.

His grandfather's death, at least, had left tangible memories - the ghost of pipe tobacco, the rumble of laughter, the feeling of a hand ruffling his hair. But even those recollections had begun to fade, time eroding their edges like waves against a shoreline. Ishmael felt the loss of Henry Cattell more keenly than that of his mother, and the realization often left him feeling guilty and somehow fraudulent in his grief.

As he sat there, caught between the graves of two people who had shaped his life through their absence as much as their presence, Ishmael couldn't help but feel like an interloper in his own family history. He was a man composed of others' stories and expectations, forever reaching for connections that remained just beyond his grasp.

"There's something I should, I should mention," Osborn said, snapping Ishmael out of his thoughts. "Ray and Melody will be joining us, will be joining us for Christmas Eve dinner."

Ishmael stopped short, his heart skipping a beat. "Father, I'd rather you had told me sooner. I'd rather not. It would still be too difficult to see her. To be in the same room, pretending everything's fine."

Osborn nodded, understanding in his eyes. "Of course. But I was going to say, I was going to say that Dierdre will not be there, not be there, no. She will not be here. Ray and Melody will be spending Christmas Eve with us and collecting Dierdre Christmas morning at the train station, at the train station Christmas morning to accompany her back to their home in Pittsburgh, yes." Osborn pushed the brush away as they entered the forest behind their home.

Ishmael followed him in. "Even so—"

"Ishmael, please. They did what they thought best, what they thought best for the family, yes. And I, and I have not seen Ray for some time, for some time, no."

"That's because of Charlotte. I'm surprised Melody is coming. Did Charlotte remove her leg iron?"

Osborn spun around to read Ishmael's expression. "It is a joke, Father."

Osborn shrugged. "It seems so, but nonetheless, nonetheless, I would like to have Christmas Eve dinner with you and my nephew and his, and his lovely wife, yes."

Ishmael smirked. "Alright, I understand. I will have dinner and be a gentleman."

"Thank you, Son. Thank you."

"It's fascinating to me that Charlotte does not realize that you haven't been a sin eater for over two decades."

Osborn's eyes fell to the pine needles on the ground. "But she knows I pawned my soul, yes, I pawned my soul."

Ishmael shook his head in disbelief. "Father, these are modern times. I can't believe you still believe those wives' tales. That was over twenty years ago."

Osborn shrugged it off, and they stood in silence for a few more minutes, the peacefulness of the snow-covered grove broken only by the occasional chirp of a winter bird. As they headed back to the house, Osborn said, "Your mother would be proud of you, proud of you, Ishmael, just as I am. You are, you are a handsome and successful man, Son. There will be, will be many beautiful ladies vying for your attention, yes."

"Mr. Roche, you have guests!" said David, his voice echoing through the high-ceilinged hallways, prompting Osborn to emerge from his study.

"It's your nephew and his lovely wife," David announced as Ray and Melody ascended the front steps.

Osborn's face lit up with a warm smile. "Excellent. David, please fetch Ishmael."

"Uncle," Ray greeted, embracing Osborn.

Melody stepped up from behind Ray. "Osborn, how have you been?"

"Well, very well. I was, I was hoping again to see, to see Clara and Alice, yes."

"Charlotte would never allow that," said Ishmael as he entered the room. His eyes met Ray's, and tension flickered between them. Two years had done little to ease the pain of Ray's refusal to allow Ishmael to court Dierdre.

"Ishmael," Ray said, extending his hand. "It's good to see you."

Ishmael paused before accepting the handshake. "And you, Ray."

"But I'm afraid he is right," Melody said. "My mother, you know how she is."

"Well, yes, well, yes. Maybe someday, someday." Osborn gestured toward the parlor. "Please, let's make, let's make ourselves comfortable. David, would you bring us some refreshments?"

The butler nodded. "Of course, sir. Tea and biscuits for everyone?"

"That would be perfect, perfect, thank you," Osborn replied.

As they settled into the plush armchairs and sofas of the parlor, Osborn turned to Ray. "Now then, tell me about your business."

Ray's eyes lit up. "Indeed, Uncle, I've hired two additional photographers. Business is booming."

Melody chimed in, "Ray's portraits have become quite popular. He's even received commissions from as far as Philadelphia."

"That's wonderful news," Osborn said. "And what about you, about you, Melody? How have you been and the girls?"

"Oh, the girls are thriving in their new school."

Osborn chuckled. "Is that so?"

As David returned with the tea tray, Osborn turned his attention to Ishmael. "Ishmael, why don't you tell, you tell them about your work with Eastman Kodak?"

Ishmael, who had been quiet until now, straightened in his chair. "Well, it's been an exciting time. Our new camera, the Kodak, has been selling beyond our wildest expectations."

"Oh? Do tell us more," Ray encouraged.

"Well," Ishmael began, "we've simplified the entire process of photography. Our slogan is 'You press the button, we do the rest.' It's opened up photography to the masses."

Osborn couldn't contain his pride. "Ishmael's been instrumental in developing the new roll film. He's even been made a partner in the company."

"A partner?" Melody exclaimed. "Ishmael, that's wonderful."

"Thank you," Ishmael said. "I've been fortunate to work with some brilliant minds."

"Very good. Quite an accomplishment, Ishmael," added Ray before shifting to Osborn. "And you, Uncle? What about you? Will you stay in that massive home all alone while Ishmael is in New York?"

"David, David is here. I have David here with me. And my portrait charity keeps me busy."

Curious, Melody tilted her head to the side and asked, "Portrait charity?"

"It's nothing, really," Osborn began. "I take portraits for families that cannot afford it, no."

Ishmael chuckled. "My father is too modest. Every month he will journey into Johnstown and set up his vardo in the town square. People that have never had or can't afford a portrait come from all around to get one from him. He incurs all the costs. He'll even travel if they need, or if it is for a postmortem photograph. He brightens a lot of people's lives."

"My, my," said Melody. "That's a wonderful thing. And doing what you know best."

"By the way, how's that new Romani vardo caravan of yours coming along?" asked Ray.

Osborn's eyes sparkled with excitement. "Oh, it's a marvel, yes," said Osborn before becoming even more animated. "The craftsmanship in this one is exquisite, is exquisite, yes. I've been adding, I've been adding my own touches – a perfect mobile darkroom for my photography charity, yes, and other expeditions too, yes."

As the conversation flowed, it touched on various topics, from the children's schooling to the latest news from Philadelphia, but avoided any mention of Dierdre.

David announced dinner, and they moved to the dining room. The table had a sumptuous Christmas Eve feast – roast goose, chestnut stuffing, glazed carrots, and a towering plum pudding for dessert.

After dinner, as the family retired to the parlor for coffee and brandy, David discreetly approached Ray with a telegram. When Ray excused himself to read it, Ishmael took the opportunity to head to the washroom. Hearing a discussion from the hallway, Ishmael cracked the washroom door, his ear to the opening.

Melody had joined Ray in the hallway. "What is it, dear?" she asked quietly.

Ray sighed, keeping his voice low. "It's from Dierdre. She's changed her plans for tomorrow. She won't be taking the morning train. Instead, she'll be spending Christmas with... a young man and his family here in Johnstown."

"Here in Johnstown?" asked Melody.

"That's what it says. She says she'll take the 4:15 train to Pittsburgh herself, and she's bringing this young man to meet us."

"Oh my. Did she say who he is?"

Ray replied, "No name mentioned."

Ishmael leaned against the wall, closing his eyes as a wave of emotions washed over him.

Ishmael stood on the platform, his breath forming small clouds in the chilly atmosphere. After bringing Ray and his family to the station for the morning train to Pittsburgh, he decided to stay and wait for the 4:15 to Pittsburgh. The train station bustled with activity, porters rushing to and fro with luggage while travelers hurried to their destinations.

Ishmael pulled out his pocket watch. The 4:15 to Pittsburgh was on the tracks, steam hissing from it. Passengers stepped on and off it, a sea of hats and coats moving in all directions.

Suddenly, Ishmael's heart leapt into his throat. Dierdre strode toward him from the far end of the platform. Ishmael ducked behind the porter's booth, pressing himself against the rough wooden planks. Peering around the corner, his eyes drew to Dierdre like a magnet. She stood alone with her luggage, looking radiant in a forest green traveling cloak, until a man approached her. Taking her into his arms, he kissed her. When a porter came to collect their bags, the man turned in Ishmael's direction. "Jefferson," hissed Ishmael quietly. Her presence alone made his pulse race, but the sight of Jefferson True by her side sent a jolt through him.

The train sounded its whistle, and Ishmael watched as Dierdre and Jefferson boarded it. "Why did I have to do this to myself?" Ishmael admonished as he shook his head.

The train lurched forward with a screech of metal on metal. After most of the train had left the platform, he emerged from hiding. Walking alongside the train, he saw her through the window. Their gaze locked for a fleeting moment, her expression unreadable as it faded into the distance.

Ishmael's shoulders slumped, feeling as though all the air had been knocked from his lungs. The realization that Dierdre was now with Jefferson True – an old neighbor, schoolmate, and fraternity brother- was a bitter pill to swallow.

It had been two years since he'd seen her last, but seeing her now felt as fresh as their last day together. It was Christmas, a day for new beginnings, but as each turn of the train's wheels carried her further from him, Ishmael could only feel the gravity of an ending. The Christmas present he wanted most would be a ticket to the next train back to New York.

CHAPTER 19

Ray guided the carriage, setting the brake in front of his house. He climbed down and walked around to his front door. Opening it, he leaned in and called, "Are you ready?" Charlotte and Melody, dressed in their Sunday best, came down the stairs. "Can you grab my top hat, Melody?" he asked. She handed it to him as they came outside.

Melody climbed up into the carriage, settling next to Ray. Charlotte took the seat behind them. Ray slapped the reins and headed down their street. On the other side of their street, another carriage headed toward them.

Lines of confusion deepened on Ray's forehead. "What? They're early. I was supposed to pick them up from the 4:15 train," he muttered, pulling the reins to halt their carriage.

Her face glowing with excitement, Dierdre sat beside a young man driving the carriage.

Dierdre's hand waved as her voice rang out. "Mother! Father!"

Melody said, "Darling, what a surprise!"

"You are here early," said Ray.

"We just decided to take an earlier train," Dierdre replied.

Charlotte studied the young man as Melody asked, "We're just on our way to the Christmas service. Won't you join us?"

Dierdre beamed, turning to her companion. "Of course! Oh, let me introduce you. This is Jefferson," she said, her eyes shining as she looked at the young man.

"Nice to meet you, young man," said Ray. "Why don't you just turn your carriage around and follow us to the church? We'll greet you proper there."

"Certainly, sir," said Jefferson.

The expanded group made their way to the church, the two carriages forming a small procession through the snow-dusted streets. The young man appeared very handsome, tall with sandy brown hair, but something else Charlotte couldn't quite put her finger on. Something familiar.

As they arrived, other parishioners filed in, their excited chatter filling the air with festive spirit. The group made proper introductions and shook hands before entering the church.

Ray and Melody engaged Jefferson in quiet conversation in the church vestibule, their voices low.

"And where did you two meet?" Ray asked, watching his daughter beam at the young man beside her.

"We met at Swarthmore," replied Dierdre, squeezing Jefferson's hand.

"Of course."

Melody appeared around Ray and asked, "And where are you originally from, Jefferson?"

"Johnstown, ma'am."

Melody's hand tightened on Ray's arm. "Is that so?" she said, her voice carefully controlled. "Ray's uncle, Osborn Roche, lives up there. Do you know him?"

Jefferson's face lit up with recognition. "Of course - everyone in Johnstown knows Mr. Roche. I went to lower school with his son, Ishmael - though he was four years ahead of me. Small world, isn't it?"

"It seems too small for us," Charlotte hissed under her breath.

"Yes. So it seems," Melody agreed, though something in her tone had shifted.

Charlotte leaned forward and asked, "And what does your father do, Jefferson?"

"He's in the mortuary business," Jefferson replied, oblivious to the sudden tension that seemed to ripple through Charlotte and Melody.

Barely above a whisper, Melody asked a question she didn't want to hear the answer to, "Jefferson, what's your last name?"

Just as the church bells began to toll, he said, "True," with a smile. "Jefferson True."

The name slapped their ears like a thunderclap. Ray watched as Melody's and Charlotte's faces paled in unison, a fact that went unnoticed by the happily chatting Dierdre and Jefferson. At first, their anxiety confused Ray, until a moment later, he put two and two together. Ray's face fell as he contemplated the cruel irony: Augustus True fathered both Dierdre and the boy beside her, a truth known to him but not to them.

The preacher stood at his pulpit, signaling the start of the service. Charlotte caught Melody's eye, seeing her shock and panic reflected there. Ray clenched his jaw, his eyes darting between the two women as if seeking guidance.

The hard wooden pews suddenly felt like islands in a stormy sea. The preacher's voice rang out with the joy of Christmas Day, but the words were a distant hum for Charlotte, Melody, and Ray. Their minds raced, grappling with the implications of what they'd just learned. As the congregation around them sang hymns of peace and goodwill, the three sat rigid, their faces masks of polite attention while inside, a tempest raged.

Dierdre and Jefferson sat close, their hands intertwined, blissfully unaware of the turmoil their presence had caused.

As the sermon continued, Charlotte focused on the stained glass windows, their colorful depictions of biblical scenes suddenly seeming like a mockery of the tangled web of secrets threatening to unravel before her eyes. She knew this Christmas Day would mark the beginning of a potentially heartbreaking journey for all of them, a journey she had traveled before.

After the service, Charlotte, Melody, and Ray exited the church in silent anguish, wondering how they could navigate the treacherous waters ahead. They greeted the preacher before stopping with Dierdre and Jefferson at the bottom of the stairs.

"Meet you two back at the house?" Ray asked.

"Certainly," replied Jefferson as Dierdre wrapped herself around his arm.

"Wait!" said Dierdre, beaming. "I must tell you now. I have such wonderful news!" Ray, Melody, and Charlotte froze with fake smiles on their faces. "Mother, Father, Grandma," Dierdre announced before facing Jefferson, beaming. "We're betrothed!"

A stunned silence enveloped them before Melody found her voice. "Betrothed? But darling, we've barely met this young man."

Jefferson stepped forward, extending his hand to Ray. "I know I should have asked you for her hand—"

"But this is the modern era, and women have rights now," interrupted Dierdre.

"But sir, I know this is sudden, but I assure you, my intentions are honorable," insisted Jefferson.

Ray shook the offered hand with a surprised expression. "Well, this is certainly unexpected. Perhaps we should all get home to discuss this further."

Dierdre's expression fell. "What with all the somber faces?"

Ray shook a smile onto his lips. "Oh, darling, we are just surprised, is all," he said, pulling her into a hug. "Just a surprise."

Jefferson and Dierdre took the lead on the way home. Ray purposely held back. As soon as the young couple was out of earshot, Melody turned to Charlotte, her eyes wide with panic. "Momma, what are we going to do?" she hissed.

"We need to tell her," said Ray.

"We need to break them up without telling her," said Charlotte.

"What is so wrong with telling her who her real father is?" asked Ray.

"There's a lot to unpack in that question, Ray," Melody said with tears filling her eyes. "A lot I never told ya, and I don't wanna never tell ya."

Ray slammed his foot on the floorboard. "Why?" he demanded.

Charlotte slapped Ray's shoulder. "Hush your mouth, Ray. They's just ahead."

Melody threw her face in her hands. "'Cause I'm ashamed."

Ray's head whipped around to Charlotte. "Was she raped by him?!"

Charlotte spun away from his searing eyes. "Some truths should remain buried, Ray. Not for your sake," Charlotte said as she motioned her head to Melody, "but for hers."

"He didn't rape me, Ray," Melody said, wiping her tears.

"It's a curse it is," Charlotte said calmly. "What I did when I was young and foolish caused all this. Can't ya see it?"

Melody shook her head. "It wasn't your fault, Momma. No one knew better."

Charlotte shook her head. "It has to be a curse on me. Same thing happening again, right in front of us, right in front of me. Should'a been a better weeper, I believe."

"What are y'all talking about?" demanded Ray.

"Nothing's happened yet, Momma. We can stop this before it does. Just have to think on how."

Ray yanked the horse to a stop in the middle of the street, whirling to Melody. "I'm your husband, and you're my wife. I need you to tell me this buried truth right here and right now, or I'm gonna tell Dierdre what I know. She's my daughter too, and I'll do what I gotta do."

Reading his dead-set expression, Melody shifted to her mother for support. She gave none. Melody swallowed hard. "My momma—"

Charlotte stopped her. "Oh, now you're going to be divulging my secrets too, are ya?"

"Looks like we all have a price to pay," said Ray.

Ray slapped the reins as Melody said, "My momma, when she was young, met Augustus's father, and things happened, and Augustus came out of that union. A few years later, so did I. We didn't know each other, and so—"

"Oh, my," said Ray, slowly beginning to understand.

"I was trapped in Petersburg during the war," Charlotte began. "I didn't know what was happening. When I made it home after the war, I found them together. Augustus never knew I was his mother. Some other woman raised him. It was the curse that brought them together. Outta all the people in the world, they met and—"

A sigh escaped Melody's lips, one heavy with the weight of uncomfortable truth. She and Augustus had been victims of their parents' secrets, their feelings poisoned by truths hidden away in dusty letters and whispered confessions. If only they had known sooner, if only their parents had spoken the truth, she and Augustus would never have wandered down that path. The life she had built with Ray was not just her destiny but her salvation, a proper future unmarred by the shadow of forbidden kinship.

"Augustus and I were married and had Dierdre by the time my momma came home from the war. She told us, and she forced us apart."

Charlotte crossed her arms. "Just like you gotta do now, child, I 'spect."

Ray slapped the reins, and the carriage lurched forward. "Just like we gotta do," he said.

Charlotte's heart clenched. Sitting beside Dierdre was her grandson - the word echoed in her mind with a bittersweet ache. How many times had she thought of him yearning to reach out, to be the grandmother he never knew he had? Charlotte pulled a tissue out and dabbed her eyes. Melody turned to her. "Momma?"

"Ah, nothing. Just thinking. That boy, that boy is my grandchild."

Melody thought about it, nodding. "Yes, yes he is."

"Maybe I should pay a visit to Augustus," said Ray. "He should know what's happening. He could tell Jefferson to stop seeing her."

Melody's hand snatched Ray's arm as she stared off in thought. "Wait! Augustus already knows."

"How's that?" asked Ray.

"She was just visiting his house. He knows her name is Dierdre, and he knows you, Ray. Dierdre Roche ain't a far throw."

"They's still together," added Charlotte. "So, he didn't say nothing to them."

Melody shook her head. "I believe he's in the same pickle."

Ray veered the wagon down Crape Street. "Y'all better be thinking fast. We're almost home."

Charlotte's mind raced through possibilities. We could invent some scandal about his family, something offensive that would make her reconsider the match."

Melody shook her head. "Are you kidding? You saw how happy Dierdre is again. She won't give him up after we forced her away from Ishmael."

"She's right. We can't use that card twice. After breaking her and Ishmael up, she won't listen to us," said Ray.

"Then we'll have to be clever," Charlotte said, a determined glint in her eye. "We'll find a way to make Jefferson lose interest in her. Make him want to break the engagement himself."

"But how?" Melody asked.

"We could... emphasize Dierdre's less appealing qualities to him. Make her seem high-maintenance, difficult to please."

Ray's head snapped back to Charlotte. "And what if she found out we said that about her? And she will, Jefferson will tell her. That ain't being clever. Now, shush now. They's up ahead."

Dierdre stood on the sidewalk, her arm linked with Jefferson's. Her engagement ring caught the weak winter sunlight as Melody, Ray, and Charlotte pulled up, their faces masked with forced cheer.

"I'll make us some lunch, and we'll get acquainted," said Melody.

Inside the warmth of the family home, they took off their coats and removed their boots. The fragrance of pine and cinnamon mingled with the crisp outdoor chill that clung to their clothes.

"Ray, why don't you show Jefferson to the guest room?" Melody suggested, her voice tight despite her smile.

Ray nodded, leading Jefferson up the creaking stairs. The guest room was small but cozy, with a patchwork quilt draped over the bed. After Jefferson set his bag down, the pair silently returned to the living room.

In the kitchen, pots clattered as Melody and Charlotte prepared lunch. Charlotte's hands shook as she chopped carrots, her mind racing with the implications of their secret.

Ray settled into his favorite armchair as Jefferson perched on the edge of the sofa, his posture stiff. "So, Mr. Osborn Roche is your...?"

Ray lit a pipe as he stared at Jefferson. Puffs of smoke rose into the air. "My uncle, yes."

"Oh, alright," Jefferson replied as he nervously picked at his fingernails.

Dierdre breezed into the living room and nestled next to Jefferson on the sofa, oblivious to the tension crackling in the air.

As the family gathered around the dining table for Christmas lunch, the interrogation began in earnest. Ray asked, "Jefferson, is this your senior year?"

"No, I am in my sophomore year, sir."

Lines formed on Ray's forehead. "Oh, how old are you?"

"I am twenty, sir."

Ray seized the opportunity. "But as a sophomore, graduation is still quite a ways off, and marriage is quite a commitment."

Jefferson straightened in his chair. "With all due respect, Mr. Roche, I may be young, but I'm ready for the responsibilities of marriage. "

"And I know he is," added Dierdre.

Melody passed the roast turkey to Jefferson, her smile barely reaching her eyes. "But how, Jefferson? You do know you have to provide."

Jefferson beamed. "I do. My coursework is in mortuary science, Mrs. Roche. It's a two-year program, and I have completed it all. I only have general education classes remaining to complete my degree."

"Well, exactly," Ray chimed in. "You won't be working while completing those courses."

"Well, I had intended on achieving my degree, but since I've met Dierdre, I believe it will not be necessary. I intend to join my father's mortuary business post haste. Your daughter will be provided for."

"You know, there's no need to rush into anything. Perhaps you should focus on finishing your coursework first," Ray said before turning to Dierdre. "And you too, Dierdre. Wouldn't you like to complete what you have started?"

Dierdre's fork clattered against her plate. "Daddy, I'm twenty-two. I'm practically an old maid already. Almost all of my friends from Swarthmore are married now."

Charlotte chimed in, her voice syrupy sweet. "Now, dear, your education is important. There's no shame in waiting a bit longer."

"Grandmother," Dierdre sighed, exasperated. "I can always return to my studies later if I choose."

Dierdre reached for Jefferson's hand. "I think it's admirable. Jefferson will be providing an important service to the community, just like yours does,

Daddy."

Melody, Ray, and Charlotte exchanged glances, knowing the fragile happiness before them was built on a foundation of sand – and they held the tide that would wash it away.

CHAPTER 20

The bell above the door chimed as Ray unlocked and entered his office. The streets were quiet as most businesses were closed for the holiday season. He had barely stepped inside when a familiar voice called out behind him.

"Ray Roche."

Ray whirled around to find Augustus True standing in the doorway, his face etched with worry. The years had been kind to Augustus, but today, he looked every bit his age, the reality of the circumstances evident in the slump of his shoulders.

"Augustus," Ray said, nodding in recognition. "Come in."

Augustus followed Ray in, shutting the door behind him. "You remember me?"

Ray gestured for Augustus to take a seat. "Of course, please take a seat."

Augustus sagged into the chair. "Ray, it's very important I speak with Little Miss. Now, I know y'all are married and all, it ain't about that..."

"I know what it's about, and we've been expecting you."

Augustus' eyebrows shot up in surprise. "You have?"

"I was going to see you, but you got to me first."

"Jefferson and Dierdre?" Augustus probed.

"Unfortunately, yes. Jefferson and Dierdre."

"I know Little Miss knows, but do you understand why they can't be together?"

"My wife's name is Melody now. Melody Roche. And I do. She told me."

Augustus leaned forward, his eyes intense. "I pulled Jefferson aside and told him he shouldn't be fussin' with her. I told him there's some bad blood with your family. It's the only thing I could think of that quick. I told him I didn't want him seeing her, courting her, nothing." Augustus rose and began pacing the room. "That's why they ran outta my place early yesterday morning. Jefferson wasn't happy with me."

"Dierdre didn't know anything about that. Her tongue was plumb tuckered going on and on about the both of them."

"We have to stop them, Ray. Before it's too late."

"Agreed," Ray said, moving to his desk. "I'll be taking Jefferson to the train station at noon. Dierdre will be going with us to see him off. Go on over to my house and speak to Melody about it. Think of how to do it. She'll be expecting you."

Ray pulled out a piece of paper and jotted down an address. "Here's our home address. Just around the second corner, down Crape Street. Go see Melody while we're away. You'll have about an hour before I return with Dierdre."

As Augustus left, Ray sank into his chair, his shoulders sagging, the enormity of it all pressing upon him. He wondered, not for the first time, how their lives had become so entangled in secrets and half-truths.

The knock on the door came precisely at the time Ray had specified. Melody and Charlotte exchanged glances, steeling themselves for their own reason. Melody opened the door to Augustus standing there, looking as if he'd aged a decade since she'd last seen him. Melody smiled at him, and he replied with a smile of his own, sharing a moment of recognition for the time they spent together in their younger years.

"Augustus," she said softly, stepping aside to let him in.

He entered, his eyes darting around the room before settling on Charlotte.

There, too, a flicker in his eyes laden with unspoken history before he acknowledged her. "Mrs. Fenn," he said with a polite nod.

Charlotte didn't expect his greeting to hurt, but it did. She wouldn't expect him to ever call her 'mother,' but not hearing it felt like a stab in the gut. "It's been some time," she said.

"It has," he replied.

Charlotte gestured for him to sit. "Augustus, please sit."

All three sat in the large living room, falling silent, each lost in thought, grappling with the impossibility of their situation. The ticking of the clock on the mantle seemed to grow louder, a reminder of the limited time they had to find a solution.

Charlotte rose. "Can I get you some lemonade, Augustus?"

"That'd be fine, thank ya. I feel a bit dry in the throat."

Charlotte nodded and went into the kitchen.

Augustus turned to Melody, his voice hoarse. "You ain't Little Miss no more, I heard."

"Melody, yes."

"Melody Ann Roche," he repeated.

"Yes."

"Ray, he's a good one. I like him. I like him a lot."

"He's been a good father."

Augustus's eyes twitched, and he looked away. "I'm certain he has."

"What I mean is, he's been a good father to your daughter. I didn't mean to imply—"

"No, no," he insisted.

"With the circumstances and all—"

"I, I understand what ya meant."

Charlotte came back in with a tray of lemonades, handed a glass to Melody and Augustus, and took one for herself. "When did you find out about this?" Charlotte asked.

"So, Jefferson just showed up with her at my house Christmas Eve. Arm in arm, they were. And he introduces her. Dierdre, he says. I knew those eyes, that hair. I had to steady myself," he said as he attempted to wipe the emotion off his face. "When I saw her...after all these years..." Both Melody and Charlotte nodded understandingly. "And now..."

"We understand, Augustus. We're all in a difficult position."

"As Melody knows, I know Mr. Osborn Roche. We met him at the same time back then. Anyhow, he's now living outside Johnstown, living in the Cattell mansion. What do ya know? Yessir, his son, Ishmael, and Jefferson, they went to school together. Anyway, when I heard Dierdre's full name...Roche photography in Pittsburgh ain't too hard to find."

The room fell silent as Melody lifted her chin to Augustus. "I can't tell Dierdre, Augustus. I told Dierdre her real father died in the war. She can't know the awful truth."

"We're wrestling with the same bear."

"We realize that, but perhaps," Charlotte began, "we don't need to tell them anything. Maybe there's a way to separate them without revealing the truth."

Augustus looked up, a glimmer of hope in his eyes. "What do you mean? I already pulled Jeff aside and told him he shouldn't be courtin' her. I said there's some bad blood with the Roches."

"That didn't work," said Melody.

"We could... create a reason for Jefferson to break off the engagement," Charlotte suggested. "Something that would make him reconsider."

"But wouldn't harm Dierdre's feelings too deeply," added Melody.

Charlotte frowned. "Harm her feelings, please, child. Letting them marry would be a might more harmful."

"I'll do whatever it takes," Augustus said. "Even if it means never seeing my daughter again." Augustus leaned forward. "There was a day... I came to the farm, and you were all gone. Vanished without a trace. I had no way to find out where you'd gone. I thought I'd lost my daughter forever." His voice broke. "And now that I've found her again, I must send her away." Augustus sank into a chair, his hands clasped tightly in his lap. "I watched her grow up, you know, those years back. From the treeline behind your farm. All these years, never able to speak to her, to tell her who I am..."

A bitter laugh escaped Charlotte as a sad smile rose on her lips. "As did I with you, Augustus. Watching you from afar as another woman raised ya."

The room fell silent before Melody said, "My momma thinks it's a curse. A family curse."

"A curse," Charlotte began. "Yes, I suppose that's as good a word as any for the poison that's seeped through our family tree."

The moonlight filtered through the lace curtains of the bedroom. Ray lay next to Melody, running a hand through his hair. "Now I understand why you and your mother didn't want Ishmael to court Dierdre. It's because of what happened to you and Augustus?"

"Yes."

"Hmm."

"What?"

"Don't you see that as a mistake now?"

"Mistake?"

"Yes, a mistake."

"Not letting Ishmael court Dierdre was a mistake?"

"They aren't related by blood, Mel. What harm would it have done? Look where we are now," Ray replied.

Melody tensed beside him. "Ray, we've been over this—"

"Who cares how it would've looked to others? They were in lo—"

The floorboards outside their room creaked, and they both froze. After a moment, Ray relaxed but lowered his tone. "They were in love, and we let yours and your mother's foolish fears get in the way." Ray's words resonated in the silence stretching between them, broken only by the distant hoot of an owl. "You and Augustus need to tell her the truth."

Melody inhaled sharply. "No, we can't. There's got to be another way."

"Augustus is waiting for us to figure out what to do. I let him stay at the shop. I'll get him in the morning and bring him by."

The old grandfather clock in the hallway ticked steadily as Charlotte and Melody sat in tense silence. The sound of gravel crunching under tires broke the quiet, and both women straightened in their seats. Moments later, the front door creaked open.

Ray's hushed voice carried from the entryway. "This way, Augustus."

Footsteps approached, and the two men entered the parlor.

Charlotte stood, gesturing to an empty armchair. "Please, sit. Would you like some coffee?"

Augustus nodded, sinking into the offered seat. "Thank you."

Melody poured a steaming cup, her hands trembling as she passed it to him. Charlotte stood by the hearth, her silhouette stark against the flickering flames. Melody sat in her chair, her knuckles white as she gripped the armrests. The air between them crackled with tension, heavy with unspoken words and long-buried secrets.

"I can't tell her, Augustus," Melody insisted. "It would destroy her."

"And what of the destruction that lies ahead if we don't?" said Charlotte. "This secret... it's a cancer, Melody. It will eat away at all of us until there's nothing left."

Melody shook her head vehemently. "She's too young, too innocent. How can we burden her with this knowledge?"

"Innocence," Charlotte scoffed, the word bitter on her tongue. "Innocence is a luxury our family can ill afford. We've paid for it dearly, time and time again."

"I think she's right, Mel," said Ray.

"Listen to me, child. Dierdre comes from weeper blood. Our line has borne witness to the deepest sorrows, the darkest secrets of others. It's in her very marrow to shoulder such burdens."

Melody's eyes welled with tears. "But she's my daughter. I should protect her."

"And you will," Charlotte assured her, her voice softening. "By arming her with the truth. By trusting in her strength. By showing her that even in the face of unspeakable truths, we endure." Melody rose, moving to the window. The early morning sun hid behind the mountains to the east. "I've watched you struggle with this secret for years, Melody," Charlotte continued. "I've seen how it's eaten away at you, how it's shaped every decision you've made. Would you condemn Dierdre to the same fate?"

"She won't take just any reason. We already used the 'it's best for the family reputation' reason," said Ray. "We gotta tell her she's blood related to Jefferson. He's her half-brother. It's not only the truth; it's the only reason she will accept. I promise you that."

Melody's resolve wavered, uncertainty flashing across her face. Charlotte pressed on, her voice low and urgent. "Think of the alternatives. If we don't tell her, and she discovers the truth on her own... or worse, if she and Jefferson..."

Melody considered all of their faces, each one steadfast in agreement. She stood, smoothing her skirt. "I'll wake her."

The room fell silent as Melody's footsteps faded up the stairs. Minutes later, she returned with a sleepy-eyed Dierdre in tow. She guided her daughter to the sofa, her movements slow and deliberate, as if prolonging each second could somehow forestall the inevitable. As they sat, the air in the room seemed to thicken, charged with unspoken truths.

Dierdre blinked, taking in the solemn faces around her. Seeing Augustus, she rubbed her eyes. "Mr. True, what are you doing here? Is it Jefferson? Has something—"

Augustus raised his hand to her. "No, no, Dierdre. Nothing like that. Jefferson is fine. Back at home."

Dierdre's eyes darted between her mother and the others, confusion and apprehension etching lines across her young face. "Then, what's going on?"

Melody's hands trembled as she clasped them in her lap. She opened her mouth to speak, then closed it again, the words sticking in her throat like thorns. Finally, Melody drew a shaky breath, her voice low. "Sweetheart, there's something... something we need to tell you." She paused, swallowing hard. "It's about your father."

Dierdre stiffened, her spine straightening as if bracing for a physical blow. "What about him?" she asked, her voice small and uncertain.

Melody's gaze flicked to Augustus, then back to her daughter. The years of secrecy pressed down upon her, threatening to crush the breath from her lungs. She licked her lips, her mouth suddenly dry. "What we've told you... it's not...

it's not the whole truth."

Dierdre's eyes widened, curiosity swirling in their depths. "What do you mean?" she pressed, her words coming out in a rush. "What haven't you told me?"

Melody closed her eyes briefly, steeling herself. "Your father," she began, "he didn't die in the war. That was... that was a secret I kept from you till now."

Dierdre's brow furrowed, her mind struggling to process this revelation. "What?" she breathed, the single word laden with disbelief and dawning realization.

Melody's hand gestured to Augustus, who stood frozen like a statue, his face a mask of regret. "Mr. True," she said firmly. "He's... he's your real father."

Dierdre shook her head, confused. "Mr. True?"

"Augustus and I... he was my first husband. He's your daddy."

"Jefferson's father?" Dierdre asked as her eyes widened, darting between the adults in the room. Realization dawned on her face, followed quickly by horror. "But that means... Jefferson..."

She broke off, tears welling in her eyes. Ray moved swiftly to her side, wrapping an arm around her shoulders.

"Sweetheart, I'm sorry this happened. So sorry. You'll have to break it off with him, but he can't know the reason. He can't know Augustus is your true father."

Dierdre pulled herself back, wiping her eyes. "Why can't he know?"

"It'll destroy my family, Dierdre," said Augustus.

"It'll destroy your family that you were married before and had a child with that person? You were married, right?"

"We were," added Melody. "But there's more to it. Much more."

"What?"

Charlotte stepped forward. "Your mother and Augustus, due to circumstances they could not see... when your mother and Augustus met, just like you and Jefferson, they had no idea that they were, in fact, brother and sister. Augustus is my son." Dierdre's mouth fell open. "Yes, child, it's a family curse, it seems," Charlotte murmured. "But you must be strong now. Jefferson can't know about this. You have to end things with him."

Dierdre nodded, her body shaking with silent sobs. The clock chimed, its sound echoing through the heavy silence of the room.

"I can't do it. I can't tell him," pleaded Dierdre. "It's not fair. You made me break up with Ishmael, and now this?" She spun around to Ray. "You tell him, Daddy. Tell him you don't approve of him or he ain't right for me, something. Tell him anything, but you do it."

"I'll do it," replied Ray.

CHAPTER 21

WESTERN UNION TELEGRAM

TO: JEFFERSON TRUE
AUGUSTUS TRUE AND SONS MORTUARY
JOHNSTOWN, PENNSYLVANIA

FROM: RAY ROCHE
112 CRAPE STREET
PITTSBURGH, PENNSYLVANIA

MESSAGE:
JEFFERSON STOP

AFTER CAREFUL CONSIDERATION MY WIFE AND I HAVE CONCLUDED THAT THE MATCH BETWEEN YOU AND OUR DAUGHTER DIERDRE IS NOT SUITABLE STOP

WE HAVE DISCUSSED THIS MATTER WITH DIERDRE AND SHE AGREES WITH OUR REASONING STOP

DIERDRE WISHES TO TERMINATE THE ENGAGEMENT AND

CEASE ALL FURTHER CONTACT STOP

WE APPRECIATE YOUR UNDERSTANDING IN THIS DELICATE MATTER STOP

RAY ROCHE

END MESSAGE

The acrid smell of developing chemicals mingled with the odor of fresh paint as Jefferson pushed through the door of Ray's photography studio, the crushed telegram a damning weight in his hand. The bell's cheerful jingle mocked the storm brewing within him.

An employee rose from his desk. "May I help you?"

"I'm here for Ray Roche," Jefferson demanded, his voice tight with contained fury.

"Settle down, young man. Is there a problem?"

"It's fine, James. I'll take care of this," Ray's voice floated down from the staircase. He descended slowly, each step deliberate, his eyes never leaving Jefferson's face. A wisp of guilt passed across the older man's features before he schooled them into careful neutrality. Ray stopped four steps from the bottom. Looking down on Jefferson, he began, "Jefferson, I—"

Jefferson's heart pounded in his ears. "Don't," Jefferson cut him off, his voice determined and trembling. "This paltry explanation isn't enough. I deserve more than a few cryptic lines dismissing years of friendship, of... of love."

"I thought the telegram was clear—"

"Clear?" Jefferson scoffed. "It explained nothing. Why do you suddenly disapprove of our match?"

"It's your family, Jefferson," Ray managed. "There's been a long-standing disagreement..."

Jefferson's forehead creased in thought, his analytical mind kicking into overdrive. "What's the reason?" he pressed, his voice taking on the calm, reassuring tone he used with grieving families. "How did this all start?"

"That's for your father to tell you. There's been a long standing disagreement between the Roche's and the Trues. Ask him about it."

"He did mention something about bad blood..."

Ray held up his hands, already retreating. "Ask your father, son. I don't have time for this. James, show Mr. True out."

James put out his arm, gesturing to the door for Jefferson. Jefferson stared at Ray for a long moment, his jaw clenched, before spinning on his heel and storming out of the studio. The bell clanged violently behind him, a discordant note in the quiet afternoon.

Outside, the sunlight seemed harsh and unforgiving. Jefferson shuffled aimlessly down the sidewalk, his mind a maelstrom of confusion and pain. What could his family have possibly done? The Roches and Trues had been pillars of the community for generations.

What if the "bad blood" Ray spoke of wasn't metaphorical? What if there was some dark secret lurking in his family's past, some sin committed by a long-dead ancestor that now reached across the years to taint his chance at happiness?

The full impact of the situation bore down on him, hunching his shoulders. Jefferson leaned against a nearby lamppost, his breath coming in short gasps. The future he'd imagined with Dierdre seemed to crumble before his eyes.

But beneath the pain and confusion, a spark of determination flickered to life. He couldn't let this go. If he loved her enough to ask her to marry him, he needed to speak to Dierdre first. He wasn't going to take the word of Ray's telegram. If she still wouldn't have him, he surely would search for whatever secrets lay buried in his family's past. He would unearth them and clear the air so he and Dierdre could be together again.

The carriage wheels clattered against the cobblestones as Ray urged his horse homeward. His mind raced, replaying the confrontation with Jefferson. As he rounded the corner to his street, his heart sank.

Jefferson and Dierdre stood on the front porch, locked in a heated argument. Dierdre's face was streaked with tears while Jefferson gesticulated wildly.

Ray pulled the reins, bringing the carriage to an abrupt halt. He leapt down, his boots hitting the ground with a thud.

"What's going on here?" he demanded, striding toward the pair. Ray pushed between them, placing a firm hand on Dierdre's shoulder. "Inside. Now," he ordered, guiding her toward the door.

"But Father—" Dierdre protested.

"Now, Dierdre," Ray repeated, his voice leaving no room for argument.

He whirled around to Jefferson, standing defiantly on the porch steps. "Leave now, or I'll call the constable. I won't ask again."

For a moment, Jefferson looked ready to argue further. Then, with a final, anguished look at Dierdre, he stormed off the porch and crossed the street. He spun around and faced them from the opposite sidewalk, crossing his arms defiantly. "We don't need their permission, Dierdre!" he called out.

Ray slammed the door shut and faced his daughter. Dierdre stood in the entry, her arms wrapped tightly around herself.

"What were you thinking?" Ray hissed. "You can't speak to him anymore. Do you understand?"

"He came here. What can I do? Mother and Grandma are out shopping."

Ray's expression softened. "Alright," he said, peering out of the transom window at the top of the door. "If he does this again, just don't talk to him."

An hour later, Melody and Charlotte approached the house laden with grocery bags, and Charlotte nudged Melody.

"Look," she whispered, nodding across the street.

Charlotte's heart broke at the sight of Jefferson sitting hunched on the curb, his head in his hands. She longed to comfort the grandson she could claim only in the silence of her own heart. Her long-held secrets pressed down upon her, heavy as gravestones as they hurried inside.

Ray stood at the transom window, his posture rigid. Dierdre peeked out from behind lace curtains, her eyes red-rimmed.

"What on earth is happening?" Melody demanded, setting down her bags.

Ray whirled around to them. "Jefferson showed up at the studio. Then here. He's not accepting our resolve."

Dierdre stepped forward. "He wants me to elope with him. Please, let me talk to him one last time. I can convince him it's over."

"Absolutely not," demanded Ray.

"Let her try," Charlotte interrupted. "It might be the only way to end this cleanly."

After a moment of tense silence, Melody faced Dierdre. "Be careful," she warned before Dierdre slipped out the door.

Jefferson's head snapped up as Dierdre approached, stopping on her side of the street. He scrambled to his feet.

"Dierdre, please," he pleaded. "I don't understand. Why are we ending this? This family disagreement or whatever it is isn't between us. It's their problem, not ours."

Dierdre wrapped her arms around herself, fighting back tears. "It is between us, Jefferson. I can't explain why."

Jefferson shook his head, bewildered. "We can elope, start fresh somewhere else."

"No," Dierdre said firmly, though her voice quivered. "I can never do that, Jefferson."

"This doesn't make any sense!" Jefferson exclaimed, taking a step toward her. "If you know something, then tell me!"

Dierdre retreated, shaking her head. "I'm begging you, Jefferson. Please go home. Please accept that this is over."

Jefferson stared at her, hurt and confusion etched across his face. "I'll go home, but I want to talk to you when we go back to school."

"No, please, Jefferson. I'm begging you."

"I love you, Dierdre, and I know you love me. We'll talk at school," Jefferson called out.

Without another word, Dierdre fled back into the house, leaving Jefferson alone on the street. He stood there, staring at her front door for a few moments before walking away.

Dierdre's face was pale, her eyes distant as she entered the foyer. Ray sat in his armchair, running a hand through his hair, frustration evident on his face. Melody perched on the edge of the settee while her grandmother stood by the fireplace, one hand resting on the mantelpiece.

"Mr. True is wrong," Dierdre said, her voice flat and emotionless. "Jefferson needs to be told like I was told. He said he'd talk to me at school. I don't want to go back there."

Without waiting for a response, Dierdre spun around and ascended the stairs, her movements mechanical. The click of her bedroom door echoed through the suddenly silent house.

Melody rose, exchanging a worried glance with Ray before following her daughter. After a few moments, Charlotte stood, her eyes glinting with determination. She made her way up the stairs, her skirts rustling softly. Pausing outside Dierdre's room, Charlotte could hear the murmur of Melody's voice through the door, suggesting various remedies – a trip to the shore, perhaps, or a visit to her cousins in Philadelphia. Charlotte gave a soft knock before entering.

Dierdre lay on her bed, staring blankly out the window. Melody sat beside her, gently stroking her daughter's hair. Both looked up as Charlotte entered.

"I know what to do," she said, her voice firm. All eyes turned to her as she continued, "We'll take her to your uncle. That big mansion of his is in the country, with lots of land, and it's practically a fortress."

"Ishmael's house? I can't go there," Dierdre said.

Melody continued to stroke Dierdre's hair. "Ishmael doesn't live there anymore, sweetheart. Only Uncle Osborn. And a change of scenery might be just what you need. And there's plenty to explore there – the gardens, the library. You could even continue your studies privately if you wish."

Dierdre sat up. "The Cattell mansion?" she asked.

"She'll have space to breathe, to heal," added Charlotte.

Dierdre centered herself with a slow breath. "I... I think I'd like that."

Melody and Dierdre exchanged a look, a silent communication passing between them. After a moment, Melody said, "If that's what you want, sweetheart."

"I'll have your father take you up there tomorrow—"

"No," Charlotte interrupted. "I'll take her."

Intrigue etched itself across Melody's features. "But Momma, you've always—"

Charlotte held up a hand. "It's about time I had a change of heart about him. He may be full of sin, but I'm cursed. We're two peas in a pod, really," Charlotte said firmly. "Ray's got a business to run, and you've got the girls to look after. I'll do this. I need to right things. This is all my fault, after all."

Dierdre turned to her grandmother. "When do we leave?"

Charlotte crossed her arms and sucked in a breath through her nose. "First light tomorrow. Pack only what you need. We'll slip out before the town wakes up."

CHAPTER 22

Osborn sat in a high-backed leather chair in the vast parlor of the Cattell mansion, his gaze moving between Charlotte and Dierdre. "I must say, I must say this is quite unexpected, unexpected, yes," Osborn said as he twisted the brown cloth around his fingers.

Charlotte shifted in her seat. "We didn't have time to send a telegram. The situation... developed rather quickly."

Dierdre stared at her hands, folded tightly in her lap.

"I see," Osborn replied, his tone neutral. "And what, may I ask, may I ask, is this situation?"

Charlotte glanced at Dierdre before responding. "Dierdre has ended her relationship with Jefferson. She needs some time away from Pittsburgh, somewhere secluded to... heal."

Dierdre looked up, her eyes glistening. "I just can't be there right now. It's too painful."

Osborn shrugged. "I understand. You needn't explain, explain further, no." He leaned back in his chair, a small smile on his lips. "You're both welcome to stay as long as you need, yes, yes. This old house has plenty of room. I, I enjoy visitors. I am all alone, all alone, except David, of course, yes."

Relief washed over Charlotte's face. "Thank you, Mr. Roche. We appreciate your hospitality."

"Yes, thank you, Mr Roche," added Dierdre.

"Please, please, call me Osborn, Osborn, yes."

"Alright, well, then, thank you, Osborn," replied Dierdre.

Charlotte cleared her throat. "As for myself, if I may, I would very much appreciate it if you would allow me the courtesy of referring to you as Mr. Roche for the time being. It is a sign of respect, and respect you deserve for your hospitality and for allowing us, especially me, to stay in your lovely home."

"If you must, if you must."

"Thank you, Mr. Roche. I do expect you are surprised by my visit due to my previous transgressions—"

"Yes, I would not, would not expect a visit from you, Charlotte. No, no, I would not. Quite surprised, quite surprised, yes."

"I expect you are, Mr. Roche, and I would like to apologize for those transgressions. I, I have had a change of heart on… well, she who dwells in frail circumstances should not point out the flaws of others."

"Oh, oh, yes. Or, or as the good book says, those who dwell in glass houses, glass houses should be wary of casting stones, yes."

A small smile rose on Charlotte's lips before she said, "Amen."

"I have no idea what frail, frail circumstances you are referring to, referring to, no."

"In the past, I have criticized you for being a sin eater, but now I believe I am packed full of more sin than you ever consumed, Mr. Roche. All gathered by living a shameful life when I was young. That is why I'd like to apologize for my past trespasses."

"I, I accept your apology, yes, but, but how is it that you are as full of sin, full of sin as I am?" Osborn laughed. "I've eaten a lot of sin, a lot of sin."

Charlotte smiled while nervously smoothing down her dress on her knees. "I'm sure you have, but with me, my sins ripened into a curse."

"A curse?"

"Tish-tish," said Dierdre. "Don't go on saying such, Grandma."

"I'm certain of it. Sins so shameful that they cursed me and my kin after me."

"Oh, no," Osborn said with concern.

"Yes. A curse so powerful it lasts through generations."

Osborn's eyes grew wider. Noting his concern, Dierdre slapped at the arm of her grandmother's chair. "Grandma, now, don't be go scaring our host, now."

"The man's a sin eater. The curse can't do nothing to him."

"I, I have not been a sin eater for, for over, over two decades, yes."

"You mean you haven't eaten sin for over two decades, but, no offense, but you're still a sin eater. Like the curse on me, time don't take that away," Charlotte said as she sat in the wingback chair across from him. "You do clean up nice, though. You certainly don't look like a sin eater anymore."

"And with this place," Dierdre said as she gestured to the room. "If you have them, I believe the Lord may have blessed those sins you ate away."

"Thank you, thank you," said Osborn as he picked up and rang a small silver bell on the side table. David appeared at the parlor entrance. "David, please show our guests to their rooms."

Charlotte and Dierdre glanced at each other as they rose from their chairs. "Please follow me, ladies," David told them before they followed him through the winding corridors of the mansion. Both Charlotte and Dierdre found themselves in awe. Massive oil paintings hung on walls covered in rich brocade. Crystal chandeliers cast rainbows across marble floors.

"This wing houses our guest suites," David explained, his voice echoing in the cavernous hallway. "Each room has its own sitting area and private bath."

He opened a door, revealing a bedroom larger than the first floor of their house back in Pittsburgh. A four-poster bed dominated the space, flanked by intricately carved nightstands.

"This will be Miss Dierdre's room," David said. "And Ms. Charlotte, if you'll follow me..."

He led them further down the hall, opening another door to an equally opulent chamber.

Charlotte stepped inside, her eyes wide. "This is... remarkable."

David nodded, a touch of pride in his voice. "The Cattell mansion has hosted royalty and presidents. I trust you'll find everything to your liking."

As David excused himself, Charlotte and Dierdre exchanged glances. In awe,

Dierdre silently mouthed to her grandmother, "Royalty and presidents?"

The morning sun streamed through the towering windows of the Cattell mansion as Charlotte, her silver hair neatly pinned, wandered about the hallways, finding undiscovered rooms and art. Walking into the two-story library, she perused the books and paintings. "Oh, hello," said Osborn, surprising her to the point that she jumped.

"Oh!" she screamed, making Osborn flinch and toss the book he held into the air as he sat in a high wingback chair. "Oh, I'm sorry, Mr. Roche," she said, reaching down for his book and handing it back to him. "I did not see you there. This house is so large."

Dressed impeccably in a crisp suit, Osborn said, "Oh, yes, no, no, I apologize, apologize for not disclosing myself."

"No, it was me, please. I will leave you to your book," she said as she stepped toward the doors.

"No, please, please, Charlotte. Please sit, sit, yes."

A little taken aback, Charlotte returned and sat in a plush chair across from him.

"Did you sleep, sleep well?" he asked.

"I did very well."

"Did you, did you find everything you need, yes?"

"I did, thank you."

"If there is anything, anything you need, pull the rope, the rope next to your bed, and David, David will assist you, yes."

"You are far too kind, Mr. Roche."

"Would you, would you like a book?" he asked, gesturing to one of the hundreds of books in the room. "To read, to read, yes."

Charlotte looked about the room, not knowing where she would start. "Uh—"

"Breakfast is served, sir and madam," said David, entering the room.

Osborn rose. "Feel free to take, to take a book whenever you like, yes."

Covered breakfast entrées sat at the far end of the dining table. Already seated, Dierdre, still adjusting to the grandeur around her, perused each one. Charlotte and Osborn entered, their footsteps echoing across the marble floor. Dierdre said, "Good morning," her voice echoing in the cavernous space.

"Good morning, dear," Charlotte replied as she sat across from her.

Osborn sat at the head of the table as David took his plate, dished a portion from all the selections, and placed it before him. Osborn methodically cut his eggs into perfect squares.

David did the same for Dierdre and Charlotte as they sipped their tea quietly.

As David poured coffee into Osborn's cup, he leaned down and quietly said, "Sir, the mule has been hitched, and your Romani Vardo is prepared out front."

"Thank you, David. Mathew, Mathew will want to see my new, my new vardo. "

"Would you like me to come along or attend to our guests?"

"Oh, oh, please, please attend to our guests. Thank you."

"Very well, sir."

Dierdre perked up. "Where are you going?"

Osborn smiled, setting down his fork. "A book signing event in Johnstown. Of my first book—"

"Portrait of Shilo," finished David, spreading his hands across the sky.

"Yes, yes. Thank you, David."

"Really? That sounds wonderful!" Dierdre exclaimed. "May I come along?"

Charlotte's eyebrows pulled together in a frown. "I'm not sure that's wise, dear. You know Jefferson lives just outside Johnstown."

Dierdre waved her hand dismissively. "He's in Philadelphia now, at school. It'll be fine."

"We can't be certain of that," Charlotte argued. "He could be visiting home or on a break like you."

"The school break isn't for another month."

"Are you at school?" Charlotte asked with raised eyebrows. "He's just as hurt as you are. He could be taking a break as well, for all you know."

Osborn, sensing the tension, interjected. "Perhaps, perhaps you could play croquet with David instead? He's quite skilled, skilled indeed, yes."

David, who had been refilling coffee cups, agreed. "It would be my pleasure, Miss Dierdre."

Dierdre's face brightened. "That does sound fun. I'll go change into something more suitable." She hurried from the room, her footsteps fading down the long hallway.

Charlotte turned to Osborn, her expression softening. "If you don't mind, I'd like to accompany you to Johnstown."

Osborn's face lit up. "Of course, of course! I'd be delighted, delighted to have you along, yes."

Osborn's Romani vardo waited beyond the front entrance, a rolling palace of wood and color, its curved roof a bold arch against the sky. It was his second one after he lost the first one in a river. It stood twelve feet in length and roughly eight feet tall as a masterpiece of craftsmanship, with intricately carved woodwork tracing patterns along the sides. Rich, jewel-toned paints adorned its panels—deep crimson, emerald green, and sapphire blue—blending harmoniously with golden scrollwork that danced in the sunlight. Osborn's vardo was more than a wagon; it was a home on wheels, one he had used as a traveling war photographer in his past adventures.

"Let us be off, be off," Osborn said, climbing onto the wagon bench. Charlotte stuck her foot on the step, about to climb up, but faltered. She tried again with her hand out to him. "Mr. Roche, can you give me a hand?" Osborn stared at her hand without moving. "Mr. Roche, please."

"I, I, I do not, do not like to touch, no."

She stepped back, surprised. "Oh, OK, well then…" she said as she tried again, this time able to pull herself up. The wooden seat creaked as they settled in, and Osborn clicked his tongue, urging the mule forward. "You always been that way?" she asked.

"Yes, yes. I have only enjoyed the touch, the touch of my mother and Lou, yes. Oh, and Ishmael, my son, Ishmael and I, I embrace Ray every time I see him, but I suffer through it, yes."

"Suffer through it?"

"A little, a little. It seems easier as I age, age, yes."

The wagon lurched to a roll, its wheels rumbling over the uneven road. A playful headshake betrayed Charlotte's amusement. "You are a very peculiar one."

"I've been told, yes, yes. Peculiar, the word with a strong consonant c."

Johnstown materialized on the horizon. Charlotte leaned forward, her eyes widening at the sprawling expanse before her. Gone was the sleepy hamlet of her youth, replaced by a bustling town that pulsed with life. "It's grown so much," she said.

Osborn nodded, his hands steady on the reins. "Yes, yes, Johnstown has changed, changed a lot, it has, yes."

The vardo rattled past newly erected storefronts, and townsfolk hurried along wooden sidewalks. A cooper hammered rhythmically at a barrel, while across the street, a milliner arranged vibrant hats in her window display. Drinking in the unfamiliar sights, Charlotte's gaze darted from building to building. "The old general store is gone," she murmured, more to herself than to Osborn.

"Progress, they call it, they do, yes," Osborn replied, guiding the mule around a muddy patch in the road. The bustling streets were alive with activity as Osborn and Charlotte approached Matthew Brady's daguerreotype shop.

Osborn strode with purpose, his steps quick and precise. Charlotte found herself having to quicken her pace to keep up with him. As they drew near the shop, she noticed a long line of people stretching around the corner, each clutching a copy of his book, 'Portrait of Shiloh.'

"My word, Osborn," Charlotte remarked, her eyes widening. "Ray had mentioned your book, but I had no idea it would be so popular after all these years."

"Yes, yes. People still want to see, to see, and to remember." Osborn said, his face impassive. "The war, the war, it left marks on us all, it did. yes."

Matthew burst out as they neared the shop's entrance, his face alight with excitement. "Osborn, my old friend! So good to see you again," he said, sticking out his hand with a grin on his face.

Osborn turned to Charlotte. "He, he knows I do not shake hands. He, he always does this to trick me."

Mathew burst into laughter as he withdrew his offered hand. "You know me, Osborn!" He shifted to Charlotte, offering a warm smile. "And who might this lovely lady be?"

"Charlotte Fenn," she replied, extending her hand. "I'm visiting Mr. Roche for a time."

Matthew's eyes twinkled with interest. "Is that so? Well, you're in for a treat today, Mrs. Fenn. You'll get to see the great Osborn Roche in action," he said before his eyes caught a sight down the street. "Did you bring the vardo? I see you did!"

"It's, it's a new one."

"Really? Hard to find they are. You'll have to show me after. You better be off, boy, your audience awaits."

As they entered the shop, Charlotte marveled at the walls adorned with photographs. Matthew leaned in close, speaking in a low voice.

"You know, he's quite particular about his work. Always insisted on taking every photograph himself, unlike myself who enjoys collaborating with other artists."

Charlotte's face came alive with keen interest. "Is that unusual?"

Matthew chuckled. "For someone of his fame and demand? Absolutely. But that's Osborn for you – stubborn as a mule but with an eye like no other."

Matthew continued as Osborn settled behind a table, ready to begin signing. "You should have seen him years ago, always correcting me when I used the term 'daguerreotype.' Insisted 'portrait' was the proper word. Drove me mad at the time, but I've come to appreciate his... unique perspectives."

Charlotte watched as Osborn interacted with his admirers. His responses were brief, often abrupt, but his eyes lit up when discussing the technical aspects of his work. She noticed how he seemed to relax when talking about his craft, his usual rigid posture softening.

"He's different here," Charlotte mused aloud.

Matthew nodded sagely. "Photography is his language, Mrs. Fenn. It's where he truly shines. The camera lens allows him to see the world in a way that makes sense to him, and in turn, he helps us see it, too. We used to be competitors, him and I. But with age, I've come to see his genius," he said before gesturing to the line of waiting book buyers. "And, as you see, I'm not the only one."

As the afternoon wore on, Charlotte found herself intrigued by this side of Osborn she hadn't seen before. The man she knew as reserved and often difficult was, in this setting, respected and even revered. It was a glimpse into a depth she hadn't realized, sparking a curiosity she couldn't quite name.

When the last book was signed and the shop emptied, Osborn approached Charlotte, a rare hint of uncertainty in his eyes. "Was it... was it alright? My being here, I mean?"

Charlotte smiled warmly, "It was more than alright, Osborn. It was quite enlightening."

As they headed out of town, Charlotte asked, "Do you know where the undertaker is in this town?"

"The undertaker? Yes, yes, on Bedford, Bedford Street, yes," Osborn replied, his hands gripping the reins of the carriage.

"Is it far from here?"

"A few, a few blocks."

Charlotte hesitated momentarily before asking, "Would you be so kind as to pass by it? I would just like to see the building."

"Of, of course," Osborn nodded, steering the horse toward Bedford Street.

As they drew near *True and Sons, Undertakers,* Osborn slowed the carriage. "Would you like, like to stop? Go in?"

Charlotte's eyes widened as she caught sight of a familiar figure in front of the building. Augustus stood there, carefully adjusting a funeral flower arrangement. Her heart skipped a beat when she saw Jefferson emerge from the building, approaching his father.

"No, no," Charlotte said hurriedly, ducking down in her seat. "Just drive by, please."

Confused by her sudden change in demeanor, Osborn continued driving. Once they were safely past, she straightened up, her cheeks flushed.

Osborn glanced at her, his face pinched with concern. "Why did you, did you hide? Do you know them?"

Charlotte smoothed her skirts, avoiding Osborn's gaze. "Oh, it's nothing really. I just... I remembered I had some dirt on my face from our outing. Didn't want to be seen looking unladylike, you understand."

Not fully comprehending her explanation, Osborn's forehead creased in thought. "The Trues, I, I know them, yes. Ishmael went, Ishmael went to school with their children."

Charlotte forced a smile. "Another time, perhaps. I'm feeling rather tired after our busy day. Shall we head home?"

CHAPTER 23

Charlotte pushed open the mansion's oak doors, her quick steps echoing through the foyer. She paused briefly to catch her breath, then made her way to the parlor where Dierdre usually spent her afternoons. As expected, she found Dierdre seated on the velvet settee, an open book resting in her lap.

"Dierdre," Charlotte said, her voice tight.

As Dierdre's eyes rose from her book, she took in Charlotte's flushed appearance. She set her book aside as concern shadowed her features. "What is it? What's happened?"

Charlotte crossed the room, sinking into an armchair opposite Dierdre. "My concerns were justified. Jefferson isn't at school. He's in Johnstown, working alongside his father."

Dierdre dropped her book. "That's good, isn't it? We know where he is now, at least."

"Suppose," she agreed. "Do you want to go back to school or go back home to Pittsburgh?"

Dierdre moved to the window, gazing out at the manicured gardens. The perfectly trimmed hedges and carefully arranged flower beds seemed to mock her with their order and beauty. She pressed her fingertips against the smooth glass of the window pane. "I don't know," she told the glass. "I like it here. He won't come here. Maybe I can stay here until the start of next semester."

"If you wish, but you won't ever be able to go into town now."

"Yeah," Dierdre said, the word falling from her lips like a stone. She closed her eyes for a moment, feeling the consequences from the choices of others pressing down on her. Part of her wanted to rail against the unfairness of it all, to demand why she should be the one to hide away. But another part, a quieter, more insistent voice, whispered that this was safer, easier, in this beautiful prison of a house.

Jefferson's persistence followed her like a shadow at noon, inescapable and overwhelming. She closed her eyes, allowing herself a moment to confront the truth she'd been avoiding. Why couldn't Jefferson let go? The question echoed in her mind, a discordant note in the symphony of her thoughts. She admired his passion, his unwavering devotion—traits that had initially drawn her to him. But now, in the stark light of reality, those same qualities cast long shadows over her carefully constructed peace.

The bitter irony wasn't lost on her. Here was Jefferson, fighting with every fiber of his being for a love that, if she were brutally honest with herself, paled in comparison to what she had shared with Ishmael. The thought sent a pang of guilt through her chest, sharp and sudden as a gunshot.

Ishmael. Even now, years later, the mere thought of him could make her breath catch. Letting him go had been like severing a limb—painful, traumatic, leaving behind a phantom ache that never faded. In contrast, her separation from Jefferson, while undoubtedly difficult, felt more like the healing of a deep cut. Painful, yes, but not life-altering.

Perhaps that was why Jefferson couldn't let go. He sensed, on some level, that he was competing with a ghost, a love so profound it had reshaped the very landscape of her heart. His persistence was as much about proving himself worthy of that depth of emotion as it was about winning her back.

Charlotte rose, crossing to stand beside Dierdre. "And what if Ishmael ever comes home? He's another one you might want to avoid."

Dierdre whirled around to her grandmother. "Why would I want to avoid him? He might certainly want to avoid me because of what you did."

"Because of what *I* did? It was your father—"

"My father did what you and my mother told him to do. Ishmael and I were in love, and we were not blood related. You know this. And, then, I start courting a man I found out I am blood related to?"

"Charlotte shrugged. "I don't know what you're getting to."

"The real reason you didn't want Ishmael to court me was because of Osborn, and you know it. Because he used to be a sin eater, admit it."

"Because he still is one."

Dierdre slapped her hips. "Oh, alright, then there you go. And now you are here, living with one. A little two-faced, don't you think, Grandma?"

Charlotte sat and took a deep breath. "You are right, it was. I was wrong about Osborn, and I see that now. He is a good man."

"And you were wrong about Ishmael and I. If you hadn't forced me away from him, I'd be married by now and living here or in New York, happier than a boardinghouse pup, but no apology from you is gonna change that."

"No, I suppose not. But I do apologize anyhow. I see I've been wrong about a number of things in my life."

The wagon's iron-rimmed wheels clattered against the cobblestones, echoing through the quiet streets of Johnstown as David approached True and Sons Undertakers. He set the brake and climbed down. Straightening his waistcoat, he made his way inside, the bell above the door announcing him.

Augustus stood behind a polished mahogany counter, his attention fixed upon a ledger of new orders.

David cleared his throat. "Mr. True?"

Augustus looked up. "Yes."

"Mr. Augustus True?"

"I am. How may I be of service?"

David withdrew a note from his breast pocket. "I've been entrusted to deliver—"

At that moment, Jefferson and another man emerged from the back room, carrying a finely crafted oak coffin. Jefferson's keen eyes caught the exchange, his gaze fixed upon the note in his father's hand.

"Easy now," Augustus told them as they guided the coffin onto two saw horses for display. Turning back to David, he asked, "How can I help you today, Mr...?"

David looked around uncomfortably as Augustus looked down at the note in his hand. "David, sir. A personal matter, sir."

Augustus's forehead creased. "Personal?"

"Yes, sir," David said before spinning around and exiting.

Augustus stared at the note in his hand as Jefferson wiped the beaded sweat from his face. "Who was he?"

"Don't know."

"What's that say?" Jefferson asked, pointing to the note in his father's hand. "Open it."

"This ain't business; it's personal. So, go on, get back to work."

Jefferson shook his head, wiping his hands on his work apron, and left the back room. With Jefferson gone, Augustus opened it. The note, a three-inch by three-inch crumpled piece of paper, read,

My Dear Augustus,

I write to you on a matter of the utmost urgency and delicacy, the nature of which I dare not commit to paper for fear of prying eyes.

There are matters of great import that must be discussed between us and require the utmost discretion.

I shall be waiting at the old mill along Solomon Run Creek as the clock strikes eight in the morning.

I am fully aware of the impropriety of my request, and I assure you I would not make it were the circumstances not so pressing.

Charlotte

Augustus contemplated the crumpled note in his hand, his mind reeling as to why Charlotte would summon him. Had someone discovered their shared past? Was this about Dierdre? Little Miss? Or worse, had Jefferson somehow stumbled upon a truth he was never meant to know? The carefully constructed facade of his life, built over decades of half-truths and omissions, teetered on the brink of collapse.

He folded the note and slipped it into his pocket. Tomorrow at eight, he would face whatever ghosts Charlotte had summoned. And perhaps, in doing so, he might finally lay to rest the restless spirits of his own past.

Osborn perched atop his horse, his weathered hands resting on the worn leather of the saddle. David secured the straps on a second mount, giving the animal a gentle pat. Charlotte approached, her boots crunching on the gravel path. "Those old pants suit you well," Osborn remarked, his eyes crinkling at the corners.

Charlotte smoothed a hand over the fabric. "Yes, though I need a tight belt to keep them up."

"They, they look good."

A faint blush colored Charlotte's cheeks. "Thank you," she murmured as David offered his hand, helping her into the saddle. She settled herself, adjusting her posture. "So, where did you say we were headed?"

"The old sin eater's cabin." Osborn's calloused palm stroked his horse's neck. "Lived there, lived there once, I did. Half hour's ride from here, yes."

"I remember it."

They set off at a leisurely pace, hooves stirring up small clouds of dust from the trail. The warm breeze carried the sweet scent of late summer wildflowers, their vibrant colors dotting the landscape.

Charlotte inhaled deeply, savoring the fresh air. "Dierdre's staying until her next college semester. Do you mind, Mr. Roche?"

"I do not mind, mind a bit."

"Tiring of my company, perhaps?" A glimmer of teasing laced Charlotte's tone.

Osborn tugged on the reins, bringing his mount to a halt. He twisted in the saddle to face her fully. "Stay, stay as long as you want, Charlotte. I enjoy, enjoy your company, I do, yes."

Charlotte's eyes widened, and a faint smile whispered across her face. "You mean that?"

"Yes, yes, I do," Osborn nodded emphatically, spurring his horse back into motion.

They resumed their ride for a while, the rhythmic clip-clop of hooves filling the air. Charlotte's voice eventually broke through. "Augustus hasn't come to see me."

Osborn glanced back at her, noting the disappointment etched on her face. "No, no, he hasn't. Busy man, Augustus is, yes."

"You think he will, Mr. Roche?"

"I do, I do. Now, come, cabin's not far, not far now." The forest gradually thinned as they came upon a small clearing. The sin eater's cabin stood before them, its weathered logs and sagging roof in a state of neglect.

Osborn dismounted, securing his horse to a gnarled oak. "Wait here, wait here, Charlotte." He approached the cabin cautiously, his voice rising in a gravelly call, "Hey bear, hey!" After a careful inspection, he waved Charlotte over. "It's safe."

Charlotte slid from her saddle, boots sinking into the soft earth. "I've been here many times." A drop of rain landed on her nose. Two more hit her cheek as she turned her eyes to the sky. "I believe it's about to rain."

"Hurry, hurry," Osborn urged Charlotte, his words tumbling out. They hastily tied their horses to a gnarled oak that looked as though it had weathered a thousand such storms. The poor beasts snorted their displeasure, tails swishing in irritation at this unexpected turn in their afternoon constitutional. "Inside, inside. Before we're soaked through, soaked through, yes."

Charlotte, fighting to maintain her composure, couldn't help but smile at Osborn's distress. His aversion to rain bordered on the comical, like a cat suddenly doused with water.

"This way, this way," Osborn insisted, ushering Charlotte toward the cabin with fluttering hands.

The cabin's door creaked open with a sound like arthritic joints protesting movement, revealing an interior that smelled of dust, memories, and forgotten dreams. Charlotte stepped inside, her eyes adjusting to the gloom. "After all these years, I've never been inside," she said as she locked eyes with the boar's head still hanging on the wall.

"Six years," Charlotte murmured, running a finger along the edge of a table thick with dust. "You lived here for six years?"

Osborn's gaze darted about the room as if seeing it for the first time. "Yes, yes. Six years, six long years. Not so bad, not so bad. Quiet. Peaceful. No one to bother me, bother me, no."

Struck by the melancholy in his voice, Charlotte asked, "Were you happy here, Osborn?"

He paused, considering the question with the gravity of a philosopher contemplating the nature of existence. "Happy? Happy... I'm not sure. Content, perhaps. Safe, yes. Safe from the world, the world, and its noise, its chaos."

A crack of thunder made them both jump, startling a nervous laugh from Charlotte. "Well, it seems the chaos has found us anyway," she quipped.

Osborn's lips twitched in what might have been a smile. "Indeed, indeed. But we're dry now, dry now, yes. That's the important thing." As if to contradict him, a steady drip-drip-drip began to emanate from the far corner of the cabin. Osborn's face fell, his shoulders slumping in defeat. "Oh no, no, no. Not again, not again."

He moved to the leaking corner with purpose, his hands running along the junction of wall and floor with the practiced ease of long familiarity. "There are tools, tools in the old chest," he muttered, more to himself than to Charlotte. "Perhaps I can..."

His words trailed off as his fingers caught on something - a loose floorboard, barely noticeable unless one knew exactly where to look. With a grunt of effort that seemed to surprise even him, Osborn pried up the board. There, nestled in the dark space beneath the floor, was a battered tin can.

"Trash?" Osborn asked himself before carefully extracting the can. "Trapper Billy," he said, his voice filled with a wonder that transformed his features. "He told me once, told me the Indian had a can of coins hidden away somewhere. I never thought, never thought..."

Osborn pried off the lid and tipped the contents onto a relatively clean patch of floor. Tarnished coins clinked together, rolling across the worn boards.

"Shitting in high, shitting in high cotton!" he happily exclaimed before his face fell. "Oh! Forgive me, forgive me for that bad word."

Charlotte grinned. "It's fine, Mr. Roche. I've heard worse."

"Billy told me that, yes. It's a metaphor, of course," he added as he started to count.

After he finished, his shoulders slumped. "How much is it?" she asked.

"Not enough, not enough to shit in high cotton."

Charlotte rolled her eyes. "My word, you're already shittin' in high cotton, Mr. Roche."

Osborn nodded. "I suppose, suppose you are right…" Osborn's words trailed off as his eyes went to the gun rack that used to hold the cursed rifle.

Charlotte followed his gaze to the empty space. "Mr. Roche? Are you—"

Osborn's frown suddenly vanished, replaced by an excited grin. He thrust a finger into the air. "Your curse! Your family curse! Would you like me to remove it?"

Charlotte cocked her head, a curious expression creeping upon her face. "Remove it? But how—"

"I've done it before, before, yes. To a gun, to the gun that hung right there, yes. As a sin eater, sin eater, I removed the curse from it, yes, I gave it to a friend, yes."

"The curse or the gun?"

"I removed the curse and, and, and gave the gun, yes."

Charlotte sat back in the chair. "It worked?"

"It worked, yes. I'll be happy to do it for you, for you, yes."

"Well, then yes, of course."

"I believe the rain, the rain has stopped, yes."

"Let's go, then," she replied before they headed out of the old door.

Charlotte approached her mount, placing a foot in the stirrup. She grasped the saddle pommel, hesitating. "Mr. Roche, would you mind giving me a..." She shook her head, a wry smile tugging at her lips. "Oh, never mind. You don't like to touch." With an awkward heave, she pulled herself up. "Shall we?" she asked, settling into the saddle.

"We shall."

As they trotted down the overgrown path, Charlotte's forehead creased in thought. "Wasn't there some other reason for coming here?"

Osborn shook his head, his gaze fixed on the trail ahead. "There was, there was, but I can't seem to remember, remember what it was."

Dierdre hurried down the wide corridors of the mansion on her way to dinner. David had told her that they dress for dinner. The ornate double doors of the dining room stood open, and Dierdre stepped in but froze at the bizarre scene before her.

Charlotte lay at the far end of an impossibly long table draped in crisp white linen. Her hair fanned out around her head like a silver halo against the stark tablecloth. Osborn hunched over her, his weathered face a mask of intense concentration. Across from him stood David, perfectly poised despite the bizarre tableau, holding a steaming plate of food aloft.

"What in the world is going on here?" Dierdre's voice rang out, bouncing off the high ceilings and wood-paneled walls.

Charlotte lifted her head, her calm at odds with the situation. "Don't worry, dear. I know this looks strange—"

"Ah! I hate that word!" Osborn interrupted, a troubled expression flashing in his eyes. "Please use peculiar. It's a better word, better word. Strong consonant 'c,' yes."

Charlotte let out a long-suffering sigh, her head dropping back onto the table. "Fine. It looks peculiar, Dierdre, but please hold on. Osborn needs to do what he needs to do."

Osborn nodded to David, who handed him the plate over her body. Osborn inhaled deeply, the aroma of roasted meat and herbs filling his nostrils. His voice took on a solemn tone as he intoned, "I give, I give peace and rest to you, rest to you, dear woman. This curse, this curse shall go now, go now from you. And for thy leaving, I pawn my own soul. I pawn my soul, yes."

With that, Osborn began to eat. Charlotte rotated her head toward him. "May I get up now?" A faint flush colored her cheeks, betraying her awareness of the absurdity of her position - a woman of her age and station sprawled across a dining table like some pagan sacrifice.

"Yes, yes, you may," Osborn replied between bites. "David, please help her."

David hurried around the table, offering Charlotte his arm. She slid off the table with surprising dignity, smoothing her dress.

Dierdre remained rooted to the spot, her fingers gripping the doorframe for support. "What... what was that? Have you all gone mad?"

Noting the oddness of it all, Charlotte fixed her hair with her hand and sat across from Osborn, placing her napkin on her lap. "It's not madness, dear. Osborn was removing my curse."

"Removing curses, yes," Osborn chimed in from the table. "Like the gun, the cursed gun. But people too, people too, yes."

Dierdre's gaze darted between her grandmother and Osborn, her mind struggling to process the scene. "I think," she said, spacing out the words, "I need to sit down."

David pulled out a chair for her, his expression betraying nothing of the oddity of the situation. He unfurled her napkin with a flourish, draping it delicately across her lap. He retrieved a crystal decanter and silver ladle from a nearby sideboard and leaned down to her. "Soup, Miss Dierdre?"

CHAPTER 24

Charlotte's smile deepened as Augustus arrived at the old mill. She descended the steps and approached him as he tied his horse.

"Thank you for coming, Augustus. I'm very happy you came. "

"Your note said it was important, so I came."

"Shall we walk the grounds?"

"You lead, I'll follow."

"Would you let me take your arm?" she asked, a wisp of hesitation in her voice.

"Course," he replied, offering it to her. The fabric of his well-worn jacket was rough beneath her fingers.

"I've always wanted to tell you, Augustus...I've wanted to apologize for sending you away back then."

Augustus ran a hand through his hair. "I was angry for a long time, Charlotte. But I understand now. You did what you had to do, and it was the right thing to do."

"Yes, like what we had to do with Jefferson and Dierdre."

"Yes."

Charlotte grinned. "You know, I knew you were coming back to the farm every month for a time to be with Dierdre. Middle of the month, as I recall."

Hearing that, Augustus dropped his head, a wry smile on his lips. With a chuckle, he said, "You knew?"

"I even spied on you once. I remember one time that little girl burst into laughter so loud it scared you. You thought I would hear from the house. Instead, I heard it from only a couple yards away!" Augustus and Charlotte both laughed. "I almost burst into laughter myself. Had to keep a hand over my mouth, or you would'a known I was there."

"I had no idea."

"Ya know, after you were born, Mrs. True took you away from me. I spent my life watching you from the trees," she said before Augustus turned to her. "Yessum, just as you did with Dierdre. Same thing, wishing to be close to you, to hold you. I was secretly in your life all until the war. Do you remember meeting me when you were at the Academy?"

A deep line etched across Augustus's brow as he shook his head. "No."

"You know the gunsmith across from the main gate?"

"I do. I slept in that place after my brother and I left the Academy."

"I lived there. I watched you from the second-story window that faced the grounds."

"You did?"

"I did. I even had supper with you. It was a formal supper that your commander set up for local businesses."

"The Commandant, yes. I think I remember the event."

Charlotte smiled at the memory. "You were about seventeen, I believe. Standing there, all soldier-like, with your brother. I was so proud of you, seeing you like that."

"Those were good days for me, there at that Academy."

"I'm sure. You rose the ranks so faster than small town gossip. Sorry to hear about your brother, though. Real sad day, that was. I see you named your son after him."

"Yes," Augustus replied in a far-off tone. Having meandered back around to the mansion's front steps, Augustus asked, "Was there something else? More than just. . .recalling the past?"

She let go of his arm and faced him. "Yes, yes, there is. I would...Well, I'm living here for a while, at the Cattell place, and I, I would like us to become better acquainted, if you will."

Augustus's eyes widened, and mixed emotions played across his face. "I, I couldn't let my family know. You understand?"

"I do. It'd be just between you and I."

"Well, yeah. I'd guess I'd have to come here. Couldn't get away a lot, though, otherwise..."

"I understand. We'll come up with something."

"Alright, well, I should be going. I never thought I'd say this, but it was nice talking to ya, Charlotte," he said as he untied his horse from the step's marble column. "You know, I would, I would also like to get better acquainted with Dierdre on those occasions. As long as Jefferson don't catch on. Is that possible?"

Charlotte smiled. "It would. I will speak to her."

Augustus's features softened into the beginnings of a smile. "That'd be fine."

Mounting his horse, Augustus settled his hat atop his head. He gazed into the distance, his voice tinged with wonder. "Never too late for both of us to get what we so badly desired all those years ago. Never too late."

Charlotte stood at the window, her hand resting on the cool glass. Outside, Osborn's figure strode across the back lawn to a place beyond the trees.

"Ma'am, can I bring you something? Tea perhaps?" asked David.

Still staring out the window, she asked, "Where does he go?"

"He goes to his late wife's grave. Just beyond the trees."

"Would he mind if I followed?"

"I believe he would enjoy your company, Ma'am."

The grass whispered beneath her feet as she approached. Osborn knelt before a mound with a weathered cross at its head, his lips moving in silent conversation. Charlotte paused, allowing him a moment of privacy before she spoke.

"Hello," greeted Osborn, his back to her.

"I hope I'm not interrupting you."

Osborn rose to his feet, brushing dirt from his knees. "No, no. Not at all, no." Osborn's gaze drifted back to the grave as he sat on a log worn down by years of his sitting on it.

"May I sit?" she asked.

"Please do, please do."

She sat next to him and fixed her dress. "Tell me about your wife," she said softly. "If it's not too much. What was she like?"

Osborn's shoulders stiffened, then relaxed. "Lou. My Lou. She was... extraordinary. A brilliant, brilliant embalmer, yes, yes. Even, even worked on Willy, Willy Lincoln, the president's son. Just as, just as I photographed him."

"True love, the kind you shared with Lou - I've come to realize it's as rare as a perfect diamond and just as unattainable for some of us." She paused, her fingers absently tracing the worn fabric of her dress. A wistful smile grew on her lips. "In my youth, I fancied myself in love once. I clung to that belief with the fervor of the young and naïve," she pronounced, using the knowledge of years and hard-won wisdom. "But time has a way of stripping away our illusions, doesn't it? What I thought was love turned out to be... something else entirely."

They sat in silence for a moment, the breeze carrying the scent of fresh-cut grass.

"I've seen a photograph of her. The one in the library."

"The one of her by, her by our old Romani vardo, yes, yes. I remember taking that photograph. That was a good day on the, on the great plains of the west, yes."

The memory made him smile as she recalled. "Wearing those denim trousers and flannel shirt. She sure did look like a cowgirl."

"She, she never wore a dress, wore a dress. Never. Well, she would on occasion, on occasion."

"Nonetheless, a real special photograph. Are there more photographs of her?"

"Yes, yes. There is one in the parlor, and I have three tintypes in my bedroom, in my bedroom, yes. I lost many, lost many when my first vardo sank, sank in the river. But that one, that one is a special one, yes."

"Sure is. I wish I had a special photograph of me like that. You know, I ain't never had a photograph taken of me before."

Osborn's eyes lit up. "Never?"

"No, never."

Osborn stood and stuck his finger in the air. "My, my dear, we must remedy, must remedy that at once. I am, after all, a world-famous photographer!" Osborn exclaimed. "Let's set up in the conservatory. The light there is perfect this time of day." Osborn quickly strode across the broad green lawn toward the mansion.

Charlotte followed. "But this isn't my best dress. Osborn, please, another time," she pleaded, but before Charlotte could protest further, Osborn was already far ahead.

Charlotte smirked and said, "Well, I suppose... if you'd like to," to herself as he disappeared in the distance.

Changing course for the conservatory, Charlotte felt a flutter in her stomach. She was about to become a subject for one of the world's most renowned photographers, and the thought both thrilled and terrified her. She walked in as Osborn set up his equipment and ordered David around to help.

"Would you like me to set up the background canvas, sir?" David asked.

Osborn's eyes, typically darting and evasive, now held a laser-like focus. They scanned the room with the precision of a master painter, seeing not just what was there but what could be captured, immortalized. The conservatory, with its play of light and shadow, became his canvas, and Charlotte could almost see the composition forming in his mind.

"No, no. We will use the room as a background and the fireplace as the focal point. Place a chair right next to it, yes."

David placed it where he had been told, and Charlotte sat in it.

"Perfect," he told her. "Stay, stay right there."

As Charlotte watched Osborn work, she was struck by the transformation that came over him. The nervous energy that usually animated his movements seemed to evaporate, replaced by a focused intensity that was almost palpable. His hands, often fidgety and uncertain in social situations, now moved with a fluid grace as they adjusted the camera's intricate mechanisms.

Osborn ducked under the camera shroud, his hand on the lens. Osborn's other hand gestured to her. "Lean back, back a little, chin up… stop, good."

The artistic soul that Charlotte had glimpsed only in fleeting moments now stood fully revealed. Osborn moved about the space with the assurance of a conductor before his orchestra, every gesture purposeful, every decision informed by an internal vision that she could sense but not fully comprehend.

As she sat, poised for her portrait, Charlotte realized she was seeing Osborn in his element for the first time - not just the sin eater or the eccentric recluse, but the artist whose name was whispered with reverence in galleries and drawing rooms across the country. It was a revelation, one that added yet another layer to the enigma that was Osborn Roche.

David walked in with a plate for the camera, handing it to Osborn. "I will leave you to it, sir."

"Thank you, David," he replied, turning to Charlotte. "And now, and now if you would please, like I told you about, about Lou, tell me, tell me about Melody's father?" he asked as he slid the plate in and dove back under the camera shroud, his fingers on the lens cap.

Charlotte hesitated, her fingers twisting in her lap. "Well, that's a tough one," she said sadly. "I never had what you had. I... I married a man I didn't love and loved a man I didn't marry."

"Tilt your face just a bit to the, to the window. Yes, yes, right there," Osborn directed, focusing the camera. "Now, tell me, what's your favorite time of day?"

Charlotte smiled. "Dawn, when the world is still quiet."

"Good, good. Now, what's your deepest regret?"

Charlotte's smile faltered. "I have so many."

"Your deepest, deepest."

Charlotte swallowed hard and looked away. Osborn popped out from under the shroud. "No, no, you moved," he said. "Face to the window, chin up, yes."

She did as told. Osborn continued, "Stay there, stay there while I continue. Don't think about, think about the questions as I, as I ask them. Tell me the first thing, the first thing that pops in your head, yes."

"OK, I'll try."

"What is your proudest moment before the age of twelve?"

"Barrel racing, I'd say. Barrel racing my horse. Not in competition or nothing. Just at the farm. I was good at it."

"Good, good. Now, quickly now. Tell me, what is your deepest regret?"

"Letting my son be taken from me."

Osborn came out from under the camera shroud, his brows knitted. "I'm, I'm sorry to hear, to hear that, Charlotte. I didn't know, didn't know Melody had a brother."

Charlotte's shoulder slumped as she said, "The most unfortunate thing is, neither did she."

"Oh, oh, yes, I am sorry, yes, but don't move." His fingers on the lens cap, he asked, "What was the boy's name?"

Charlotte's chin trembled. "Augustus is his name," she said. "Augustus True."

The lens cap slid off as Osborn said, "Please hold still."

Candlelight bathed the dining room in warm light. Osborn sat at the head of the table, his fingers drumming an erratic rhythm on the polished wood. Charlotte occupied the seat to his right, her gaze fixed on her barely touched plate. Dierdre, seated across from Charlotte, glanced between the two with growing unease.

The clinking of silverware against fine china punctuated the heavy silence.

Dierdre cleared her throat. "The roast is particularly good tonight, don't you think?"

Osborn grunted in response while Charlotte nodded, not looking up from her plate.

"Did your photography session go well this afternoon?" Dierdre tried again.

Osborn's fingers stilled. "Yes, yes. Quite... illuminating."

Charlotte's fork clattered against her plate. "Excuse me," she murmured, reaching for her water glass with a trembling hand.

Dierdre's expression tightened with concern. "Is everything alright? You both seem... out of sorts."

"Everything's fine, dear," Charlotte said, her voice strained. "Just a bit tired, that's all."

Osborn waved a dismissive hand. "A bit tired, A bit tired," he repeated.

The silence descended again, broken only by the ticking of the grandfather clock in the corner.

After several more minutes of stilted attempts at conversation, Dierdre set down her napkin. "I think I'll retire for the evening. Thank you for dinner."

With Dierdre's departure, the tension in the room seemed to double. Osborn and Charlotte avoided each other's gaze, the unspoken words hanging heavy in the air between them.

David entered. "Will there be anything else this evening?" he asked, moving to clear the plates.

Osborn shook his head. "No, David. That will be all, be all."

As David left the room, Charlotte asked, "David, would you please close the doors behind you?"

"Certainly, Ma'am."

The doors closed, and Charlotte looked up at Osborn. "I'm sorry if my revelation today disturbed you," she said.

"No, no. Not at all. I was, I was worried that it may have, may have disturbed you."

She smiled. "You are a sweet one, Mr. Roche."

"The Trues, they are why you asked about the undertaker in town, in town, yes?"

"Yes, I wanted to speak to him, but I saw his son come out. Do you know his son, Jefferson True?"

"Yes, yes, their first son, I believe, I believe, yes."

Charlotte chuckled sadly and said, "That's why we're here, Osborn. Dierdre brought home Jefferson True to meet us at Christmas. When we learned his last name was True, and he was from Johnstown, we knew we had to break them apart."

Osborn's eyes widened. "Good heavens, his father is Augustus. Jefferson is Dierdre's half-brother, half-brother, yes."

"Yes," Charlotte confirmed.

"Does Augustus know about Dierdre?"

"Yes. Augustus came to our home in Pittsburgh to warn us, but we already knew."

Osborn's fingers dove for the brown cloth in his pocket before he asked,

"Charlotte, does, does Dierdre know? About Augustus being her father and Jefferson being her, being her half, half-brother?"

Charlotte's hands tightened in her lap. "She does now. We had to tell her and make her end things with Jefferson." Charlotte's voice cracked slightly. "But Jefferson, he wouldn't give up on Dierdre. He told her he would speak to her at Swarthmore. That's why we came to live with you. To recover from the pain of the breakup and to avoid him. I just wish he'd give up. Truth is, I'm thinking, Dierdre, she didn't love this one as much as your son."

Osborn popped his head up. "Ishmael?"

"Yessum. It just seems to me, this one? He's a might easier for her to let go than Ishmael was. Ishmael broke her."

"She broke, she broke Ishmael, Ishmael. I remember. I was, I was sad for him. Very sad, and I know sadness."

"We all know sadness."

"And they were only related by marriage, by marriage, yes?"

"Yes."

"Ishmael and Dierdre would have, would have been a better choice, yes."

"I see that now," said Charlotte as she fixed her gaze out the window. "It's part of my curse, you see. Augustus was taken from me when I was young. I had to watch him grow from the woods outside the True farm."

Osborn's jaw dropped. "I did too, yes. I had to, had to watch Ishmael for the first six, first six years of his life. From the trees, from the trees, in back of where we live, yes."

Charlotte faced him. "Really?"

"Yes, yes."

Charlotte's mouth parted slightly as the realization dawned. "Of course, that's when you were sin eating and living in the cabin. That's why you came to live there, and that's why you became the sin eater, so you could watch your son."

"Yes, yes."

Amazed, Charlotte let out a laugh before saying, "Just like me."

"Yes, yes, like you, like you, yes."

"Now, that's a revelation, that is."

"It is, it is, yes."

"But you ended up with Ishmael in your life. I had to send Augustus away. It was the curse. It surely was."

"But, I, but I took the curse from, from you, yes."

"You did indeed, I am certain of it. Since then, I have spoken to Augustus. I apologized for everything, and we have agreed to get better acquainted."

"I'm, I'm very happy, happy for you, Charlotte."

Charlotte let out a long, controlled exhale. "It's what any mother would want, I believe. Have their children and grandchildren in their life."

CHAPTER 25

The smell of lemon oil, lilies, and beeswax filled the air of the front office of the mortuary, a futile attempt to mask the underlying scent of death that permeated from the back of the shop. Jefferson moved methodically between the coffins, his dusting cloth gliding over polished wood. Pausing to wipe the sweat from his face, his gaze drifted to the street outside, where his father, Augustus, stood in animated conversation with Mrs. Holloway, no doubt discussing arrangements for her recently departed husband. Jefferson watched the exchange, noting how his father's face shifted between sympathy and businesslike efficiency.

After Mrs. Holloway walked away, a man in a finely tailored suit replaced her, the same man who had handed his father the "personal" note two weeks ago. After the quick exchange, his father read it, his gaze distant before heading toward the shop's door.

The door swung open, and Augustus strode in. Without thinking, Jefferson ducked behind the broad mahogany counter, wedging himself between stacks of ledgers and boxes of candles.

"Jefferson!" Augustus called out, his voice booming in the quiet shop. Jefferson held his breath, hearing his father's footsteps draw nearer. He pressed himself further into the shadows, praying he wouldn't be discovered. Augustus went to the back room's doorway, calling, "I'm heading out on an errand. Mind the shop while I'm gone!"

One of the workers in the back called back to him, "Got ya, Mr. True!"

The door slammed shut, and Jefferson slowly emerged from his hiding place and walked to the window. Peering out, he saw his father untying a horse from the hitching post. Augustus swung into the saddle and set off at a brisk trot, disappearing around a corner.

Jefferson's mind raced. *Who is that guy, and what urgent business could pull him away from the shop in the middle of the day?*

Making a split-second decision, Jefferson bolted for the back door and out to the stable behind the mortuary. He saddled a dappled gray mare and rode out.

He set off at a steady pace, looking down each street from the main street. Reaching the edge of town, he stopped. The open road stretched before him, winding through golden fields and patches of dense forest without a soul on it. Jefferson pulled the reins on his mare. "Let's get on back."

With the Cattell mansion's sprawling lawn before them, Charlotte and Dierdre sat on the veranda, the gentle clinking of ice in their lemonade glasses punctuating their conversation.

"He's my son, and you're his daughter. He'd like to see you if you don't mind," said Charlotte.

A young doe emerged from the woods at the beginning of the treeline. It paused, ears twitching, before cautiously making its way across the manicured grass. Dierdre's eyes widened at the sight, her question momentarily forgotten.

"Look," she whispered, pointing. "Isn't she beautiful?"

"Yes," replied Charlotte, waiting for her answer.

"I would be interested in seeing him. Speaking with him."

"Alright, then. I'll set that up."

"How with Jefferson not knowing?"

Charlotte's forehead creased in thought. "We'll need to think of something for that. Another way."

"Jefferson will eventually move on and go back to school or something," said Dierdre.

"Yes, and it won't be hard getting to know Augustus. He wants it, too. I just wish I could get to know all my grandchildren. They's all my grandchildren."

Dierdre nodded understandingly. "I know."

Osborn stepped out onto the veranda. "I, I, I believe I know how to solve the problem, yes."

"How?" asked Augustus.

"It will. It will solve two problems, yes."

"What is it?" asked Charlotte.

"A way, a way Charlotte can, can meet the rest of the True family, the family. Her grandchildren, yes."

Charlotte shook her head. "Whatever it is, it won't work. Jefferson knows me. Dierdre introduced him to me."

"Yes, yes, but he knows you as Dierdre's grandmother. If Augustus were to bring you to his house, that would be peculiar, peculiar. Why, why, would he bring Dierdre's grandmother? But, I am, I am well liked in this community, yes. I am world-famous, world-famous. If he were to bring you with me, as my wife, he is simply, simply inviting a prominent couple, couple to supper, yes?"

Charlotte's head snapped toward him, her eyes wide with shock. "Osborn, what are you saying?"

"If Charlotte and I were married, were married, Augustus could invite us to supper, yes."

Charlotte and Dierdre's jaws fell open. Dierdre asked, "Are you asking my grandmother to marry?"

Osborn continued, his words coming out in a rush. "We wouldn't have to, have to truly marry, just say we are, we are, yes. And Charlotte, Charlotte could live here, be part of Augustus's family openly, openly. As my wife, that becomes a family friend, family friend of the Trues. Meet Augustus's other children, watch her, her grandkids grow up, and be with them instead of watching them from afar."

Charlotte considered the proposal, but doubt gnawed at the edges of it. What of Osborn? The man was eccentric, to be sure, but he had shown her kindness. Was it fair to entangle him in her web of familial complexities? And what of her own heart? She had long ago resigned herself to a life without romantic love, but to enter into a marriage, even one of convenience, was no small matter.

"That's a fine idea, Osborn," Dierdre said as the idea in her head grew. "But I'm thinking you would have to truly marry. As a matter of fact, it should be a grand affair, one that the whole town is invited," Dierdre said. "Including Augustus, his wife, and his family. Everyone would know the both of you are together."

Charlotte realized that this decision would reshape not just her future but the very foundation of who she was. The weeper, the watcher from afar, the keeper of secrets - all of these identities hung in the balance. And beneath it all, a question whispered insistently in the depths of her heart: after a lifetime of sacrifice and separation, did she dare to reach for happiness, even if it came in such an unconventional form? "That... that could work," Charlotte mused.

"At the wedding, you could speak to his wife and suggest getting to know the True family better. Invite them over for supper," Dierdre added.

"Yes, it is the perfect way to meet her and get my foot in the door."

Dierdre jumped out of her chair, grinning ear to ear. "Let's shoot out the lights! There's gonna be a wedding! Grandma and Osborn!"

Charlotte put up her hand. "Don't get your tail up, child. Sit on down." Unable to wipe the smile off Dierdre's face, Charlotte sat back, her mind reeling. "I... I need to think on this."

Osborn shook his head. "It would be no, be no different than how we're living now, yes, with you as my guest. You know I don't like, don't like to touch or be touched, no, no. And I have my own bedroom. Nothing would change except in name, except in name, no."

"But a Fenn never changes their last name. Weeper tradition says it's so."

Dierdre wiped the smile off her lips, sat down, and faced her grandmother. "They do now, Grandmother. They do now."

Once again, the morning sun streamed through the dining room windows.

Charlotte and Dierdre sat at the far end of the table. David entered and moved silently around the table, refilling coffee cups. As he placed a steaming cup of coffee before Dierdre, she looked up at him.

"David," Dierdre asked, her voice carrying a note of curiosity, "where is Osborn this morning?"

"Mr. Roche was up quite early, Miss Dierdre. He's currently in the vardo, preparing his equipment."

Charlotte looked up from her newspaper, interest piqued. "The vardo? What for?"

"Today is Mr. Roche's monthly journey into town for his photographic charity, madam."

"Charity?" Dierdre asked.

"Yes, Miss. He takes free portraits for those who cannot afford them otherwise."

Dierdre's eyes widened with surprise and admiration. "I had no idea he did such a thing. How wonderful."

With a hint of pride in his voice, David said, "Indeed, Miss. Mr. Roche has been doing this for years now. It's quite popular in town." He turned to Charlotte, his tone becoming more formal. "Which brings me to a message, Mrs. Fenn. Mr. Roche has asked me to inquire if you would like to accompany him into town today for this event."

Charlotte's eyebrows rose in surprise. She faced Dierdre, a question in her eyes.

Dierdre smiled warmly and gave an encouraging nod. "You should go, Grandma."

Charlotte hesitated for a moment, then smiled. "Very well, David. Please inform Mr. Roche that I would be delighted to accompany him."

"Very good, madam," David replied with a slight bow. "I shall inform him at once. He plans to depart within the hour."

As David left the room, Charlotte and Dierdre exchanged excited glances.

Dierdre smiled, her eyes twinkling. "A charity? It seems there's always more to Osborn than meets the eye. Do tell me all about it when you return."

A large banner greeted them as they drove the vardo by the town square, 'FREE PORTRAITS BY WORLD-FAMOUS OSBORN ROCHE' hung between two maple trees. A line of people waited patiently under it. Charlotte's jaw fell open. "Even more people than the book signing," she said.

"Yes, yes."

As Osborn parked the vardo, setting the brake, two nicely dressed teen girls approached them. "Good morning, girls," said Osborn.

"Morning, Mr. Roche," they replied in unison.

"Go, go ahead. You, you know where the equipment, equipment is."

The girls opened the vardo's door and went inside as Osborn climbed down. They came out with arms laden with photographic equipment.

"Careful, careful with the camera, yes," Osborn cautioned, his voice tinged with nervous energy.

"Who are they?" asked Charlotte.

"They, they are from the church. They volunteer for me, for me."

Together, the girls began assembling his portable studio. Charlotte held one side of the backdrop as they unfurled it, the fabric catching the late morning breeze.

"A little higher on your side, your side, Charlotte," Osborn directed, gesturing with his free hand.

Charlotte adjusted the heavy canvas. "Like this?"

"Perfect, perfect, yes," Osborn replied before stepping back to survey their handiwork.

"Mr. Roche!" A man wearing a thick brown beard and spectacles called out as he crossed the street. "Mr. Roche, good to see you this beautiful day."

Osborn turned to him. "Mayor, Mayor Storey, good day." Charlotte stood aside as Osborn adjusted his camera for the first subject. "Oh, oh, let me introduce Charlotte Fenn, yes, Charlotte Fenn. This is the mayor, Mayor Storey, yes," he said before busily setting things up and walking back into the vardo.

Charlotte nodded to the mayor. "Pleased. Nice to meet you, Mayor."

"The pleasure is mine, Ms. Fenn. Any friend of our most famous Osborn Roche is a friend of mine. Osborn is one of our most prominent residents, he is."

Osborn popped his head out of the vardo. "I, I am."

"And one of our most humorous," added the mayor. "So, he's setting up for his charity day, is he?"

"Yes, he is."

"Wonderful, wonderful," replied the mayor as he stood beside her, watching Osborn prepare.

"Uh, how often does he…" Charlotte began to ask.

"Oh, once a month. The second Saturday of each month. The city puts out the banner for him and the registration desk over there," he said, pointing.

"Is that so?"

"Least we can do. You know, he's also the largest benefactor to practically all of the city's charities."

"He is?" Charlotte asked as she felt a twinge of shame, recalling her initial judgments of him. How quick she had been to dismiss him as an oddity, a relic of superstition best avoided.

"Oh, yes. Honestly, instead of the General over there," he said, pointing to the bronze statue, "we should have commissioned a statue of him for this town square. Well, I know he's busy," the mayor said as he began walking away. "Please send one of the girls over to our office if he needs anything. We are always at Mr. Roche's disposal."

Exiting the vardo, Osborn said, "Thank you, Mayor," and called to the girls sitting at the desk, "First family, first family, please."

A tired-looking older woman approached with two young children, their clothes threadbare but clean. Osborn smiled warmly, gesturing for them to sit.

"Hello, hello. Now, I will, I will ask you some questions, questions, yes, but when I say, 'please hold still' you know to do that right, right?"

The grandmother bent down to them and whispered in their ears before they simultaneously said, "Yes."

As Charlotte watched them, images flashed through her mind of herself, seated at a family dinner, surrounded by the warmth and laughter of her own grandchildren.

"Now, now, tell me," he began, peering at them from behind his camera, "what brings you joy, joy in your life?"

The woman hesitated, then spoke with a shaky voice. "My grandchildren's laughter."

Osborn nodded encouragingly. "Good, good. And you, you lad, what, what food do you think awful and, and yucky, yes?"

The older child piped up, "Cornmeal mush, yuck!" he said before they all laughed.

"Ah, yes, yes, yuck!" Osborn replied, his eyes twinkling. "And you, little one," he addressed the younger child, "what's your favorite game to play?"

"Hide and seek!" the child exclaimed, grinning widely.

"Please hold still." Osborn removed the lens cap, capturing the family's brief moment of shared happiness. "Good, good. It'll be just a few moments."

Osborn set the darkboard in the camera and pulled out the plate. "Would you, would you like to, to see how I develop it?"

"Very much so."

Charlotte followed him into the vardo with its cozy interior, where every inch of space was carefully considered and richly appointed. The whiff of photographic chemicals mingled with wood smoke from the small cast-iron stove in the corner. "It's quite comfortable. I used to sleep here, and Ray would sleep here below me on the floor. We bring out that mattress over there."

"I am surprised. It seems very interesting and comfortable."

"Yes, yes. The Romani vardo can float across any water. I sealed all the joints with tar, with tar, yes." Osborn shut and draped the door, eliminating sunlight from the cracks. "Not a speck of light comes in," he said as he fit a red glass plate into the small window above the counter. "The red light will not affect the silver nitrate of the photograph, but I have become familiar with working in total darkness." Osborn set the photographic plate gently into the developer bath, moving the fluid back and forth over it. "See the image of them coming through? Now, I take it and rinse it with water in this bath."

As Osborn rinsed the photograph, Charlotte thought in this element, surrounded by the tools of his art, Osborn exuded a quiet confidence that was both captivating and a bit unsettling. It was a side of him that few were privileged to witness - the artist beneath the awkward exterior, the visionary behind the stammering speech. Charlotte felt a newfound respect blooming within her, tinged with a curiosity to understand this complex man who could transform so completely when in the grip of his passion. "Your questions to them, why do you ask them?"

Osborn looked up from his work, his eyes meeting hers in a rare moment before they had to look away. "That's how I get what I want. Just what I want. I wait for that perfect instant—the point where I capture the essence, the essence of who they are."

The explanation caught her breath. He's not just an eccentric photographer, she thought, but rather an artist with a profound understanding of human nature. "Yes, I see. It reminds me of when I was a weeper. As weepers, we ask the family to tell us about their loved one before we mourn. We like to see any pictures, paintings, photographs. We like to read anything they wrote, letters and such. It helped me connect, to mourn as if I had known them."

"Yes, yes. I see how it is similar," he said as he moved the photograph from the wash bath to the fixer bath. "It's my questions, my questions, yes. I've always done it. Ray says it's genius, yes. I agree, yes."

Charlotte giggled at his lack of modesty. "I agree, too. It is genius." Her eyes followed his fingers as he pulled the photograph from the fixer bath and held it up to examine it. "It's mighty curious how we both use questions to unveil the essence of a person - you for posterity, me for a final farewell."

Osborn held the photograph over a lamp to dry it. He cocked his head and added, "Yes, yes. Isn't it ironic, ironic, yes? I preserve, I preserve people's happiest moments while you help preserve their final ones."

As the day wore on, Charlotte watched Osborn work his magic with family after family, each time capturing not just their image but a glimpse of their souls. She admired his patience, skill, and genuine care for each person sitting before his camera.

At the end of the day, they packed up the vardo and started the journey home. The rhythmic clop of the horse's hooves and the gentle swaying of the wagon lulled her into a contemplative mood.

Looking over at Osborn, his profile illuminated by the setting sun, Charlotte made a decision. Her voice was soft but sure as she spoke. "Mr. Roche?" He turned to her, a curious gleam in his eyes. "That offer you made... about marriage. Is it still open?"

Osborn's eyes widened slightly, but his voice was steady as he replied, "Yes."

Charlotte sat back, crossing her arms. "You would truly do that? You would marry me only so I can be in my grandchildren's lives?"

Not understanding why anyone wouldn't do that if they could, Osborn's confused face swiveled back and forth from the road to her and back again. He stiffened and replied, "Why, yes, yes, of course, I would, yes."

She shook her head with amused disbelief before asking, "Since the offer is still open—"

He nodded. "Yes, yes it is."

Charlotte smoothed her dress before letting out a soft sigh and said, "Then I accept. I'll marry you, Osborn."

He flinched with surprise. "Osborn! You said it! The first time you called me by my first name," he said with a laugh.

Charlotte's face lit up with a smile before she repeated it, "Osborn, Osborn Roche." The words made him laugh again. Charlotte stared off at the snow-covered mountains in the distance. Under her breath, she murmured, "The most intriguing Osborn Roche."

CHAPTER 26

Dierdre brushed a chestnut mare in the mansion's stables as Charlotte stood, her arms resting on the stall's worn wood rail. "You gonna do it?" asked Dierdre.

"Do what, dear?"

"Marry him?"

Charlotte's expression grew serious. "You're perceptive, my dear. Just what I was thinking about."

"I could tell," said Dierdre before she put down the brush and put her hand on the gate. Charlotte stood back as she came out, shutting the gate behind her.

Walking back to the house, Charlotte took her granddaughter's arm and, in a happy tone, replied, "The answer is yes."

Dierdre's eyebrows pulled together in a frown. "You look quite giddy over it. I thought this arrangement was simply to see Augustus's family."

"It was," Charlotte said with a tug on Dierdre's arm.

Dierdre giggled. "But…?"

A grin rose as Charlotte said, "I have grown fond of him."

"You are marrying for love now?!"

"Maybe not love yet. But I have grown *very* fond of him."

"Oh, my! I never would have thought…" Dierdre said as she shook her head in disbelief. "The weeper and the sin eater." They both burst into laughter as they drew near the rear doors.

"Another thing you should be aware of, Dierdre… Jefferson might be there."

"I thought of the possibility."

"You do not have to attend if you don't want to."

"Who could miss the wedding of a weeper to a sin eater?"

Charlotte released her arm as they entered the salon from the rear doors. Dierdre plopped herself into a wingback chair before asking, "Ishmael? Will he be coming?"

Charlotte stood. "Yes," Charlotte said, "Osborn received his telegram."

A small frown creased her forehead as she thought about Ishmael. At school, they had fit together so seamlessly that two pieces of a puzzle found their match, only to have been divided by a poorly made decision by her grandmother and parents. Would they even fit into each other's lives anymore? Ishmael's world had expanded beyond their small town, filled with experiences and people she knew nothing about. And she, too, had changed, grown more independent, more sure of her own mind. Dierdre shrugged. "I mean, I wouldn't mind seeing him, but I don't believe he feels the same. He ignored all of my letters."

Charlotte sighed. "You know, your father was on your side concerning Ishmael. He believed as long as you weren't blood related, it was fine for you to court him. Osborn agreed with him. It was me," Charlotte said, walking to the window to avoid Dierdre's gaze. "I convinced your momma, who convinced Ray."

"I know all this, Grandma. I knew it was you."

"I know you did, but I needed to confess it. And there is something else I must confess." Charlotte's face fell to the floor before she began, "The letters…" The words left her unfinished.

"What about the letters?" Dierdre asked in a demanding tone. "You took them, didn't you?"

Her face still to the floor, Charlotte offered a reluctant nod.

"I knew it," Dierdre said as she shook her head, her gaze spearing her grandmother. "Mine and his? Did he try to reach me?"

Charlotte offered another reluctant nod. "I'm sorry and. . .well, now I know I was wrong. It was the curse, or what I call the curse, that made me believe that—"

"Even my letters from school? How did you—"

"The administration, Ray called them and warned them." Tears fell from Charlotte's eyes after she said it.

Dierdre shook her head and rose, pulling a handkerchief from her pocket. She put an arm around her grandmother and handed it to her. "It's alright, Grandma. It's a while ago now. Don't cry, or you'll make me cry. I'm not holding a grudge. Maybe it was for the best, I don't know."

Charlotte wiped her eyes and pulled the handkerchief away, revealing a severe expression. "It wasn't. It was a misstep. Ishmael was a good boy. Is a good boy."

Dierdre's eyes widened. "You surely have changed, Grandma. Things you thought just a minute ago, you aren't thinking them anymore. And now you're getting married. . . to Osborn. Come on. Let's go get you some tea."

Dierdre's arm still around her grandmother's shoulder, they made their way to find David.

Charlotte sighed and said, "It feels like I've seen things and learned things more in the last year than all my other years combined."

Walking down the hall, they abruptly stopped at the entrance to the dining room. Osborn lay flat on his back, stretched out along the length of the polished mahogany table. David sat where she usually would, eating a plate of food before him. A strange scene for most, but Charlotte knew what was taking place.

Charlotte blinked. "Osborn, what do you think you are doing?"

Osborn's head popped up from the table with a lopsided grin. "Charlotte! Good, good, you're here. David and I, we had an idea, we did. He could sin eat my sins away, away for you. The thing, the thing that kept you from liking me all these years, yes?"

Charlotte approached the table, a bemused smile tugging at her lips. "Osborn, this is... well, it's certainly unexpected. But you do realize you're not dead, don't you? Sin eaters take sins from the deceased, not the living."

Osborn cocked his head, recalling. "But, but I removed the curse from you, I did. And the gun, gun for Trapper Billy, years ago. Why not sins, sins too?"

Dierdre leaned against a chair, amusement dancing in her eyes. "Sounds logical to me."

Charlotte smirked. "Yes, but now David is a sin eater."

David looked up from his plate, a forkful of roasted potatoes halfway to his mouth. He glanced between Osborn on the table and the women, then said with perfect deadpan delivery, "Shall I prepare the table for myself next?"

Charlotte flashed a look of incredulity. "I don't believe it works that way, David."

Osborn popped his head up again. "Then, then, how do you believe it works, Charlotte? We, we, we will do it that way, yes."

Charlotte took a seat opposite David. "I don't know how it works."

Dierdre stepped up. "Exactly, you do not know how it works, Grandma. I believe that is what they are getting at. It's an old superstition that I'm shocked you still adhere to."

Charlotte smirked. "I know what they are getting at."

Raising his head from his plate, David told Charlotte, "Madam, fear not that this becomes a regular part of the dinner service. The silverware placement alone would be a nightmare."

Charlotte burst into laughter. Dierdre joined in, and even Osborn chuckled from his prone position.

As the laughter subsided, Charlotte wiped a tear from her eye. "Oh, Osborn," she said. "You didn't need to do this. Curse or no curse, sins or no sins, I—"

She paused, realizing the weight of what she was about to say. The room seemed to hold its breath, waiting.

"Well," Charlotte continued, "I suppose I've grown rather fond of you, just as you are."

Osborn sat up, his legs dangling off the end of the table. "You have? You have, Charlotte?"

She nodded, a gentle smile on her face. "I have. Now, shall we have a proper supper? Though perhaps with fewer people on the table?"

As Osborn scrambled down, his foot caught in the tablecloth. He stumbled, nearly taking the entire setting with him. David deftly steadied a teetering candlestick while Dierdre rescued a bottle of wine.

As David returned the candle stick, he said, "I must say, sin eating is a rather unconventional way to season the food."

The iron-rimmed wheels of Osborn's buggy clattered against the cobblestones as they made their way through Johnstown's bustling streets. David held the reins, guiding the horse while Osborn sat beside him, his fingers nervously tapping an erratic rhythm on his knees.

"Are you, are you certain Ishmael will be on this train, this train, David?" Osborn asked.

"Yes, sir," David replied, his eyes focused on the road ahead. "The telegram confirmed his arrival time."

"Are you excited to see your son again, sir?"

"Yes, yes, very excited. It's been, been too long, yes."

"Indeed it has." Around the corner from the undertaker's shop, David stopped. "Will you hold the reins, sir, while I discreetly deliver the note to Augustus?"

"Yes," replied Osborn, taking the reins as David got out and straightened his coat before disappearing around the corner. A few minutes later, Osborn saw him as he reappeared, and a few seconds after that, he saw Jefferson following him. As David climbed into Osborn's buggy, Jefferson and Osborn locked eyes.

"Oh, dear," said Osborn as Jefferson spun on his heels and disappeared back around the corner.

"What's that, sir?" asked David.

"You, you were just followed."

"Followed, sir?"

"Yes, Jefferson. Did he, did he see you?"

David shook his head. "I don't believe...Even if he did, I was quite discreet."

"We should, we should go, yes."

"Yes, sir."

Running into the shop, Jefferson called out, "Father?" Without a response, he went to the back room door, yelling, "Father?"

"He went on an errand," a worker called back.

Jefferson grabbed his hat off the rack as he headed for the door. Under his breath, he murmured, "And I have an idea where that errand is."

Jefferson urged his horse forward past the outskirts of town. The rhythm of his horse on the packed dirt road matched the pounding of his heart.

Steam billowed across the platform as the train screeched to a halt. Osborn stood on tiptoe, craning his neck to peer through the haze of smoke and bustling travelers. His fingers nervously twisted the brim of his hat, the fabric worn smooth from the habit.

"Do you see him, sir?" David asked, standing tall beside Osborn.

"Not yet, not yet," Osborn muttered, his eyes darting from face to face.

As Ishmael's familiar figure materialized through the fog, Osborn felt a surge of pride so intense it nearly overwhelmed him. His son, his brilliant boy, returning triumphant from the bustling world of New York City. Osborn's hands fluttered at his sides, torn between his usual aversion to touch and the overwhelming desire to embrace his child.

"Ishmael!" he called out, his voice carrying the excitement he couldn't quite express physically. "Over here, over here, yes!"

Ishmael's face broke into a wide smile when he spotted his father. He strode toward them, his suitcase swinging at his side. "Father," he said warmly, embracing him. "It's good to see you." Osborn stiffened for only a moment before melting into the contact, his usual discomfort forgotten in the joy of reunion. He breathed in the scent of his son - a mixture of tobacco, cologne, and something indefinably New York - and felt a curious mix of pride and nostalgia wash over him.

"Good to see you, sir," said David.

"And you, David," replied Ishmael before they settled in the buggy and headed off. Osborn sat beside his son, his hands fidgeting in his lap.

"Father," Ishmael began, breaking the silence, "I must admit, I was quite shocked by your telegram. You and Charlotte Fenn? The same woman who once regarded you with such disdain?"

Osborn nodded, a ghost of a smile rising on his face. "Yes, yes, it is quite, quite unexpected, isn't it? Charlotte and Dierdre came to stay, to stay at the mansion two months ago. Over time, we grew, we grew close, yes."

"Dierdre? Is she still involved with Jefferson True?"

Osborn's head snapped toward his son, eyes wide with surprise. "How do you, how do you know about that?"

"I saw them together at the train station last Christmas."

Osborn shook his head. "No, no, they are not together, not together anymore. That's why, why they wanted to stay at the mansion, yes. Because of their, their break-up."

The buggy rattled over a small bridge, the sound of rushing water momentarily drowning out their conversation. When they emerged on the other side, Ishmael asked, "Is Dierdre there now?"

"She, she is, yes."

Ishmael felt a sudden rush of conflicting emotions, each vying for dominance in his mind. Dierdre was there, just a short distance away. A part of him, the part that still clung to the memory of their shared past, surged with anticipation. Would she still have that mischievous glint in her eye, the one that had first captured his heart? Would her laugh still sound like music, light and carefree as it had been in their youth? He found himself wondering if she still tucked her hair behind her ear when she was deep in thought, a habit he had once found endearing.

Yet, alongside this excitement came a wave of trepidation. She had chosen her parents' wishes over their relationship. The memory of that still stung, a dull ache that had never fully subsided. He had thought her decision ridiculous, a capitulation to outdated notions of class and status. But she had obeyed, leaving him to pick up the pieces of his shattered heart.

"Is she dreading seeing me?"

Osborn chuckled. "Not at all, not at all. In fact, she worries you might be thinking, thinking that about her."

"I harbor no ill will toward her. When are Ray and Melody arriving? And the girls?"

"They'll be here, be here in two days, just before the wedding," said Osborn. "And they'll head home with Dierdre the day after."

Ishmael leaned back, his gaze fixed on the passing landscape. He shifted in his seat, his mind racing. He was not the same young man she had left behind. In the years since their parting, he had thrown himself into his work, channeling his pain and frustration into ambition. Now, he stood as an executive at Eastman Kodak, his name known in boardrooms across the country. He had courted other women, even actresses whose names graced theater marquees. He had built a life for himself, one of success and acclaim.

And yet...

Something about Dierdre still called to him, a siren song he couldn't quite ignore. It wasn't just nostalgia for their shared past, though, that certainly played a part. No, it was something more elusive, a quality he couldn't quite define. Perhaps it was the way she had challenged him, pushed him to be better. Or maybe it was the depth of understanding they had shared, a connection that went beyond mere attraction.

Ishmael turned to his father. "Well, Father, it seems you've orchestrated quite the family reunion. I'm intrigued to see how it all unfolds."

CHAPTER 27

The iron gates of the Cattell mansion loomed before Jefferson, their intricate scrollwork casting spidery shadows across the sun-dappled lawn. He pulled his horse to a sudden halt, the animal's breath coming in sharp snorts. He leapt from the saddle and peered around the corner. His father's horse stood tethered near the front steps, its tail swishing lazily at flies.

Heart pounding, he crept toward the house, each step careful and measured. Jefferson's eyes darted from window to window, searching. A flash of movement caught his attention. There, in the grand parlor with its gilt-edged mirrors and velvet drapes, stood Dierdre. And beside her, his father. Jefferson's chest tightened, a vise of confusion squeezing the air from his lungs.

He pressed his ear to the cool glass, straining to catch their words. The voices drifted to him in muffled fragments, each a dagger to his heart.

"...I wish things had been different... that we had more time together from the start..."

"...And now that we've met, I hardly know what to say..."

"...I want to make up for the years we haven't been together..."

The words ignited a fire in Jefferson's veins. He bolted for the door, taking the marble steps two at a time. The heavy oak door gave way beneath his hands, swinging open with a resounding crack.

Racing down the hall, he skidded to a stop at the parlor entrance, chest heaving. Augustus rose slowly from his seat, his face a mask of shock and something Jefferson had never seen—raw vulnerability. Father and son stood frozen for a heartbeat, the air crackling with unspoken truths between them. Like an actor who had forgotten his lines, Jefferson felt like he had stumbled onto a stage where the play was already in full, tumultuous swing.

"Jefferson?" Augustus whispered, his voice rough as sandpaper. "What are you—"

Dierdre's eyes widened as she took in the scene before her. "Oh God," she breathed.

"What in God's name is going on here?" Jefferson demanded, his voice echoing in the sudden silence.

Charlotte ran in from the other room. "Jefferson?! What are you—"

Walking up to Dierdre, Jefferson pointed at his father. "You with him? You're with him, aren't you?"

Shocked, Dierdre replied, "With him? What do you mean?"

Jefferson whirled around to Augustus, betrayal etched on his face. "Father, why?"

Augustus opened his mouth to speak, but no words came out. He looked helplessly at Charlotte, searching her calm face. She stepped forward. "She's not having an affair with your father if that's what you're suggesting," she said before spinning back to Augustus.

"Augustus, he needs to know. Just as you needed to know all those years ago."

Jefferson clenched his teeth. "Need to know what?" he demanded.

"The boy is in love with the girl. It's cruel. It's time for the truth to come out," she continued. Augustus gave her a reluctant nod.

"Yes, tell me. I want the truth."

Charlotte calmly walked past Dierdre, running a hand across her shoulders. "You alright, Dear?"

"I am," replied Dierdre, sitting down in a chair.

Walking about the room, Charlotte drew air in deeply, steeling herself. "What I'm about to tell you, you can't repeat to anyone. It would hurt a lot of people if this got out. People in your family." She paused, her eyes locking with Jefferson's. "Jefferson, your father is Dierdre's father too."

The words reverberated through the room, heavy with implication. Jefferson shook his head, disbelief written across his features. "What?... How?"

Jefferson stood rooted to the spot, his body a taut wire of conflicting emotions. The initial shock of Charlotte's revelation had given way to a storm of feelings that threatened to overwhelm him. Jefferson faced his father. "You were with Dierdre's mother?"

"It was before I met your momma. Melody and I were married, but…it didn't work out."

Charlotte's eyes darted to Augustus. "Didn't work out?" Is that what you're going with? He's gotta know the rough side of the plank—"

"No, he doesn't," Augustus said firmly.

Jefferson's fists clenched and unclenched at his sides, knuckles white with the effort of maintaining control. "I do! Tell me!"

Eyes still on Augustus, she said, "If I don't tell him, he'll never know me, never get to know me, and neither will all his brothers and sisters."

"Don't listen to him," Jefferson told Charlotte, his voice steady despite the tremor in his heart. "I deserve to know the truth." The words tasted of bitterness and vindication on his tongue.

Charlotte nodded. "You do. Well, circumstances fell on the unlucky side of the coin when Augustus and Melody met. You see, like Augustus is both Dierdre's and your father, I am both Melody's and your father's mother."

"I don't…"

"It's true. I am Augustus's real mother, and Jefferson, I'm your grandmother. Is it all fittin' together for ya?"

Charlotte's eyes flickered to Augustus for reassurance. She took another deep breath. "Augustus and Melody were both unknowingly the children of myself and Archer True, your grandfather."

A confused expression on his face, Jefferson looked over at his father for answers. Augustus replied, "You getting this, son?"

Charlotte continued, "Your father didn't know I was his mother until after he met Melody, who also didn't know he was her brother. This all happened long before he met your momma, but your daddy and Melody did get married and Dierdre came from that union. You follow?"

Jefferson nodded before he flopped into a chair and put his head in his hands. In a gentle voice, Charlotte continued. "I believe it was a curse. A curse on me that affected all my kin, and you are my kin. The same thing that happened to your father and Melody was happening with you and Dierdre. Dierdre is your half-sister. That's why you can't be together."

Jefferson looked from Charlotte to his father, searching for any sign that this was some elaborate, cruel joke. As the torrent of revelations subsided, Jefferson's gaze finally found Dierdre huddled in the corner of the room. She had been unnaturally still throughout the entire ordeal, her face a mask of conflicted emotions.

Jefferson took a hesitant step toward her, his movements jerky and uncertain. "You knew," he said, his voice barely above a whisper. It wasn't a question.

Dierdre's eyes glistened with unshed tears. "I found out just before... before I ended things between us."

The realization hit Jefferson like a physical blow. All those weeks of anguish, of desperate attempts to understand why she had pushed him away so suddenly.

"Was it easy for you?" The painful question escaped him before he could stop it, laced with a bitterness that surprised even him. He knew the answer. "To walk away, knowing what we were to each other?"

Dierdre flinched as if he had struck her. "Easy?" Her voice cracked on the word. "Jefferson, it was the hardest thing I've ever done."

Jefferson's eyes narrowed, the suggestion of bitter recognition crossing his face. "Or maybe the second?" he said as more of a statement than a question. "I wonder, Dierdre, did you say those exact words to Ishmael too? The hardest thing you've ever done?"

Dierdre's face paled, her composure cracking before she regained control.

Augustus stepped forward, placing a hand on his son's shoulder. "Jefferson, that'll be enough."

Jefferson pivoted on his heel and strode across the hall to the solitude of the study. Dierdre followed him, catching him in front of the windows overlooking the back lawn and gardens.

"I've always known, you know," Jefferson said, his back to her. "That your heart belonged to him first. That I was... what? A consolation? A distraction?"

Dierdre took a shaky breath, her eyes glistening. "Jefferson, that's not fair. What I felt for you was real—"

"But not as real as what you felt for him," Jefferson interrupted, his voice sharp with pain. "Tell me, was it easier to walk away from me?" Jefferson felt a pang of regret at causing her pain, but it was overshadowed by the bitter satisfaction of finally voicing the doubts that had plagued him for so long.

"I never meant to hurt you," Dierdre asserted. "I didn't break up with you. Circumstances around us broke us up."

Jefferson's shoulders sagged, the fight draining out of him. "I know," he said with a hollow laugh devoid of any real mirth. "It's almost poetic, isn't it? To find out I'm your brother."

For a moment, they stood there, two people who had once been so close, now separated by an ocean of unspoken words and shattered dreams. The love that had burned between them was still there, transmuted into something painful and unresolvable. Dierdre watched Jefferson as he walked out of the room, leaving her alone in it.

As Jefferson exited the front door, Osborn, Ishmael, and David pulled in on the buggy. Ignoring them, Jefferson passed by them without a glance or a word. "Jefferson?" Ishmael asked himself before shifting his attention to his father. "I thought you said they were—"

Suddenly, Charlotte ran out from the front door and past them. "Jefferson!" she called out.

"What is going on here?" Ishmael murmured as he watched Charlotte chase after him. "Suppose we should let them be," he said before continuing into the house. Osborn shrugged and followed him in.

Walking down the hallway, they stopped at the parlor. Dierdre stood by the window, watching as it all played out. Augustus sat with his head in his hands.

"What's going on here?" Ishmael asked.

Augustus looked up, shaking his head, before walking between Osborn and Ishmael. "Excuse me," he sighed.

By the window, Dierdre stood, sunlight streaming through the lace curtains.

Their eyes met and, for a moment, the world seemed to hold its breath.

"Welcome home, Ishmael," Dierdre said, her tone distant and unemotional.

"Thank you," he replied, the words catching in his throat. Unspoken words and shared history filled the silent space between them. Not sure what to do or what to say, he asked her, "Are you. . .alright?"

Dierdre let out a soft sigh from the sad smile on her lips. Understanding, he nodded to her before leaving the room. Dierdre's gaze followed him as he went.

Charlotte caught up to Jefferson as he slowed to a stop in the front gardens. Surrounded by meticulously pruned hedges and vibrant flowerbeds that seemed to mock the chaos in his mind, Jefferson sank onto a stone bench, burying his face in his hands. She stood before him, her eyes filled with empathy. "I know this is a lot to take in," she said softly, settling onto the bench beside him.

Jefferson laughed bitterly. "A lot to take in? You've just turned my entire world upside down. Everything I thought I knew about my family, about myself... it's all a lie."

Charlotte reached out to touch his arm, then thought better of it. "Not a lie, Jefferson. A curse. One that's caused a great deal of pain over the years." Jefferson shook his head, trying to make sense of it all. "And everything you knew about your family is still true," Charlotte continued. "Only now, you have a new grandma and half-sister you never knew about. That could be a good thing, don't ya think?"

Jefferson pulled his head from his hands, gazing out into the garden. Charlotte understood his pain. "We should've told ya from the start like we did Dierdre. It wasn't fair to keep it from you, now was it? I had to tell your daddy and my daughter, too, when I found out about them. Told them too late, I did."

Jefferson turned to her. "A curse?" he asked.

"A curse," she repeated. "Caught you and Dierdre just in time." She paused, a wistful smile playing on her lips. "I want to know you, Jefferson. You and your siblings. You're all my grandchildren. Like you said, you miss her. And that's just like how much I miss all of you, all of my grandchildren. And I missed out on watching your daddy grow into a man. And Augustus, your daddy... he deserves the chance to know his daughter, Dierdre, to be a father to her in whatever way he can. I'm gonna make that happen. I'm gonna see to that. Her childhood, seeing her grow up, was stolen from him, like he was stolen from me."

Jefferson and Charlotte made their way back to the house. Augustus waited for them on the porch steps. "Son," he began, "I know this is a lot to ask, but you have to keep what you heard today a secret and never repeat it."

"Your brothers and sisters, your mother," said Charlotte, stepping close to him. "They can't know who Dierdre or I really are to ya. As for me, I don't know if there's a way I can be in your sister and brother's lives, but I surely would like to be in yours, if you'd have me."

Jefferson looked at them in turn – Charlotte, with her hopeful smile, and his father, looking more vulnerable than Jefferson had ever seen him.

"I understand," he said. "I won't say a word."

The morning sun filtered through the heavy velvet curtains of Ishmael's private study, and the air smelled of leather-bound books and freshly polished wood. Ishmael stood before the ornate mirror, his fingers working the silk of his tie into a perfect Windsor knot.

A gentle rap at the door broke the silence. "Come in," Ishmael called, his eyes never leaving his reflection. David's reflection appeared in the mirror. "Pardon the interruption, sir, but there's a workman at the door. Something about a telephone, he says."

"Ah, yes. Please show him in, David. I'll be down in a moment."

David nodded, then added, "Also, sir, I'll be taking the buggy to retrieve Mr. Ray and Mrs. Melody from the station shortly."

"Very good, David. Thank you."

As David retreated, closing the door behind him, Ishmael finished with his tie and shrugged on his waistcoat. He took one last look in the mirror, smoothing an errant lock of hair, before going downstairs.

Colored light streamed through the stained-glass transom above the front door in the foyer. Osborn stood engaged in animated conversation with a man in workman's clothes. His father's hands moved in their characteristic pattern, fingers tapping against each other as he spoke.

"Ishmael, Ishmael," Osborn called as he spotted his son descending the stairs. "This man, this man says he's here about, about a telephone. A telephone, yes. What do you, what do you know about this?"

Ishmael approached, offering a warm smile to the workman. "Father, have you noticed the men working in the trees along the road these past few weeks?"

"Yes, yes, I have. Curious business, curious business indeed."

"Well," Ishmael continued, his eyes twinkling with excitement, "I've arranged for telephone lines to be brought all the way out here. We're to have our very own telephone installed today."

Osborn's eyes widened. "A telephone? Here? But how, how does it work? I've read about them, read about them, yes, but to have one in our home..."

"It's really quite simple to use, Father. I'll show you once it's installed." He turned to the workman, who had been waiting patiently. "We'd like it installed in the hallway, if you please. Father, would you be so kind as to show him the way?"

Osborn nodded eagerly, his earlier apprehension giving way to curiosity. "Yes, yes, of course. This way, this way, sir. Tell me, how long have you been, you been installing these marvelous devices?"

As Osborn led the workman down the hallway, his voice faded as he peppered the man with questions.

From down the hall, Charlotte approached him, her eyes meeting Ishmael's. "Ishmael, welcome home. Forgive me. I must have missed you at supper last night."

"I had something in my chambers. I was simply exhausted."

Charlotte stood before him, studying his face until she asked, "Ishmael, might I have a word?"

"Of course."

She gestured to the door. "It's such a lovely morning. Shall we go for a stroll?"

"Certainly," he replied with a curious expression before falling into step beside her as they stepped out of the house.

The crunch of gravel beneath their feet filled the silence until Charlotte spoke again. "Is it good to be home again?"

Ishmael considered the question before answering, "I don't feel it's my home anymore. New York is more my home now. I believe it'll be more my father and your home now, Mrs. Fenn. Or should I say, soon-to-be Mrs. Roche? I must say, this is quite the unexpected turn of events."

"Life is full of surprises," she replied. "Yesterday was quite a surprise. I'm sorry you had to witness that during your homecoming."

Ishmael shrugged. "A lovers quarrel is none of my concern."

"It wasn't a lovers quarrel. Jefferson and Dierdre have not seen one another for some time now. But what I told Jefferson yesterday is what you need to do today. You will hear of it sooner or later, and I need you to hear of it from me first."

As they entered the rose garden, Ishmael replied, "If you must," before she told him the whole story about Dierdre and Jefferson and why they could not be together.

The garden paths had all been traversed by the time Charlotte finished her tale. Ishmael, his mind reeling, could only muster a single word: "Shocking."

Charlotte's hands clasped at her waist, her gaze falling to her feet like autumn leaves. "We don't know each other very well, do we, Ishmael?"

A wry smile played across Ishmael's lips. "That's because you disliked my father for so long."

Charlotte's sigh was heavy with regret, her shoulders sagging. "It wasn't dislike, Ishmael. It was fear. Fear because he was a sin eater."

"And apparently, you've had a change of heart about that?" Ishmael's tone was carefully neutral, a tightrope walker balancing between curiosity and caution.

"Yes. I was the pot calling the kettle black. As much a sinner as he ever was." They paused beside a rose bush in full bloom, its perfume hanging thick in the air. Charlotte turned to face Ishmael directly. "Do you approve of your father marrying me?"

Ishmael weighed his words carefully before answering. "It was surprising, certainly. But my father is a very smart man. If he approves of you, then so do I." His expression hardened. "Although both of you, being a part of the same family, others may disapprove, but with no blood relation, I see no harm in it." A wry smile rose on his lips after he said it, mirrored by a painful one on hers.

"I deserve that," she admitted. "Again, I'm a sinner casting the stone. And that's the other reason I wanted to talk to you, to apologize for that." She took a deep breath, squaring her shoulders. "I was the one who instigated your breakup with Dierdre, not Ray. And it was wrong of me. A terrible mistake." Ishmael nodded in agreement but remained silent, waiting for her to continue. "The letters, your letters…we intercepted all of them."

His jaw fell open. "Really?"

"Yours and hers to you," Charlotte said, her voice thick with regret.

"That makes sense. I always…" his words faltered as he stared off in thought.

"I was wrong, and I'm truly sorry for the pain I caused you both." Charlotte's eyes softened, a glimmer of hope sparking within them. "You know, Ishmael, it's never too late to right a wrong. Even if others created that wrong, it's never too late."

A sad smile appeared on Ishmael's lips. "After all this time?"

"Love, true love, doesn't fade so easily. And if what you had with Dierdre was real, well... sometimes the heart needs a second chance to get things right."

CHAPTER 28

At the front of the First Presbyterian Church of Johnstown, Osborn Roche stood nervously adjusting his cravat. His fingers, usually steady behind a camera, fumbled with the silk fabric. The scent of roses mingled with the musty odor of old hymnals, creating a sensory assault that threatened to overwhelm him. He longed for the quiet solitude of his study and the comforting weight of a book in his hands. The church's double doors stood wide open, welcoming the townsfolk dressed in their Sunday best. The air hummed with excitement and the rustle of starched collars and crisp skirts.

Ray stepped up to fix his cravat for him. "Steady now, Uncle," Ray murmured. "It's almost time."

Osborn's eyes darted to the back of the church. "Yes, yes, almost time. Charlotte, she'll be here soon, soon, yes?"

In the front pew, Melody sat with her daughters, Clara and Alice. The girls fidgeted in their new dresses, eyes wide as they took in the grand spectacle around them. Melody gently shushed them, smoothing Clara's unruly curls with a practiced hand.

Wearing a black tailcoat, Mayor Storey made his way up the front steps, stopping to shake hands and exchange pleasantries with various townspeople. He offered Osborn a handshake. "Fine day for a wedding, Mr. Roche," the mayor boomed.

"He does not shake hands, Mayor," said Ray. The mayor shook his head. "Oh! How can I forget? I forget every time, don't I, Mr. Roche?"

"You do, you do."

"It's a part of my line of work, it is."

"It is, it is, yes."

The mayor looked around at the crowd. "The whole town's turned out to wish you well."

Osborn managed a smile, his hand diving for the brown cloth in his pocket. "Thank you, thank you, Mayor. It's good of you, good of you to come, yes."

Coming from the church, Ishmael approached them. "We should go in, Father."

Entering the church, Augustus sat in a back pew with his wife and children, his face a mask of careful neutrality. Osborn and Ishmael walked down the aisle and stood before the pulpit.

As the organist began to play, a hush fell over the congregation. All eyes turned to the back of the church, where Charlotte stood framed by the church entrance. She wore a gown of pale ivory silk, its high collar adorned with delicate lace. In her hands, she clutched a bouquet of white roses and forget-me-nots.

Dierdre stood behind her grandmother in a gown of deep blue. Her eyes scanned the crowd, settling on Ishmael, who stood near the front with his father. Their gazes locked for a moment before Ishmael looked away.

A fleeting shadow crossed Dierdre's face, her composure wavering for just an instant. She felt the sharp pang of disappointment. Was he still angry? Or perhaps just nervous? The questions swirled in her mind, threatening to overwhelm her carefully maintained facade.

As Charlotte began her stately procession down the aisle, Dierdre fell into step behind her. She kept her eyes fixed ahead, but she could feel Ishmael's presence, a magnetic pull she struggled to resist.

With each step, Dierdre's mind raced. She longed to look at Ishmael again, to search his face for any sign of softening, any hint that he might be willing to bridge the chasm between them. But pride kept her gaze forward, her chin lifted in a show of indifference she was far from feeling.

As she drew closer, Dierdre allowed herself a quick, sidelong glance. To her surprise, she found his eyes already upon her. Ishmael stood motionless, his gaze steady and unreadable, until she saw something flicker across Ishmael's face—a ghost of an emotion that might have been regret or longing; she couldn't tell. As quickly as it had appeared, the look vanished, replaced by the mask of neutrality that Ishmael wore like armor.

Osborn's face lit up as Charlotte approached, and he released his fingers from the brown cloth in his pocket as his earlier nervousness melted away. "Beautiful, beautiful," he murmured as she took her place beside him.

The minister stepped forward, his voice filling every corner of the church. "Dearly beloved, we are gathered here today to witness the union of two souls..." he began, going on until he asked each of them to exchange vows. Finally, the minister's booming voice said, "I now pronounce you man and wife. You may kiss the bride."

A hush fell over the church as all eyes turned to the couple. Osborn stiffened visibly, his eyes slamming shut as if bracing for impact. With a gentle smile, Charlotte leaned in and quickly placed a soft kiss on Osborn's cheek. The kiss, over in an instant, rippled through Osborn like a stone cast into still water. He recoiled and scrunched his face, breaking the tension in the room. Laughter and applause erupted, filling the church. Charlotte leaned to his ear and said, "I'm sorry, I had to. Everyone was watching. But now I need you to take my arm and escort me down the aisle."

Her words jolted Osborn from his stupor. "Oh, OK," he muttered as he awkwardly linked his arm with hers. As the newlyweds made their way back down the aisle, rose petals rained down upon them. Osborn twisted and ducked away from them. "Why, why are they throwing these, these?"

Charlotte's reply came through gritted teeth, her smile never faltering for the benefit of their audience. "They are simply rose petals, Osborn. Stop jerking about. You look like a madman."

"I am not, am not. I am simply looking peculiar—"

Rolling her eyes, Charlotte finished it for him. "Peculiar, with a hard consonant 'c.'"

The Cattell mansion's back lawn sprawled out before Dierdre, a sea of emerald grass dotted with blue tablecloth-covered tables. The sweet scent of roses mingled with the earthy aroma of freshly cut grass, creating an intoxicating perfume that seemed to hang in the warm afternoon air. The wedding reception was in full swing, a celebration that contrasted with the tumult of Dierdre's inner world.

She moved through the guests, a sea of faces chatting and laughing with one another. Her eyes, however, sought out only one. With a flute of champagne held loosely in her hand, her eyes found him as he stood tall and handsome in his tailored suit, conversing with the mayor across the lawn. The sunlight caught the auburn highlights in his hair, reminding Dierdre of autumn afternoons spent walking arm in arm when they were in school. Her heart raced, and she silently chastised herself for the girlish flutter in her stomach. They were past all that now, weren't they?

As she watched, Dierdre noticed the subtle changes in Ishmael that spoke of his time in New York. His posture was straighter, more assured, and he gestured with a confidence that hadn't been there before. The way he engaged with the mayor – all easy smiles and articulate responses – revealed a polish that came from moving in sophisticated circles. Already the wealthiest man in the county before working at Kodak, he had become even wealthier and lived in a second mansion in New York. The distance between them seemed a bit impossible, a chasm carved by years of separation and change.

Dierdre took a sip of champagne, using the moment to collect her thoughts. This Ishmael was different from the boy she had known. He carried himself with the air of a man who had seen more of the world, who had faced challenges and emerged stronger for them. She found herself both drawn to this new version of him and unsettled by it.

The champagne bubbles tickled her nose, grounding her in the present moment. Dierdre realized that any future between them couldn't be built on nostalgia alone. It would require accepting who they had become, bridging the gap between their shared past and their individual presents. The thought both thrilled and terrified her.

As if sensing her gaze, Ishmael looked up, his eyes meeting hers across the crowded lawn. For a moment, Dierdre saw a trace of the boy she had known, a softening around his eyes that spoke of shared memories. But it was quickly replaced by something else – a questioning look, an invitation perhaps, to discover who they were to each other now.

Dierdre felt her pulse quicken. Her past was comforting in its familiarity, but it was the unknown future that beckoned. Could they forge something new from the raw materials of their changed selves? She drew in a long, steadying breath and began walking toward him. There was only one way to find out.

"Ishmael," she said, slipping her arm around his. Like a little girl pouting for candy, she said, "Please, please fetch me a glass of punch?"

The mayor chuckled as he stuck out his hand to Ishmael. "Duty calls, young man. Wonderful speaking with you."

After they walked away from the mayor, Dierdre said, "I don't want punch. You simply needed to avail yourself away from that boring old man."

Ishmael raised his brows. "I did?"

"You did. You should thank me."

"I will. Thank you."

"You are welcome. Now, perhaps we could take a walk through the rose garden?" Her arm in his, she tugged at the crook of his elbow, leading him to the garden. The air filled with laughter and the strains of a string quartet.

"Quite a turnout," Ishmael said.

"Indeed," replied Dierdre. "Your father is a popular fellow."

Arm in arm, they ambled along the gravel path until she asked, "Do you remember that summer picnic by the lake?" Dierdre asked as the hint of a grin played across his lips. "When you tried to show off your rowing skills and ended up tipping us both into the water?"

Ishmael chuckled, the sound warming Dierdre to her core. "How could I forget? I've never lived that down. You were furious about your ruined dress."

"I was," Dierdre agreed, her eyes twinkling. "But it was worth it to see the look on your face when you came up spluttering." A burst of laughter from the party interrupted them.

"We should probably head back," he said, gesturing toward the house. "They'll be cutting the cake soon."

Dierdre nodded, trying to hide her disappointment. "Of course. We wouldn't want to miss that."

The Cattell mansion's grand ballroom sparkled with candlelight, the soft glow reflecting off crystal glasses and polished silver. Osborn and Charlotte stood near the ornate fireplace, accepting well-wishes from a steady stream of guests. Osborn's fingers fidgeted with his cufflinks, a nervous habit that hadn't abated even in the joy of the moment.

"Lovely, lovely evening, yes?" Osborn murmured to Charlotte, his eyes darting across the room.

Charlotte patted his arm reassuringly. "It's perfect, my dear. Absolutely perfect."

As the crowd thinned, Augustus approached, his wife Rachel and their children in tow. Augustus's face was a careful mask of polite interest.

"Mr. and Mrs. Roche," Augustus said. "Congratulations on your nuptials. It's been a beautiful ceremony."

Osborn bowed. "Thank you, thank you, Mr. True. We're so pleased, so pleased you could come, yes."

Augustus moved through his introductions: Rachel, his wife; their daughters Wendeline and Terry Ann, eighteen and sixteen; nineteen-year-old Nicholas with his sweetheart Ginny at his side. The space where Jefferson should have stood remained painfully empty.

Rachel stepped forward, a warm smile gracing her features. "It's a pleasure to meet you both. The wedding was lovely."

Charlotte's eyes sparkled as she took in the True family, her heart swelling with a secret joy. "The pleasure is all ours, Mrs. True. We're so glad you could all attend."

Augustus's gaze flickered briefly to Charlotte before addressing his wife. "You know, Rachel, Mr. Roche here was quite helpful to me years ago when I was just starting out in the mortuary business. His skill as a post-mortem photographer was invaluable during one of my first funerals."

Osborn grinned. "Yes, yes, I remember. A difficult case, that one. But we managed, we managed well, didn't we, Mr. True?"

Rachel's eyes widened with interest. "Is that so?"

"It was, it was Mr. Parker who put us together, yes."

Augustus turned to Rachel. "You remember, I purchased his business from Mr. Parker's son when he passed."

"I do."

As the conversation flowed, Charlotte found herself studying the True children. In Sarah's thoughtful expression, she saw echoes of Augustus in young Thomas's stance. Her heart ached from secrets and lost time.

Seizing the moment, Charlotte spoke up. "Mrs. True – Rachel, if I may – I was thinking how lovely it would be to get to know your handsome family better. Perhaps you'd all like to join us for supper sometime soon? Say, next week?"

Rachel glanced at Augustus, who gave a nod. "Why, that would be delightful, Mrs. Roche. We'd be honored."

Charlotte beamed, her eyes meeting Augustus's for a fleeting moment. "Wonderful! We'll send a proper invitation, of course. I do hope you'll all be able to attend."

Osborn leaned in close to Charlotte as the True family moved on to mingle with other guests. "Seems, seems you attained your goal, goal, Charlotte. My plan, plan worked, yes. My plans always work."

"We've done more than work a plan, my dear. We've opened a door to a future I once thought impossible."

CHAPTER 29

The day after the wedding, Dierdre sat with Osborn in the parlor room, the morning sun streaming in.

"Uncle Osborn, thank you for having me," Dierdre said, her voice warm with genuine affection.

"My pleasure, my pleasure. It appears to have been, have been quite a fruitful few months, yes? I, I am married now, yes," he said with a chuckle.

"Will you, will you, will you be returning to school? To your studies, yes?" Osborn asked, leaning forward in his chair.

"Yes, I'll be going back next semester."

As the words left her lips, Dierdre felt a familiar tug of uncertainty in her chest. She gazed out the window, her mind drifting to the future that lay before her like an uncharted map. Returning to Swarthmore meant stepping back into a world of academic rigor and intellectual pursuits, a path she had chosen with such conviction not long ago. Yet now, in the wake of the wedding and her encounter with Ishmael, that future seemed somehow both more complex and less defined.

What did she truly want for herself? The question echoed in her mind, persistent and unyielding. She envisioned herself graduating, perhaps pursuing further studies or embarking on a career. The image of herself as a teacher or perhaps a writer flickered in her mind's eye, appealing yet somehow incomplete.

And then there was Ishmael. His presence at the wedding had stirred something within her, awakening feelings she thought she had long since buried. She couldn't deny the spark that still existed between them, the way her heart had raced when their eyes met across the reception lawn. But could he fit into the future she had planned for herself?

"Dierdre?" Osborn's gentle voice pulled her from her reverie. "Are you, are you all right, my dear?"

She turned back to him, offering a more genuine smile this time. "Yes, Uncle Osborn. I was just thinking about what the future might hold."

"Ah, the future, yes. Full of, full of possibilities, it is."

Dierdre squared her shoulders. "Indeed it is," she agreed, a new resolve settling over her. Whatever the future held – whether it included Ishmael or not – she was determined to face it on her own terms, to shape it with her own hands.

Ray, Melody, and their young daughters entered from the hall. "Time to go, sweetheart," Melody told Dierdre.

Ray approached Osborn, and Osborn stood from his chair. "It's time we are off, Uncle."

"Yes, yes. I never, never like goodbyes, no," he said before putting his hands to the sides of his mouth and yelling, "Charlotte, Charlotte!"

Hurriedly walking in, Charlotte asked, "Time to go already?"

"It is," replied Ray.

As they made their way to the foyer, Charlotte stopped Dierdre and hugged her. "It's been quite an experience, hasn't it, dear?"

"It has," she replied before gesturing to Osborn as he walked away. "For both of us."

Charlotte wrapped her arm in Dierdre's and guided her to the foyer. "I'll miss you quite a bit."

"I'll be back and forth to Swarthmore. We'll still be seeing each other."

The Roche family gathered in the foyer, with Ishmael noticeably absent. As they gave hugs and said their goodbyes, David opened the front door from the outside. "All the bags are loaded, sir. Whenever you are ready."

Following David to the front porch, Dierdre scanned the grounds. "Where's Ishmael? I had hoped to say goodbye."

David cleared his throat. "He went out for an early morning ride, Miss. He mentioned wanting to clear his head before the day began."

Dierdre raised a polite smile.

As the family moved toward the waiting buggy, Charlotte pulled Dierdre aside momentarily. "My dear," she said, "don't let his absence dim your spirits. Sometimes, the heart needs time to catch up with the mind."

Dierdre squeezed Charlotte's hand gratefully, but before she could respond, Ray called out, "Come along, Dierdre! We don't want to miss our train."

The buggy creaked as the family climbed aboard, David taking his place at the reins. Little Alice and Clara waved excitedly from their seats, their enthusiasm contrasting with Dierdre's subdued demeanor.

As the buggy began to roll down the long driveway, a chorus of goodbyes and well-wishes filled the air. Charlotte and Osborn stood on the porch, waving until the buggy disappeared from view.

Osborn faced Charlotte, his eyes bright with excitement. "Have you seen, have you seen the new telephone? It's quite remarkable, quite remarkable indeed, yes."

Charlotte shook her head, a fond smile on her lips. "I passed by it in the hall, but I haven't had a chance to examine it closely."

"Oh, you must see it, must see it in action," Osborn insisted. "I'm going to try it now, try it now, yes. Perhaps call the operator, the operator."

Osborn hurried inside, leaving Charlotte on the porch. She closed her eyes, enjoying the warmth of the sun on her face and the gentle breeze that rustled the nearby trees.

Hearing the sound of approaching hoofbeats, she opened her eyes. Ishmael galloped up the drive, his horse's flanks lathered with sweat. He pulled up sharply at the foot of the porch steps, dismounting in one fluid motion.

"Have they left?" he asked, slightly out of breath. "Did I miss them?"

Charlotte nodded. "They've just gone, not five minutes ago. You could catch them if you hurried."

Ishmael's eyes darted down the drive, indecision written across his features.

He took a step forward, then hesitated, before spinning around to Charlotte.

Seeing the conflict in his eyes, she said, "Ishmael, my boy, sometimes in life we're given second chances. But you must have the courage to seize them."

Ishmael's forehead creased in thought. "But what if... what if too much has changed? What if we can't recapture what we once had?"

"The question isn't whether you can recapture the past, but whether you can build a future together." She paused, letting her words sink in. "Go to her, Ishmael. Bring her back. She can catch another train any time, but this moment... this moment won't come again."

Ishmael's expression cleared, determination replacing uncertainty. With a quick nod of thanks, he swung back into the saddle and spurred his horse into action, racing down the drive.

The buggy had just reached the main road when Ishmael caught up and brought his horse alongside. His eyes locked on Dierdre's. He gave her a nod before turning to the whole family. "Forgive me for not being there to see you off."

"You are doing that right now," replied Melody.

"It was good seeing you, Ishmael," Ray said. "Congratulations on all your success."

"Thank you, Ray. But I would like to ask you a favor."

"A favor?"

"Yes, would you allow Dierdre to stay just a few more days?"

Surprise evident on everyone's faces, David pulled the buggy to a stop. "Well, I..." Ray stammered, shifting to Dierdre. "I believe that's up to her."

Ishmael dismounted and moved to stand beside Dierdre. He extended his hand to her. "Come back to the house with me, just for a little while. We can take a walk in the gardens like we used to. What do you say?"

"Ishmael, I..."

Dierdre's breath caught in her throat, her eyes widening at Ishmael's unexpected request. Her hand, which had been resting on her lap, twitched involuntarily toward his outstretched one. She glanced down at it, then back up to meet his gaze. As she opened her mouth to respond, a light breeze stirred a loose strand of her hair, and she reached up to tuck it behind her ear with a trembling hand. The gesture, so small and yet so telling, betrayed the tumult of emotions coursing through her. Her eyes never left Ishmael's face, searching for something – reassurance, perhaps, or a sign that this wasn't just a fleeting impulse.

The tension in her shoulders began to ease, and the hint of a smile tugged at the corners of her lips. She took a deep breath, steadying herself, before breaking the charged silence. "I'd like that, Ishmael. I'd like that very much."

Ray and Melody exchanged a knowing look. The edges of Ray's lips curled into a grin as he said, "I think that sounds like a fine idea. Dierdre, you can always catch a later train if you decide to stay."

With Ray's help, Dierdre climbed down from the buggy. Ishmael assisted her onto his horse, then swung up behind her. As they returned to the house, Dierdre twisted in the saddle to wave goodbye to her family.

"Tell me about New York, Ishmael. What's it like to live in such a bustling city?"

Ishmael chuckled. "It's a world apart from Johnstown, that's for certain. The energy, the constant motion... it's exhilarating and exhausting in equal measure."

"It sounds so interesting," Dierdre sighed. "A place full of opportunities and new ideas."

Ishmael's arms tightened around her waist. "Perhaps... perhaps you'll have the chance to see it for yourself someday. I'd be honored to show you around."

"I'd like that," she said. "I'd like that very much."

As they approached the house, Charlotte stood waiting on the porch with a knowing smile. Osborn appeared in the doorway behind her with a confused expression. "Dierdre! You've, you've come back!" Osborn exclaimed. "Did you, did you forget something?"

Charlotte crossed her arms, saying, "No, my dear. I believe they both simply remembered something."

Charlotte stood before the full-length mirror in her bedroom, smoothing the fabric of her light blue dress with intricate beadwork at the collar. Her silver hair was neatly pinned up, with a few errant curls framing her face.

Osborn entered her open door, his fingers fumbling with his cravat. "Charlotte, Charlotte, do you think this is, is straight enough?" he asked, turning to her for approval.

She smiled, stepping over to adjust it for him. "There, that's perfect."

As she straightened his lapels, a crease appeared on Osborn's forehead. "Have you heard, heard from Ishmael? About when he and Dierdre might, might return from New York?"

Charlotte's hands stilled for a moment. "I received a letter last week. They seem to be enjoying the city immensely. As for their return..." She paused, a knowing smile playing on her lips. "I'm not entirely sure they will, my dear."

Osborn's eyes widened. "Dierdre will not return, return to Swarthmore? But, but why?"

"I believe New York holds more opportunities for them both."

A knock at the door interrupted their conversation. David's voice came from the other side. "Mr. and Mrs. Roche, the buggy is ready whenever you are."

"Thank you, David," Charlotte called back before facing Osborn and giving him a final once-over. "Are you ready, my dear? This dinner with the Trues means a great deal to me."

Osborn offered his arm. "Yes, yes, I'm ready. Let's not keep them waiting, waiting, no."

Charlotte stared at his waiting arm. "You are offering me your arm?"

"It's what I am supposed to, supposed to do, yes."

"But you've never…" Surprised, Charlotte took it. "The weeper and the sin eater. Who would've thought?"

As they made their way downstairs, Charlotte couldn't help but feel a flutter of excitement in her chest. It was a moment she had dreamed of for so long, and now it was finally becoming a reality.

Charlotte and Osborn parked the buggy in front of the True family home and made their way up the gravel drive. Charlotte smoothed her skirts, taking a deep breath to calm her nerves before rapping on the solid oak door. The sound of laughter and clinking dishes drifted through the open windows. Rachel answered the door, her face lighting up with a welcoming smile. "Osborn, Charlotte, we're so glad you could join us. Please, come in."

As they stepped into the foyer, Charlotte thought, how many times had she imagined this moment? How many lonely nights had she spent dreaming of being invited into their home, into these lives?

The warmth of the house enveloped her, and with it came a flood of memories and regrets that threatened to overwhelm her carefully maintained composure. Charlotte's mind raced, years of choices and consequences flashing before her eyes in vivid detail.

But then she felt Osborn's hand, warm and reassuring, at the small of her back. She glanced up at him, seeing the love and acceptance in his eyes, and felt something inside her shift. Yes, she had made mistakes. Yes, there were things she wished she could change. But she had also done what she thought was right at the time, protecting her family the only way she knew how.

Augustus appeared in the doorway to the dining room, a dish towel slung over his shoulder. "Ah, right on time. We're just setting the table."

Charlotte and Osborn followed him into the dining room, where the rest of the family bustled about. Jefferson stood by the china cabinet, carefully selecting wine glasses. Wendeline and Terry Ann arranged flowers in crystal vases; their heads bent together in quiet conversation. Nicholas, the spitting image of his father at that age, helped his mother carry steaming dishes from the kitchen.

As she sat at the table, Charlotte's eyes were drawn to Augustus. The resemblance to his father – her Archer – was striking. The same strong jawline, the same crinkle at the corners of his eyes when he smiled. For a moment, Charlotte felt as if she had stepped back in time to a summer evening long ago when the world was full of possibility and her heart was unencumbered by secrets.

The meal progressed with the easy banter of a close-knit family. Charlotte found herself drawn into conversations about the girls' schooling, Nicholas's plans for college, and Jefferson's work at the mortuary. She listened intently, drinking in every detail, every shared glance, every inside joke.

Charlotte looked around the table, really looked, and saw not strangers or distant relations but family. She saw how Rachel's hand rested easily on Augustus's arm, the proud glint in his eye as he listened to his sons speak, and the conspiratorial giggles shared between the sisters. And she realized, with a start, that she was a part of this. Not on the outside looking in, as she had been for so many years, but here, present, sharing bread and conversation.

"More potatoes, Charlotte?" Rachel's voice broke through her reverie.

Charlotte smiled. "Yes, please. They're delicious."

As she accepted the proffered dish, her eyes met Augustus's across the table. There was a moment of understanding there, a shared secret that no longer felt like a burden but a bond.

The evening wore on, dessert was served, and still, Charlotte lingered, savoring every moment. When it came time to leave, she found herself enveloped in hugs and extracted promises to return soon.

Osborn walked off to the buggy as Charlotte stood on the porch, watching the fireflies dance in the gathering twilight. She felt a profound sense of peace settle over her as she made her way down the drive but paused to look back at the house. Light spilled from the windows, silhouettes moving behind curtains, and the muffled sound of laughter carried on the evening breeze. An epiphany washed over her like a warm wave, soothing the jagged edges of her long-held pain. She was no longer the specter from the treeline looking in; she had become a welcomed guest and a cherished addition to their circle. And that, she realized, was all she had ever truly wanted.

Thank you for reading
Sin Eater,
book three of the
Death Shall Have No Dominion,
three companion series books.
If you would like to
know more about the author,
Greg Morgan,
or the other two books in the
series, please visit
greg-morgan.com

Please show us a kindness and leave a
review of Sin Eater by Greg Morgan
on Amazon.com or Goodreads.com.

www.ingramcontent.com/pod-product-compliance
Lightning Source LLC
Chambersburg PA
CBHW020900150726
48196CB00048B/1118

* 9 7 8 1 7 3 4 9 6 5 7 7 3 *